THE LOST TRUMPET

Titles available in the Polygon Lewis Grassic Gibbon Series

Gay Hunter

The Lost Trumpet

Nine Against the Unknown

Spartacus

The Speak of the Mearns

Stained Radiance

Three Go Back

Persian Dawns, Egyptian Nights

The Grassic Gibbon Centre in Arbuthnott contains important archival material relating to Lewis Grassic Gibbon and his work. A wide variety of L. G. Gibbon publications and biographical studies can be found in its bookshop. The 'Friends of the Grassic Gibbon Centre' produces a bi-annual newsletter for sharing news and views about the author. For further information contact The Grassic Gibbon Centre, Arbuthnott, Laurencekirk, AB30 1PB. Tel: 01561 361668. Fax: 01561 361742. E-mail: lgginfo@grassicgibbon.com

http:// wwwgrassicgibbon.com

J. LESLIE MITCHELL

THE LOST TRUMPET

Introduced by
Ian Campbell

Polygon

The Lost Trumpet © The Estate of James Leslie Mitchell, 1932
Introduction © Ian Campbell, 2001

First published by Jarrold (London) in 1932

This edition published in 2001 by Polygon
An imprint of Edinburgh University Press Ltd
22 George Square, Edinburgh

Facsimile origination by Brinnoven, Livingston

Printed and bound in Great Britain by
Cox and Wyman Ltd, Reading

A CIP Record for this book is available from the British Library

ISBN 0 7486 6295 2 (paperback)

TO

COLONEL GRIGORI SALIAEFF
ON WHOM I MODELLED SALONEY
AND
ARTHUR JOHN HALL
WHOM THE PORTRAIT PLEASED

CONTENTS

PAGE

INTRODUCTION   9

CHAPTER THE FIRST
'And desire shall fail, and the grasshopper become a
burden' 15

CHAPTER THE SECOND
' "And, as the manuscript relates, the Trumpet . . .
had been stolen and carried away by a renegade
Levite" ' 25

CHAPTER THE THIRD
'I had gone down to the Warrens then, as other lost
souls go down to Hell' 39

CHAPTER THE FOURTH
' "There are many slaveries," I said. "Those of the lash
and those of the liquor ; and the little men who are
slaves of hope, and the bond-serfs of a creed of
hate" ' 48

CHAPTER THE FIFTH
'South we went towards Abu Zabel, past deserted
Helmieh and its lost block-houses in the sands, into
that quiet, pale country' 62

CHAPTER THE SIXTH
'I knew that voice. I had half-expected to hear it, yet
disbelieved I would ever hear it again' . . . 77

CHAPTER THE SEVENTH
'Aslaug Simonssen. I did not doubt her for a moment,
nor she me. With that name this could be no one
but Aslaug Simonssen' 84

CHAPTER THE EIGHTH
'I think they will live with me always, those days' . 100

CHAPTER THE NINTH
' "Only, wonderful to be alive and see and smell. And
to touch you" ' 115

CONTENTS

CHAPTER THE TENTH   PAGE
' "What can a modern of the twentieth century do, then,
to reach his essential self, and be that self ?" ' . . 128

CHAPTER THE ELEVENTH
'Sweet to dance to violins' 142

CHAPTER THE TWELFTH
' "It is . . . a Levite ornament. We're close on the
track of the Lost Trumpet" ' 161

CHAPTER THE THIRTEENTH
' "Look, I'm a wandering intestinal worm trying to find
out the truth of things" ' 172

CHAPTER THE FOURTEENTH
' "What would each of us do—if we found the Lost
Trumpet and it was as powerful as in the days of
Joshua ? " ' 195

CHAPTER THE FIFTEENTH
'He had turned aside into the entrance of the Wagh el
Berka. I caught his arm. "What, *here* ? " ' . . 217

CHAPTER THE SIXTEENTH
' "Oh, yes . . . I killed him that morning before I
left Rashida" ' 230

CHAPTER THE SEVENTEENTH
'There could be no doubt of that Shape' . . . 243

CHAPTER THE EIGHTEENTH
' "We will see if one of us can blow the Lost Trumpet" ' 258

CHAPTER THE NINETEENTH
'She set the Trumpet to her lips' 270

CHAPTER THE TWENTIETH
'Except the coming of that flash' 278

EPILUDE : UNENDING MORNING 284

INTRODUCTION

We know tantalisingly little about James Leslie Mitchell's experiences in the East, though we know that he was posted during his years in the armed forces both to the Holy Land and to Egypt. Ian Munro, who had access to both papers and recollections from friends, has some hints:

> I could live in this country for years, and never even see the pale ghost of ennui. Do you know what I did last Sunday? Rode across the desert on a camel to Hebron. It was a day of mist, of writhing ghostly shapes and the mountains of Moab (the word is a wealth of poetry in itself) loomed above us like giant breakers of a frozen sea. One might have been dead, a spirit wandering in a world of void . . . Right glad I am to be what I am without a future or a care for it, disreputable, a careless dreamer of dreams and a maker of songs that will never be sung, desiring always what I have not, wanderer and vagrant predestined.[1]

Right glad perhaps. But also driven and unfulfilled, a writer seeking a distinctive voice, a saleable format, a niche in a market he took a long time to break into. But the letter is revealing in its anticipation of the character who is given the narrative heart of *The Lost Trumpet* – disreputable, vagrant, reaching out for the unfindable. 'A child of the wanderlust I would be cramped and stifled in one position all my life,' he wrote to Ray Middleton[2] and *The Lost Trumpet* exorcises that claustrophobia by constructing a tale of wandering, drawing on the memories of Cairo which he found exotic and fascinating. It evokes, too, the emptiness around which the characters of the novel seek the lost trumpet of Biblical times which supposedly blew down the walls of Jericho.

Cairo is the heart of the book, even though much of the action takes place in the desert where the main characters do their archaeological digging. There is an overwhelming sense of colour and noise, energy and dust, history and suffering – and an attempt to transmit this to European audiences, through the medium of a Russian exile Saloney,[3] himself stranded between the Cairo he knows intimately and the world of predominantly British and American tourists he guides round it for a livelihood. Leonard Huxley had singled out Saloney as a successful device in his introduction to *The Calends of Cairo*.[4] John Lindsey, writing an appreciation of Mitchell in *The Twentieth Century*, reprinted in *The Lost Trumpet*, singled out the success of Cairo in that same book: 'Here is the Modern East: the whole book saturated in a strange, wild spirit – a spirit of unrest and yet tranquillity in the midst of that unrest; full of colour and a noble searching after meaning'.[5]

The Lost Trumpet draws together a number of recurring themes in Mitchell's work. The detached observer, Saloney, is the author himself in many guises – the sardonic Scot commenting on his own country in the 1930s; the sardonic political commentator of *Scottish Scene* looking far beyond Scotland to excoriate what he saw as the collapse of the civilisation of his time; the observing time travellers of *Three Go Back* and *Gay Hunter*, peering with wonder at societies they can barely comprehend; the chronicler of so many explorations in Africa, in South America, in the Arctic, with a fascination in who travel and seek to penetrate the mysteries of past and present (which gave rise to *Nine Against the Unknown* as well as to *Niger: The Life of Mungo Park*). Even in Arbuthnott, Mitchell can write with startling clarity from an observer's post: walking his father's fields at harvest time, in one of his most nostalgic and beautifully written essays, he cannot resist the urge to compare Scotland to other autumns he has known:

> Autumn of all seasons is when I realize how very Scotch I am, how interwoven with the fibre of my body and personality is this land and its queer, scarce harvests, its hours of reeking sunshine and stifling rain, how much a stranger I am, south, in those seasons of mist and mellow

fruitfulness as alien to my Howe as the olive groves of Persia. It is a harder and slower harvest, and lovelier in its austerity, that is gathered here, in September's early coming . . .[6]

Just such feelings course through this book. The two archaeologists who give the rather slender plot its basis – the searchers for the Lost Trumpet who are willing to engage Saloney as guide and take him out to the desert along with Abu Zabal from Cairo – are exiles, one from the USA and the other from Jerusalem. The cook is Greek. The Princess Pelagueya, a character taken over from *The Calends of Cairo* where her story begins in 'The Passage of the Dawn', is from Russia.[7] Other characters are wanderers too, from Iceland, from England; only the labourers are on their own territory, digging the sand to unearth their country's history for the benefit of foreigners.

And the search is for the Lost Trumpet, an authentic link to history, to legend, to the stories round which Christian civilisation is based. No coincidence here, for Christian civilisation is one of Mitchell's especial targets. In all his work, but perhaps most nakedly here, Mitchell is advancing the Diffusionist thesis that civilisation is a decline and a mockery, an enslavement of mankind originally free and untrammelled, without property, without shame, without religion, without the ugly baggage of the 1930s which makes the European travellers in Cairo and the desert so strange – sitting down to afternoon tea or dinner, dressing to visit the Princess in her castle, worrying about proprieties of dress or social class or sex. To the Diffusionist, these are alien growths on humanity originally nomadic, free, unencumbered – exemplified by the people he depicts in *Three Go Back*, naked, unashamed, happy. At the opposite end of the scale, the bitterly oppressed slaves of *Spartacus* are driven to rebellion by a civilisation so monstrous they simply cannot accept its dehumanising cruelty any longer. Mitchell had seen that decayed civilisation at closer hand than Rome, having witnessed the effects of a civilisation grinding to a halt in the Depression years, and written about it vividly in his essays ('Glasgow' in *Scottish Scene* and the Duncairn scenes in *Grey Granite*, based – despite his disclaimers – on the slums of Aberdeen).

Perhaps this is what excited him about Cairo,

> Cairo in horror and Cairo in loveliness – lanes and lost cul-de-sacs of
> the festering Warrens that are cloven through the heart by the bright
> sword of the Sharia Mohammed Ali, places where men and women and
> children lived hideous lives far sunk in such abyss of poverty and disease
> as no European has ever experienced; places where children had run
> after us with unclean demands and invitations; places no tourist had ever
> penetrated, dank, lost, courtyarded houses emitting screams of pain as
> we passed . . . These, and the blaze of colour and beauty unescapable
> in the wide khans of the metal-smiths and the leather-workers and the
> place of the fine mushrabiyeh work . . . (121)

The plot-lines of *The Lost Trumpet* spread out from that Cairo of
contradiction yet authentic energy, uninterested in the obvious (the
Pyramid and the Sphinx), interested in the human, the prostitute,
the policeman, the café owner, the tourist guide, the seeker for
something – justice, truth, social order. The most penetrating critic
of the book has been W. K. Malcolm, who writes with justice
of its 'artistic impoverishment', though he judges it 'surprisingly
successful' – not least since the greater part of Mitchell's creative
energy at the time was diverted to *Sunset Song* which was to be
published only a month after *The Lost Trumpet*.[8] The weaknesses
of Mitchell's book are not difficult to list. Some of the characters
are little more than sketches: the mysterious prostitute Huth Rizq
is introduced far too late, and developed far too little, for the
importance she holds in the author's scheme. Some of the minor
characters (one thinks of Georgios' trumpet) are too reliant on
one feature, and Huebsch's massive good nature is overplayed. The
convenient retreat of the Princess' Europeanised home nearby is
certainly handy for the plot to take a rest from the desert and the
digging. All true.

Yet *The Lost Trumpet* succeeds, despite its weaknesses. And
it succeeds because Saloney, like the characters he is supposedly
leading as well as describing, shares the urge to find what he calls
'our essential selves' – 'to dig down below the layers of prejudice and
habit and superficial like and hate and distaste and lust – to find the
essential human being and live with him and be him' (160). First
remove the characters from 'civilisation' and then put them equally

under pressure by harsh surroundings and unfamiliarity, with a restless quest to a short timetable . . . We are in the territory of *Heart of Darkness* and *The Lost Trumpet* veers between that search for the heart of truth, and some fairly heavy-handed philosophising on the diffusion of civilisation from the Nile Valley, its very cradle:

> Had Man indeed once walked free and unhampered of any laws – and been no raving brute of the nights and dawns, but that child of whom the poets had dreamt and sung? Was this world of the last six thousand years no more than a world diseased, a torture and enslavement of the human spirit through the chance of an accident? (159)

Maybe so. But Mitchell saw that one way to lift people out of the ordinary and the comfortable was to take them to the elemental, the land he himself had travelled in the 1920s: 'the roads . . . deserted and Cairo slept dreamlessly but for the purr of the engine. Northwards, over that age-old flowing of the Nile, Sirius crept down the sky, the Dog Star, the hunter of the morning . . . In front the scud of the road. Behind the Nile' (158). When the trumpet is found at last, the past and the present collide in the most dramatic way. Here is a link to a past known at best through distorted accounts: proof that something happened, even if exactly what is not clear, even if we do not know why Huth Rizq knew of the vanished blockhouse before the diggers found it, even if we do not know why the lightning should come at the sound of the trumpet and why it should select her for target.

Mitchell vividly gives the story its climax after its rather slow build-up. And he lets the tension run down – again, Conrad is an apt comparison – by letting the narrator muse on the events of the climactic moments. For Saloney, self-knowledge means he is going back to his own country – indeed, most of the characters find that self-knowledge takes them 'home' from a life of dissatisfied wandering. Whether that home is the topical one of a Russia in turmoil in the 1930s, or the more Diffusionist ideal of 'the golden ghosts of ancient times . . . who lie chained and prisoners, but undying and unslayable, simple and splendid, kindly and gracious, behind the walls of pride and race and creed' (286) within all of us – the novel suggests that its close is more than the tying-up of a mystery plot. History turns out to have a basis in fact, even if the fact is not immediately accessible or intelligible. The vanished generations are not mere skeletons, but have an unexplained life. The cosmopolitan atmosphere of Cairo, the struggling attempts of different peoples to understand one another, indicate some intention on Mitchell's part that mankind cannot live within the prison walls it has built for itself in the 1930s – power, influence, racial prejudice, political dogma, family pride – but that those walls must somehow, like Jericho's, be breached.

If not now, they will be in the book of Revelation, and mankind has a lot of living to do before that trumpet sounds.

Notes

1 Ian S. Munro, *Leslie Mitchell: Lewis Grassic Gibbon* (Edinburgh and London, 1966), pp. 33–4, quoting from a letter to Mitchell's future wife, Rebecca Middleton, 24 November 1921.

2 12 December 1921, quoted from Munro p. 36.

3 Munro tells us (p. 34) that Mitchell met 'a Russian White Officer, typical representative of a vanquished class' while in Egypt and the East.

4 (London, Jarrold, 1931), p. 9: 'a set of stories which would have the mysterious heart of Cairo for background, and should be linked together as the experiences of a Russian exile living in the city'.

5 'J. Leslie Mitchell: An Appreciation', unnumbered double-sided page bound in after p. 286 of *The Lost Trumpet* (London, Jarrold, 1932), reprinted from *The Twentieth Century*.

6 'Autumn', from *Scottish Scene* (1934), reprinted in *The Speak of the Mearns* (Edinburgh, Polygon, 2001), pp. 160–2.

7 Her husband is killed, victim of 'an aching restlessness that had driven Gault to his death in Mesheen, that Pelagueya herself had shared when she let him go'. (*The Calends of Cairo*, p. 282).

8 W. K. Malcolm, *A Blasphemer and Reformer* (Aberdeen, 1984), p. 106. The criticism on pp. 106–11 represents a serious discussion of what is good and bad; this should be supplemented by reading Douglas Young's *Beyond the Sunset* (Aberdeen, 1973), pp. 51–6 and its treatment of the book as an allegorical quest, and most importantly his appendix pp. 154–7 on the short stories. A brief but excellent introduction to the Cairo stories reprinted in *The Speak of the Mearns* is by Jeremy Idle, pp. 218–222.

THE LOST TRUMPET

CHAPTER THE FIRST

'And desire shall fail, and the grasshopper become a
burden.'

Subchapter i

THE night before, passing through the terrace
of Heliopolis House Hotel, I had heard two men
refer to me.

"Who's the old buffer with the beard?" had
queried one, a gay youth, albeit chinless, and with
the adenoidal accent of some little university pant-
ingly in the tongue-tracks of Oxford.

And the other, whom I took to be an English
official of customs, had replied :

"Sh. That's the posh dragoman. Saloney.
Russian. Was colonel in one of those freak little
armies the Reds chased out of the Crimea. Lived
the last ten years as a guide here in Cairo. Supposed
to know it better than the average Cairene."

The chinless youth had shaped an eagerness into
his accent. "Might hire him to show me some of
the gay doin's in the Wagh el Berka. Hwaw?
Sporty?"

"N.B.G."

Then I had passed beyond the range of their voices, a little angered, which was foolish, and very wearied from a day in tramping the Ghizeh sands, which was understandable.

'Buffer.'

That was the word which gnawed at the blankness of my mind, wakening too early the next morning. For a little I lay and looked at it, and searched for that philosophy ten years of Cairo had taught me. But it seemed I had mislaid the thing. 'An old buffer with a beard.'

I got out of bed and, while the kettle hissed above the flame of the unchancy oil-stove, looked at my reflection in the shaving-glass which I did not use for shaving. Bearded (but there *was* a chin below the beard, if I remembered). Old?

At least not young. I saw a face netted with wrinkles, some of the years and some of the sun. A face pallid still, with that Russian pallor that acquiesces not readily to sunburn. Eyes: I had been told they were grey. Now they seemed merely troubled. A kindly nose, a kindly forehead . . .

Or perhaps they were merely weak.

That wry thought abode with me, drinking my coffee, listening to the morning coming over Heliopolis. Weak—of a surety what else? Had I made the seemly grab of wealth or women, lined my soul with satieties or my stomach with the seasonable oyster? None of these things. I was a failure.

Once Adrian had said to me : "Only a man with a bank-balance can afford to look at a sunrise." And I had no bank-balance.

But my sunrises !

I leant from my window, spendthrift yet, to look on this new one. You know that stormy skyward charge of pale hosts of videttes that daylight sends across the Egyptian desert ; these, and behind them the dull-smocked storm-troops (foot-weary and remembering their wives) ; then, bannered and in chariots, the Immortals of the Sun . . .

'Akh God,' I said to myself in some disgust. 'You are becoming a little man of literature.'

And thereat my past drew its head out of limbo, brushed the dust from its hair, and regarded me with surprise.

'Dragoman and tout for the Pyramids ?—perhaps you are. But once you were I—Anton Kyrilovitch Saloney, Professor of English Literature in the Gymnasium of Kazan.'

'That was long ago,' I told my past, 'and now the chinless have inherited the earth.'

And, a little cheered at the puzzled look on the face of my past, I divested myself of pyjamas and rang my bell—no push-bell, but a sturdy instrument once property of some Mameluke. It had acquired notoriety in Heliopolis, this bell of mine, and it was told me that neighbours set their watches by it. They would set them awrong this morning.

After the surprised interval Annie Marie came

fleeting up the stairs and poked her small ferret face
round the door. I said :

"I shall want breakfast in half an hour. And
make it a seemly breakfast, Annie Marie, for it may
be the last that approaching senility will allow me to
appreciate."

She said : "Gobblimey, kurnel, wot's wrong ?"

I explained about the buffer with the beard. My
landlady's Cockney face wrinkled in disgust.

"Aw, on'y some sissy-boy, kurnel. Don't yew
worry. Yew ain't old."

And, nodding, she vanished to heed to my breakfast and the piercing howls of her infant. Of all
Heliopolis she was surely the inhabitant most incon-
gruous—the widow of an English trooper who had
betaken to herself a Greek husband. Of poor
Nicolaos Anastassiou's language she knew nothing ;
and despite much brow-corrugation over an English
text-book he had as yet been unable to identify a
single phrase that spat from the lips of his spouse.
Pursing small, shapely lips he would look upon her
with admiration and awe and remark "pif !" to her
many scoldings. Such scolding uprose to me now.
He had left the infant unattended. I turned to the
window and my dressing with a new twist to my
thoughts. . . . If I had foregone the amorous
possessions had I not foregone the scoldings
also ?

'*And desire shall fail, and the grasshopper become a
burden.*'

So I had read in the English Bible, in those days

in far Kazan. I had loved that phrase, for the beauty
of it and the pity of it. I had not dreamt I would
sometime stand, a middle-aged tourist tout in a
shabby Heliopolitan room, and know it no mere
phrase. Depression came on me again and, clothed,
I sat in the early silence of the Sunday morning
regarding my shelves and the tawdry bindings of
their books. To-morrow and to-morrow and
to-morrow . . .

And then, for the first time in many months—
for it was long since I had risen at such an hour—
there came to me that sound first heard on a morning in 1921, after night-long wandering the Cairene
streets. I had been starving then, when I heard it,
chilled with the long, dark hours, and it came to me
while I looked into the waters of the Nile from
Shoubra Bridge. I had started and listened then, in
that hasting light, and suddenly found myself weeping as I listened. Almost ten years afterwards the
sound brought again that tightness in my throat.

It was only the sigh of the morning wind. But
no such wind comes to any city but Cairo and the
little tourist-towns that squat at her feet on the
desert hem. It grew and grew, coming from the
sands—as a sleepy boy, roused in some desert lair,
uplifting a moment a sounding trumpet across the
sunrise roofs of Heliopolis. Once, twice, he blew,
and at that call of reveille I could see from my window
the marsh-birds wheel from above Zeitoun. Then
the wind had passed on to Cairo, which I could not
see, and day had come upon Egypt.

Subchapter ii

I ate a large and heartsome breakfast. I was old.
Very good. And a buffer. Good also. Shocks were
the lot of buffers. But I had still my chin and my
sunrises.

Midway breakfast Annie Marie brought up my
letters, and I sat and unfolded them while day
unfolded and brightened outside. A bill from
Sednaoui's; some day I would pay the good
Sednaoui. A bill from Simon Papadrapoulnakophitos; some day, were he not more careful, I
would cease to drink at the café of Simon in the
Khalig. Two other envelopes, one in Adrian's
fertile scratch, the other in a handwriting unknown
to me and bearing an English stamp. I regarded
the half-obliterated likeness of the good King
George in surprise, and then broke open the envelope and found this news set forth:

'DEAR COLONEL ANTON,

'You'll have forgotten me, so I'd better re-intro-
duce myself: I'm Roger Mantell.

'And you *do* remember me now, don't you? All
of it? That year that Dawn and I spent in Cairo
when you shepherded us around? And Daybreak
House?* (Who lives there now, I wonder?) And
that night when you and I walked the Nile garden
and Dawn's baby was born? Can't have forgotten

*See "The Calends of Cairo."

any of it, unless you've done so deliberately to spite us for our failure to write you.

'For that, we're infernally sorry, all three of us. The years like great black oxen tread the world, and we've been so busy keeping out of their tracks that it was only a month ago that Dawn, checking her diaries, ejaculated : "Goodness, we haven't written Colonel Saloney for over three years !" And we agreed that that was so bad we daren't attempt to re-open communications. But circumstances have forced the agreement, and we're aiding and abetting them, and quite frankly sending you a request for your favour and patronage. (Unless you're back in Russia by now.)

'And, to make as little bones about it as possible, the favour centres on Aslaug Simonssen.

'Brief biography of said female : Born I don't know when, but somewhere towards the close of the century's first decade. Of Scoto-Norwegian parentage. One of twins, the other being a male, Carl. Lived in Bergen or Edinburgh, God help her, most of her life. Pleasant-looking; beautiful upon occasion. Recently became acquainted with Dawn.

'Sails for Egypt in three days' time; and when she arrives in Cairo we want you to look after her.

'Her mission's an unusual and I think a half-crazy one. (Not that Aslaug is crazy.) Brother Carl went out to Egypt five years ago, it seems, to take up a Government job; oil-prospecting or the like.

He seems to have done it for the fun of the thing, the family being quite comfortably well off. Two years went by, during which he moved from place to place, sending home an occasional letter to Aslaug. Then, at Rashida, while in residence there, he was found one morning with a slit throat.

'Perhaps you saw in the papers something of the fuss there was about the happening? The murderer, however, was never caught. The Egyptian Government sent its condolences and a handsome cheque to Aslaug, and the matter was officially dropped.

'Aslaug, however, refuses to treat the matter officially. She is going to Egypt to investigate for herself. 'Investigate' is a mild word. She's convinced the murderer can be found and intends to find him. In fact, the conviction has become an obsession.

'Now, it's only with diffidence that I'd try to unload a monomaniac on anyone—let alone Colonel Saloney. But Aslaug's too good to waste on this insane search—potentially too good. From what little I've heard of Carl he was no great loss to this planet in his untimely demise.

'So what we want you to do—of course by way of business—is to take Aslaug round the sights of Cairo, if you've no other engagements. Show her the Nile at sunset; show her Daybreak House; and the pyramids and all the other oddities. Inoculate her with Cairo, in fact.

'Then she'll forget and come back to England, like a sensible being.

'And now, my dear Saloney, I'll retire from the field quickly, rather scared at my presumption in making all these staggering requests. Aslaug has promised to wire you when she gets to Alexandria.

'Love from us all, and do write, even though Aslaug's beyond your handling.

'Yours ever,

'ROGER MANTELL.'

I give this letter in full, because for unknown reasons I did not destroy it and it is beside me now. In the stillness of the Heliopolitan morning I remember that I sat long in reminiscence of the Mantells whom I had known and loved in Cairo, in days before the grasshopper——

I started up half-angrily at that. The insect was becoming more than a burden; a nuisance. And as I started I caught sight of the remaining envelope, that in the handwriting of Adrian.

Opened, it told me this:

'DEAR SALONEY,

'If you've nothing special to do when you receive this letter—which will be at breakfast-time on Sunday—come down to Shoubra and see me. Come about eleven o'clock. I want to introduce two people to you.

'They're Americans, both of them, and want to engage you as a guide.

'Now, don't get bored.   If they're not exactly
folk after your own heart, they are at least mildly
interesting fauna in their way—monomaniacs out on
a search they believe portentously important.   And
at least, they aren't tourists.

'Anyhow, come and see them.

'ADRIAN.'

CHAPTER THE SECOND

' "And, as the manuscript relates, the Trumpet . . .
had been stolen and carried away by a renegade
Levite." '

Subchapter i

I RODE into Cairo on a tram-car, and, as we
swerved by the bend that leads to Abbassieh,
the Gift of the River, the City of Many Colours, the
Heart of Masr, lay revealed before us. There was
the dark bulking of Abbassieh, where English
soldiers lounge in boredom and dusty khaki at
barrack-entrances and the little Greek folk of the
catering trades chatter over dank fruit in danker
alleys. There, dark-blue in the west, was Koubbah ;
and in a shimmer far to the south, Manchiet el Sadr.
The day was shining like a burnished shield over
the strange city of Mansur in which for ten long
years I had guided the curiosities of the tourist and
restrained the curiosities of myself.

So I came at last, though not by tram-car, but
walking through the sun-haze of dust-ochred streets,
to the house of Adrian in Shoubra. I stopped outside
the house, I remember, in the hot flare of the sun,
thinking of the first time I had entered it—that
morning ten years before, when Adrian had found

me starving by Nile bank and had brought me home as his guest. He had been curt and brusque then, being ashamed of himself and the human race because of that look he had glimpsed on my face.

"Hungry?" he had said, as he had stood beside me upon the bridge where I listened to the passing trumpets of the sunrise. I had turned round and regarded him without enthusiasm, seeing a small, slight man, dark-faced and pale-handed. The hands had attracted me at once. They were the hands of a surgeon—indeed, though I had not known it, of Cairo's leading gynaecologist.

He had repeated the question. I had nodded. "But damnably."

"Come on, then."

So I had gone with him, wondering and a little amused, in spite of the emptiness within me. And Adrian had fed me and listened to me and comforted me, and had been my friend in days that the locust had eaten, leaving the remains to the grasshopper——

I swore a little to myself. The insects had now doubled in number. I rang with unnecessary vehemence upon the handbell that outjuts from the wall of Adrian's house and stood in the dusty sun-shimmer till his Greek servant opened the door for me.

"The doctor is in the garden," he said, "he and the two millionaires."

"Millionaires?" I had been unprepared for that.

"But certainly. They are Americans."

With that he preceded me into the house, into

that unchanging, commingled no-smell of anti-
septics and back-wearying scrubbedness. In the
rear of the house he abandoned me on the flagged
walk that led to the garden, and going down that
walk I came into the trim floral neatness where
Adrian paces in leisure moments dreaming of new
and paradisal combinations in the game of dominoes'
—his life-passion. Or at least with such concentra-
tions I had been wont to twit him. Now he was
otherwise engaged. In the shade of a tree under the
far wall he sat with two guests. The presumptive
millionaires.

Now of millionaires I have made much study the
while I have elevated their lean or bulging persons
up the steep slopes of the Great Pyramid. Either
they writhe the many hours each day in the agonies
of stomach-ache or their necks obtrude without
pleasantness from coloured collars and tight suits.
A millionaire departing from such canons would
be stared at aghast in the tourist-quarters of Cairo.
So I knew at once that Adrian's servant had been
misled. These were no millionaires.

"Hello, Colonel," said Adrian. "Allow me :
Colonel Anton Saloney—Mr. Huebsch, Mr. Marrot."

Marrot I saw as a pale, thin, lithe man, a little
of Adrian's appearance. He had the face of a saint
but faintly recovered from the austerities of a hair-
shirt. But that, I reflected, might be rather gastritis.
He stood up and held out his hand.

"H'm. . . . Militarist, eh ?"

That was surprising enough. But before I had

time to make comment on my supposedly warlike
nature the large bulk of Huebsch was slowly upraised
behind Marrot's acidulous disapproval.

"Now, Marrot, soft on the propaganda pedal."
His hand, large as two hands of an authentic millionaire, enfolded mine. "Glad to meet you, sir.
You'll have to excuse my colleague here. He's a
communist in his off moments."

"That is interesting," I said. "I have known
other communists."

Marrot raised his eyebrows at me as he sank back
in his chair. "You fought them, I suppose ?"

I shook a deprecating head. "Not at all. I ran
away from them."

"All scoundrels, eh ?"

"On the contrary, I found them appallingly
virtuous."

Adrian had been regarding this by-play with a
school-boy grin. Now he said :

"Sit down, anyhow. Colonel Saloney, I must
explain, was the only communist in the white armies.
He fought against his fellow-believers because they
maltreated the Russian alphabet and wore disorderly
ties. . . . Something like that. But I think the
three of you want to talk about something other than
politics ?"

"Sure we do." Huebsch settled himself, largely,
spreadingly, weightily. The chair creaked below
him in frightened protest. He regarded me with
large, unwinking stare. I stroked the chin-conceal-
ing beard and made appraisal of him myself.

He was a Jew. I have been told that the characteristic features with which we associate the modern
Jew have no true Jewish associations at all; they
are later graftings from Mongoloid and Negroid
converts. But Huebsch made no attempt to slip
behind these apologetics of history. He was in
every detail of appearance the Jew of caricature and
controversy. With a large head, an ovoid head,
whence outbranched a great, curving beak of a
nose. So did his eyebrows curve also, and his lips,
which were thick and red. Almost had he the number
of chins seemly on the déclassé order of millionaire.
He stood a good six feet in height and to the unwary
was apt to seem some six feet in breadth. Also,
which went not at all with the upmake, he had large
blue eyes, deeply-lashed and calm and beautiful eyes,
the eyes of a dreamer who was, of all things, a kindly
dreamer.

"Well, Colonel?" he said.

"Very well," I agreed, for I liked this flaunter of
the oddities Hebraic. He smiled slowly, absent-
mindedly. He brought out a large pipe, apparently
rough-hewn from the bark of some tree, but which
I learnt was a corn-cob pipe. This he proceeded to
stuff with great waddings of tobacco. All three of
us watched him, as I noted, myself noting the other
watchers from the corner of an eye. It was very hot.
Adrian's roses drooped dustily. Not so Adrian
himself, with his head a little to one side, like a cool,
sardonic fowl. Marrot tilted back his chair and
regarded the pearlment of the sky, for in the glare

of the sun the true Cairene azure was now over-
spread by a filament of heat-cloud. From the pipe of
Huebsch ascended now an impressive reek.

"Dr. Adrian will have told you something about
the expedition we're planning, Colonel."

"Not a thing," cut in Adrian. Huebsch nodded.

"Well, well." He turned his gaze, that was somehow vast, and smile, that was unbelievably slow,
upon me. Fascinated, I watched the patient convo-
lutions ebb from his mouth across his countenance.
"Dr. Adrian's still of two minds whether we're
cranks or quacks."

It was now Adrian's turn to appraise the promise
of the weather. "I think you may be—a trifle over-
enthusiastic."

Huebsch pondered this, heavily, but not dully;
as I was soon to note was his unvarying habit in
consideration of all things, great or small. "Well,
well, we may be. Anyway, Colonel, we want to
engage you as our guide and general direction-
finder-in-chief in a little archaeological mission that
has brought us to Cairo."

I made speedy disclaimer. "I am no archaeologist."

"That's one of the points in your favour."

"So ?"

The great ovoid head swung forward slowly;
regained its customary elevation. "Yes. And now
we'll cut the box-string and chew on the cake. If
you'll have us, we'll have you. That so, Marrot ?"

The sky-gazing communist lowered his head to
nod assent. "But hell—a colonel !"

My colonelcy vexed him. This but mildly surprised me. In my ten years in Cairo I had met travellers and tourists by the dozen and in the gross whom the most unexpected things vexed. I had known a man who regarded the Sphinx as an insult to his grandmother's memory (he had also, as was proper to an epileptic in Egypt, believed himself to be Akhnaton); beside such obsession the militarist dislikes of the thin, acidulous American seemed negligible.

"The colonelcy need not worry greatly," I said. "And you may drop the 'colonel' when addressing me. But I beg that you will not call me comrade."

"Why not ?"

He was, I saw, if with a sense of humour in other things, prepared to do battle in defence of even the most minute curlicue on his political creed. I explained, mildly.

"Because I'm not."

Huebsch waved his colleague to silence. "Well, well, and all that's that. Colonel, we're archaeologists from Palestine. For the past three years we've been engaged in excavation in the Jordan Valley— ever been there ?"

I shook my head.

"Haven't missed much—lice, liars and lizards. We did nothing of great importance during the first two years, but you may have heard something of our work last September."

Now, by a curious coincidence, I had. "Something I read in the European journals," I said. Then :

"Huebsch and Marrot—but of course! It was you two who uncovered the walls of Jericho which Joshua overthrew."

"Pat. We discovered that Jericho had been encircled by walls, just as it says in the Bible, and those walls bore every appearance of having been overthrown by some means not accountable on the natural list of unfriendly phenomena—earthquake or the like. In fact, they had the appearance of having fallen just as it is related in the Bible that they did fall."

My interest waned. Two fanatics, it appeared; and I had thought them scientists. What did they wish me to do? Go search the upper Red Sea for chariots from drowned Pharaoh's army, probably, I reflected. Probably, indeed, they were archaeologists so overloaded with preconceived ideas that their mission was to dig up only articles likely to strengthen their preconceptions. . . . Perhaps envoys of the Fundamentalist churches, hot on the track of 'literal truth'! If so, they might bay their optimistic pursuit without my assistance. But with such nose I was disappointed in Huebsch. I had not thought he was of the type to rat to the parvenu superstitions of Christians and Nords . . .

And I regarded him with an amused regret.

He nodded. He seemed to have read my thoughts. "Can't help it. That's as they seemed to be, those walls; and, believe me, their appearance surprised me as much as anybody. Now, I know something of Jewish myth and legend in connection with this event. You may have guessed I'm a Jew ?"

"Not at all. He thought you were a Tasmanian aboriginal."

This was Marrot. Huebsch turned his head, considered his colleague and the interpolation, smiled slowly and vastly. "Well, anyway, Jew I am, and was once pretty conversant with the legendary stuff about the overthrow of Jericho. The result of our excavation raised some fuss, both inside and outside archaeological circles. We had about two tons of letters from all parts of the world on the subject of tumbling walls——"

Marrot chuckled reminiscently. "The best was a circular addressed to a Mr. Wall from some kidney-cure people—about taking pills if one suffered from dizziness."

"Yes. Well, a pretty mixed lot it was, and sent by folk with all kinds of faddist notions. But there was one letter which interested us both. It came from a co-racial of mine in Bokhara—a Samarcand Jew whose family has been resident there since the Dispersion.

"The letter was only an introductory to something else—the copy of a lengthy sheepskin document extracted from his family archives. Well, to make short work of a long story—and I'll miss you out all about my wrestlings to decipher and transliterate bad mediaeval Hebrew—this document purported to tell of the later fortunes of Jericho's conqueror and the magical rams' horns which helped to overthrow the Jericho walls."

It was my turn to make interpolation. "But I understood that, even if the Bible story were authenticated, what caused the overthrow of the good Jericho walls were the not unheavy tramplings of the marching cohorts about them."

"And I always understood it was the Faith, not the Feet, of the said cohorts."

This was Adrian, eyes half-closed to the sundazzle, head brightly cocked, making ironic play on the capital letters. Huebsch considered both of us, kindly, detailedly, massively.

"Well, it wasn't the feet. The walls would have fallen quite differently if it had been. We're a bit beyond the age which believed most things of antiquity could be explained by the shoddy rationalism of the nineteenth century."

Marrot brought down his chair-legs with a bang. "So they can."

The immense Huebsch made a rather weary and deprecating gesture. "We'll leave Karl Marx out of it. He was a Jew, anyway, and would probably have agreed with me. . . . To get back: if the walls of Jericho were overthrown in any dramatic fashion at all—as they were—all the evidence points to it having been done simply through the agency of the rams' horns employed—or, according to this Samarcand manuscript, through the agency of only one of these rams' horns, the magic Lost Trumpet of Joshua."

Nor was it apparently only the ancient and gullible scribe of the manuscript who believed this.

Huebsch himself was quite evidently convinced. I felt a little dazed, spite remembrance of the man who had considered his grandmother's memory insulted by the Sphinx.

"And *you* believe this ?"

The eyes of the American Jew lost their lazy good humour ; they made a fine snapping as of flint and steel in parturition of a flame to uplight an inward dream. "Why not ? It is a theoretical possibility in acoustics that such an instrument could be made. Variations in vibration. . . . Anyway, according to this manuscript the Trumpet of Joshua was never used again. It was kept by the Levites in sanctuary against a great day of need that might come to Israel. That day, says the MS, was Nebuchadnezzar's invasion of Palestine——"

But I could not let that pass. "Surely Jewry had known many days of need—and desperate need at that—before the time of Nebuchadnezzar ? This Trumpet would have been a most seemly instrument to blow against the gates of Gath and so have spared the perspirings of the good Samson."

Adrian stirred. "Who was himself an imported Babylonian myth."

"Being naughty in company with the pure Akkadian sun-goddess Delilah," completed Marrot.

Huebsch waited with monumental patience ; nodded to each of his interrupters ; resumed undeviatingly. "As the manuscript relates, the Trumpet was desperately wanted at the time of Nebuchadnezzar's invasion. And the writer goes on to tell of the

desperate search that was made for it—this instrument that would have blasted Nebuchadnezzar's
hosts from the face of the earth, that with three
blasts would have brought the everlasting hills
about his ears in powder and dust. . . . But no
Trumpet could be found.

"It had been stolen and carried away by a renegade
Levite who had gone to Egypt and become an
Egyptian, a worshipper of idols and a traitor to his
God and country (I'm précising the MS).

"He was followed—after Nebuchadnezzar had
passed away again. Three young men of Judah
journeyed into Egypt to track him down, kill him,
obtain the Lost Trumpet and return with it to
Jerusalem. And they came upon the renegade in
Heliopolis."

"Heliopolis?" For a moment I thought of the
tourist-city in which I myself lived and had vision
of the young men of Judah calling for refreshing
cocktails at the House Hotel bar. Huebsch nodded.

"The old city, of course, not the new. Well, to
précis a précis of what I was going to tell you, the
renegade learned that he was followed and was in
danger of his life. He knew it would be useless to
appeal to the Egyptians for protection; they would
have impounded the Trumpet. But he was also a Jew,
and knew that even though he surrendered the
Trumpet to the young men of Judah he would still
be killed. He disappeared from Heliopolis for three
days during which the pursuers, who had been
setting their snares confident of success and were

at that happening greatly perturbed, searched for
him unavailingly. Then he returned abruptly to
his house, and they entered it that night, and slew
him.

"And there was no Trumpet."

I was leaning forward in some interest by then.
Truth or an ancient fiction, this had interspun in its
texture that glamour of wonder that could still
enthrall me.

"He had taken it away and buried it ?"

"Exactly. Or so they swear in Samarcand. He
buried it about twenty-five miles out from modern
Cairo." Marrot had brought down his chair with a
bang ; had stood up, and was regarding Huebsch
and myself with acid impatience. "Sorry to spoil
the next instalment, but we've a devil of a lot of
work to get through before to-night."

Huebsch glanced at his wrist-watch. "Well, well,
and so we have. Didn't notice that the time had
gone so quickly. An addendum to the MS explains
how the three young men found out that the Trumpet
had been buried. But, of course, they were unable
to do any digging in that hostile country, with some
mile or so of ground to choose. But they left this dusty
record and from study of it and the survey maps,
Marrot and I have narrowed down that once-
indefinite territory to a mile or so again. And we're
going out to search for the cache of the renegade
Levite."

"But—in a mile of country, you said ? Nearly
every foot of Egypt has already been excavated. If

such an interment ever took place, thieves or peasants
must have come upon the treasure long ago."

Huebsch also had stood up. Now, looking down
upon me, he shook his great head.

"They haven't."

"How do you know ?"

"We'd all know. If they'd found it the Lost
Trumpet would have been used again in history."

I had not thought of that. Used ? I think that I
mused aloud, Adrian and those two watching me in
that sunlit garden.

"Titus before Jerusalem—the Jews would have
swept his army from the earth."

Huebsch's great hand came on my shoulder.
But he was not looking at me. He was looking
nowhere, unless into the spiritual mysteries enshrined
in his colossal physical garmenture.

"So you will come with us ?"

I hesitated a moment. Remote in a garden neigh-
bouring Adrian's rose the shrilling of a cicada. In
my brain the grasshopper chirped response. Anything better than to abide in Cairo till that duet
drove me mad . . .

I nodded.

"I will come."

CHAPTER THE THIRD

'I had gone down to the Warrens then, as other
lost souls go down to Hell.'

Subchapter i

THEY had gone. So had not I, for Adrian with
a twitch of his brows had signalled me to
remain. Straying round the garden paths the while
he saw the guests from the premises I put my hands
to my ears, and then laughed at myself, and dropped
them in some shame. If the shrilling of a garden
insect could drive me to this, I had better cease from
life altogether . . .

Adrian reappeared. Behind followed his servant,
tray-laden, with long glasses frostily bespeared.
Adrian sank again into the chair he had but lately
vacated.

"Here's how, Colonel. Neither Huebsch nor
Marrot would look at a spot—prohibitionists in
fact as well as theory." He held up his glass to the
sunlight. "I warned them as a medical man that
that was carrying things too far."

"How did you come to know of them?"

"They came to know of me. Fame. Marrot's
occasionally troubled with the after-effects of a
perfectly devilish stomach-wound—war-relic. He

went to consult Lugden as soon as he came down
to Cairo from Transjordania. Lugden's in Alexandria,
so he came on to me. . . . Hell, to think that he
and Huebsch excavate into life and the pits of the
ancient dead on nothing stronger than lemonade !
You'll have to lay in a private cellar when you go
down with them to Abu Zabal."

"To where ?" I set down my glass, gently, I had
thought, but it reeled and rang on the tray.

Adrian looked up at me, eyes solemn and guile-
less. "Abu Zabal. That's the region where the supposed treasure lies. . . . Is Princess Bourrin still
there ?"

The grasshopper and the cicada had both stilled.
Adrian sprang up. "What's wrong, Saloney ? . . .
Sit down, man."

"A poor plot, my dear Adrian. The Princess has
not been there these last nine months."

He started a little at that. "Hell, I'm sorry,
Saloney. I thought I was doing you a good turn by
stealth. It was time someone did it. . . . No, don't
go. Wait for a little plain speaking."

I waited. He prowled to and fro under the tree-
shade for a little. Then :

"Curious chap that you are, Saloney. And plain
speaking isn't so easy to you, after all. What *is*
wrong with you these days ? I'd thought it was this
confounded Princess of yours, but surely nine months
should have cured you. Or haven't they ?"

I picked up my hat. "My cure has been a counter-
irritant, Listen !"

We listened, Adrian with his bright bird's head on one side. "Only a cicada. What has a grasshopper to do with it ? . . . Where are you going ?"

"A little walk in the footsteps of Dante."

Subchapter ii

I was in the drained canal which is called the Khalig el Masri. To this day one may see the tide-marks on old houses. Brown men in dim shops and tarbouches, drinking of arrack and deep in interminable games of chess ; Jewesses, with imitation harem-veils pendent from brow to chin, slipping in and out the throngs, encavaliered by red-lipped, scented hes ; automobiles, with tourists and honkings, out on a day's sight-seeing ; a string of camels, burdened and ill-smelling, snarling and stately, dun hulks against the polychromatic drifts. . . . The Khalig.

So I came at last to the café of the little Simon Papadrapoulnakophitos. And there, at my wonted table, I sat with my head between my hands and heard the street-sounds die and pass and rise again.

'The years that the locusts have eaten.'

'And desire shall fail, and the grasshopper become a burden.'

I summoned the little Simon then, passing with his worried, wrinkled face.

"I am plagued with insects, my good Simon."

He made shocked motions towards my chair. I restrained him.

"No, no, not fleas. Locusts and grasshoppers."

"M'sieu' has been out in the sun?" He was palpably startled, for he had an affection for me. "I will bring him some brandy."

He brought the brandy and I sat and drank it. A prostitute, poor and painted and tattooed, went by. A sakkah passed, trudging footsore. A party of yellow-booted little Syrian men. Camels. A long emptiness of street. A scowling gendarme. . . . I stared at the street through the brandy fumes.

The Princess Bourrin?

I, the teller of tales, the romantic tourist-tout, life's spectator—to sit in sick bitterness over a story told and closed and hidden away on a dusty shelf! Because of the chance words of a meddling Englishman I must bring that story from its shelf again, and scuffle the heat-warped pages, and hear the clamour and cries of years that the locusts had eaten . . .

The brandy, of course. Out of the years and out of the Khalig, gay and unfaded as ever she came, she who had then perhaps loved me almost as I loved her—if eighteen may ever love as thirty-five. The Princess Pelagueya Bourrin; absurdly clad as were women in those days—though I had gone unaware of the absurdity; tall and dark and white and gold—all those, for somehow she had had gold colour even in the blue blackness of her hair; white with our Russian whiteness, that somehow is not pallor, though I would use that word but for the later twist of meaning that it bears in English ; long of limb—but even then she herself would have said "leg", loving to shock Kazan's starched little circle of the bourgeois-nobility ; a wide mouth, with fine and full lips and a little shading of dark down below that seemly, shapely nose. . . . That had been Pelagueya, lost from sight and hearing of me in the blur and din of the October Revolution. And, almost unchanged, almost thirteen years later, it had been the Pelagueya who had accosted me in the hall of Shepheard's Hotel in Cairo.*

But if unchanged in appearance——

I drank off a second glass of brandy, sitting outside Simon's café in the dust and glare of the Sunday afternoon, remembering then how Pelagueya had told me she was leaving Cairo as the mistress of an Englishman, Gault.

And Gault had been my friend.

Loved each other ? They had hated each other at first, these two. She had sold herself to Gault in a gay, callous desperation. As brutally he had bought her ; he, the explorer from Sahara, hungry for the touch and sight of women. They had left Cairo together, and together, by some queer accident, had fallen in love—there, at Gault's Turkish house in Abu Zabal.

And then Gault had gone away again, the explorer's urge upon him ; and he had been killed by raiding Tuareg in the mountains of Mesheen,

*See "The Calends of Cairo."

and Pelagueya, coming out of days of agony and dazed disbelief, had turned to my friendship for months, till I had remembered things older than friendship——

Spectator unmoving on the fringe of life! Fool and renegade and dreaming traitor as I had known myself. For, a morning three months after the death of Gault, I had journeyed down to Abu Zabal with but one intent and one purpose; a winter day of clarity and cold sunshine; and Pelagueya's eyes, questioning and clear. And I had looked in those eyes, and suddenly had known myself old and sick and tired, fit subject for the jeers of a tourist-tout in a later day.

Love—I could not cease to love her though I tried. And I found it a love as remote from life and reality, the touch of her and the sight of her and the sweet blood in her body, as the ghost desire that haunted still the bones of Gault in wild Mesheen . . .

Subchapter iii

It was late that night when I left Abbassieh and trudged out on the long lamp-lit road to Heliopolis. And suddenly I found myself footsore and tired enough from my long strayings in the Cairene streets after leaving the shelter of Simon's hospitable awning. For an unreasoning urge had come upon me there to revisit those streets and scenes across which the locust had flown, devouring ten years of my life.

I had had the notion that if I went cautiously and carefully, somewhere—perhaps after all I had drunk too much of Simon's brandy—I would find explanations and expiation. Even I, the frozen onlooker on life's hates and follies and loves !

I had gone down to the Warrens then, blindly, as other lost souls go down to Hell. Down the Khalig, in that late afternoon strong sunlight ; out through the dusty bazaars, by the Suq el Fahlamin, cobalt and deserted, past the frowning walls of Citadel, up and around and on to those walls on a sudden impulse, so that all Cairo lay below me. Cairo, Polis Polychrois, with no single colour of its spectrum that for me, as other men, could shine and abide and be mine . . .

Down dim dark lanes as the evening came on I had wandered—lanes overhung with crumbling balconies, lanes unknown even to me, dark corridors where the poor and rejected—the maimed and brutalized of this thing that East and West these thousand years have called civilization—lived their dark and fetid lives, and somehow found still the courage to raise those bursts of laughter that I could hear far in dim, stifling courtyards ; still to bring with hope unlessened new life to add to that ferment of pain and want, for children suckled at unshielded breasts in almost every doorway ; still to live and lust and seek——

The Cairene woman of the Warrens has ever gone unveiled ; there has been little enough for body-wrapping, far less the blinding of the face that so shocks the Muslim God and stirs amorous passion in the Muslim angel. So, in one doorway—and this had been near to sunset, when wave on wave of light, that somehow was not light but darkness with ghost-foam of light on the fringe of each wave, rolled and lapped with a soft hiss over the towering khans—I had stood a long while and looked at a woman who played with a baby in her lap. Only she was no woman; she could scarcely have been sixteen years old.

"What is he to become when he grows up?" I had asked, not idly, but in desperate earnestness.

She had smiled up at me then, already with a face anxious and lined, this child already a mother, prey and partner of that eyeless lust that haunts the hovels of the poor. And suddenly she had smiled, with the three-pointed tattoo-star below her nether lip for a moment dimly symbolic.

"A man," she had answered, and smiled again.

Subchapter iv

And out on the Heliopolis road, remembering that answer, I laughed. What hope or help for me in the mindless hope of a woman of the Warrens? The days when either a word or a phrase could enslave me were surely over. Reality or fantasy? Truth or delusion? Like Gallio, I cared for none of these things.

For me, the grasshopper. Sleep and retreat and a

clinging to safe friends and known places. For me the dragoman's whine and the dragoman's patter, and all the hum and the colour of Cairo wherein I might have no time to think. This search of the American archaeologists—to-morrow I would send them a letter resigning from the expedition.

CHAPTER THE FOURTH

‘ "There are many slaveries," I said. "Those of the lash and those of the liquor; and the little men who are slaves of hope, and the bond-serfs of a creed of hate." ’

Subchapter i

NEXT morning, to counter-balance my early stirrings on the Sunday, I overslept. Nor did Annie Marie awake me until necessity beat with urgency upon her door. In dream I heard the sound and imagined myself back again in Crimea, watching the bombardment of Perekop Fortress across the Sivash Boloto. Presently, however, half-awake, I was aware that the barrage against Perekop had ceased and that someone shook me ungently by the shoulder.

So I awoke to find my room filled by the dazzle of Egyptian sunshine and the heated presence of my landlady.

" 'Ere, kurnel, two blokes in a car lookin' f'r yew. 'Mericans."

"Americans?"

"Yers. Fat un an' a thin. 'Ere's yer breakfast. I told 'em yew'd be down in a quarter of an hour." She peered at me anxiously, concernedly, knowing that these were probably clients who awaited me. "Yew will, won't yew?"

I remembered Huebsch and Marrot then. I sat up.
"Tell them I will be down in less."

Dressing, my mind was firm in my resolve of the
previous evening. A month at Abu Zabal in company
with an incarnation of Joshua and a clipped avatar
of Spartacus—I had sooner go back to Russia !

Below, I found them sitting in an aged Darracq,
Huebsch at the wheel, the corn-cob pipe fast-gripped
between his jaws, Marrot lolling in the rear seat,
his feet upended on the prone girders of the hood.
I went out of the doorway and was greeted by them
and roar of the engine as it leapt to asthmatic life
under the force of the self-starter.

"Jump in, Colonel. Guess we want you to pilot
us through the Ministry of the Interior."

"But—" I was about to make my resignation.
Huebsch shook a worried head.

"Jump in. I can't hold her much longer. . . .
This is the first time I've driven an auto."

So I guessed. We missed dismemberment of
Nicolaos's eldest boy by a hair's breadth, almost
scraped a yawning and early waiter from the steps
of Heliopolis House Hotel, yammered wildly amid
the ruts of the tram-tracks and then found ourselves
headed erratically for Cairo.

I had gained the rear seat by Marrot's side. Now
he was sitting upright, shouting directions to the
gigantic worriedness of Huebsch. His hair was on
end, his pale face flushed. He gripped me at one
particularly lunatic lurch of the vehicle.

"Stick it. . . . This is Huebsch's first go, but

he's learning. . . . Oh, hell, not that knob ! That's
acceleration. . . .   With the right foot, man, the
right foot !"

Huebsch braked.   The two donkeys, making
Cairowards laden with vegetables, swerved in panic.
The objurgations of their master melted away behind
us. Marrot leant back with a sigh.

"He's never before had time to learn steering, so
I thought I'd put him on to it this morning."

Like a schoolboy, my spirits were rising in the
wild exhilaration of the lunatic ride.   I closed my
eyes as a tramcar rushed upon us, towered above
us, repented and flashed past.   "He appears—an
enthusiastic pupil."

"He'd learn anything, Huebsch."

The ferocity of our career through the Cairene
streets gradually lessened in degree. By the time
we came to the Ministry the great face and neck of
Huebsch though beaded with perspiration were no
longer knotted with anxiety.   He decanted himself.
We followed suit.   The automobile groaned its
relief.

Huebsch smiled at me his slow, gigantic smile,
his curving nose outjutting from his face like the
beak of a benevolent vulture. "Say, Colonel, guess
I deserve a medal."

Marrot was brushing the dust from his hair.   "If
you'd asked that donkey-driver he'd have said you
deserved shooting."

Huebsch pondered this ; shook his head. "He
wasn't in danger—much."   He turned again to me.

"And now—you're coming with us to dig up the Lost Trumpet, aren't you ?"

I hesitated only a moment. "I had intended to say no. But now—yes, I will come."

"That's good. Adrian rang us up yesterday and said you were down in the dumps and likely to resign. And we didn't want you to, Colonel. So Marrot and I plotted the little jaunt of this morning to shake your cobwebs clear."

Subchapter ii

So, through a schoolboy ruse—and on the realization of that with a shrug of indifference—I found myself committed to a month's contract to guide these two on the desert fringe of Egypt, to engage native labourers for excavation, to engage a cook, to superintend the collecting of stores and the granting of permits—"Everything, in fact," said the acid Marrot, "except lick Huebsch's boots twice nightly and once before breakfast—though that would no doubt make your position a sinecure. You are, my aristoemigré, a wage-slave. How do you like it ?"

"There are many slaveries," I said. "Those of the lash and those of the liquor ; and the little men who are slaves of hope, and the bond-serfs of a creed of hate."

He said to Huebsch : "By God, but I believe the ex-militarist is sneering at me. Put him dowd, Huebsch. You're his employer."

This was at Simon's café in the Khalig to which I had taken them sight-seeing and to complete details of the agreement. Huebsch withdrew his earnest, enormous interest from the Street of All Egypt, and viewed us with absent, titanic benevolence.

"I guess we'll get on all right. Mustn't mind Marrot, Colonel. Now we've most of the necessary permits from the Ministry of the Interior we can start getting gear together to-morrow."

I drew out my note-book, making notes of his requirements. The Khalig voices cried around us and over the roofs the sun was setting against a background like a field of dandelions. So, pausing in the list-making, I pointed out. Marrot, surprisingly, agreed. "Glorious. Fascinating city, yours, Saloney."

I had pointed out the sunset for the benefit of Huebsch. And here, upsettingly, was a communist with aesthetic appreciations ! I sought refuge in my list again.

"And the cook ? Shall I myself select him ?"

"Sure," Huebsch directed. I hesitated, for the curve of his nose had suddenly suggested caution to me. And, in the fashion which was uncannily common to him, he knew at once that I hesitated.

"Can you manage that all right ?"

"Surely," I said. "But—is there not a special meat that your nation eats ?"

Marrot's acid pipe of laughter rose. "Kosher, b'God ! Oh, hell !"

Huebsch looked from one to the other of us, a

kindly, unmoved Gargantua. "I'm a Jew, but the older type of Jew, y'understand."

"Older? You mean of the New Jews—the Reformers?" I suggested, helpfully.

Marrot explained. "Not a bit of it. Huebsch holds that the olden Jews never kept the Mosaic law in all its nonsensical details. They were merely aware of the Levites and their rules as so many handy ready-reckoners. But they themselves were too much concerned with things of the spirit to worry everlastingly over details of feeding and bedding and genuflexion like the modern Orthodox Jew. . . . The things of the spirit being David's rape of Bath-sheba and Solomon's marrying of a thousand wives——"

Now, near to us, at the single other table which the little Simon had placed outside the café that evening, a young man had lolled in a chair, a great flame of a red sombrero over his eyes, ever since we had sat ourselves down. He had sat with the immobility of a sack and something of its appearance, a bottle of the little Simon's Greek brandy almost empty near his elbow. Idly I had noted from the corner of an eye that he had lately shown signs of stirring. Now, abruptly, he did more than stir, coming to life and his feet with a swaying deliberation. He clutched at Huebsch's shoulder, steadied himself, and peered down at us.

"Solomon? Don't worry over Solomon. Used to have a spot of respect for him myself, but all that's gone. Not a spark of wisdom in the old fungus. Listen" :

He threw back his head and, still clinging to
Huebsch's shoulder, burst into a foolish scrap of
song :

> " 'Old King Solomon had ten thousand wives —
> *And the damn fool slept with his fathers !'*

"Mark that. Ten thousand of them. In gold they
were, Caucasian gold ; white Greeks and the lovely
things of Lebanon. The Shulamite was there, and
the Queen of Sheba. Love and loveliness like lilies
curled in a garden awaiting him. . . . And what
did he do ? Slept with his fathers ! He was no ancient
sage ; he was a soft-breeched little modern. Round
the door he'd peek of an evening and see them
waiting in battalions—all loveliness and all delight
and all pain and all fine-edged agony. And what
would he do ? Nip back and sleep with his
fathers . . ."

He leered down at Huebsch. "Don't take it to
heart, sonny," the great Jew advised him, placidly.

For a moment the young man seemed a little taken
aback. Then : "Haven't you any bowels of com-
passion for your ancestors ? Slept with his fathers.
Fathers, mind you. In the plural. And his mother
—what must his mother have been like."

Huebsch disengaged himself, still placidly. "Pretty
fast, pretty fast, I guess. Sit down, young man.
You're a little bit snooted."

The young man breathed heavily, swayed, and
stared at Huebsch. The three of us stared up at him :

Picturesque and amazing indeed was his attire—the red sombrero, the Greek jacket, the flannel trousers and rubber shoes. Below the hat was a wild swirl of brown hair, and below that a face like a faun's— a faun meditating incarnation as a satyr.

"Snooted? At this time o' night? D'you think I'm a damn language-murdering Jew from Volsteadia? When I *am* snooted, to quote your elegant jargon—oh, boy!"

"Well, well, well," said Huebsch. "You don't like America?"

The young man clutched at Huebsch's shoulder again, and stared round our table malevolently.

"America! Banned my books there, blast them. And why? Because the fat and frothy Middle West still believes that children come out of eggs. Exactly that. . . . America! Good God, and to think that the continent where the intelligent Mound-Builders and Maya lived gracious and seemly lives is now the spawning bed of half the transported scum of Eastern Europe, embedding its beastly jaws perpetually in the spoil of gum-forests and enunciating its ghastly sentimentalities in what it believes to be the tongue of Shakespeare! Snooted? It's just that the American boorzhoi stirs my bile, and I wanted to watch the asinine amazement on your deplorable faces. And I have. Faugh! . . . May your blasted continent sink!"

He swung uncertainly towards Simon (who bowed scaredly), handed over an Egyptian pound note, and swayed away down the Khalig, his sombrero

borne like a beacon of revolt. I had listened in some
considerable amusement, Marrot with acid contempt. Huebsch turned his immense head and neck
to follow the young man's progress with kindly
commiseration.

"Well, well, your Cairo's interesting right enough,
Colonel. What was the boy? Scotch?"

"English, I think."

"Thought he might have been from the Northern
half and couldn't touch anyone for a spot of the
home-brewed when he was over the Pond. Reminds
me. . . . More beer, Colonel?"

"Please."

He ordered more beer for me and had the glasses
of Marrot and himself recharged with a horrid mess
of bubbling, coloured waters. I drew my list towards
me again. It had grown intensely light, awaiting the
sunset.

"We had not settled about the cook. But if there
are no dietetic drawbacks, I think I might be able to
engage one here."

"From this café?"

I nodded and called to the little Simon. He came
in an ingratiating hurry to our table and his eyes
lighted at my request.

"If your cousin Georgios is still with you, will
you bring him here? I might find him work for a
short time."

"The job!" He threw up his hands. "Now Mary
Mother but grant him sense and discretion. I will
fetch him at once."

Huebsch looked a question. Marrot put his in words. "What's happening ? We've no Modern Greek, either of us. But the little man looked mightily bucked."

"It was at thought of getting rid of his cousin, our prospective cook."

Marrot raised sardonic brows. Huebsch considered the matter with heavy, just deliberation.

"Well, well. But it doesn't sound much of a recommendation."

I hastened to explain. "Georgios Papadrapoulnakophitos was cook at the Pension Avallaire, so you may have no doubts as to his culinary skill. He was dismissed from his post but a month ago, and has since then been wasting his talents in the kitchen of the little Simon."

Again, with that slow unhastingness that I was beginning to admire, Huebsch bent over the matter —like a Father of the Sanhedrin debating capitulation to the Army of Titus, said a flippant imp in my mind.

"And why was he dismissed ?"

"He knelt on the stomach of the manager, I believe, and beat the manager's head against the floor."

Marrot turned his head and surveyed his colleague's girth with interest. "Excellent. Just what you require to tone you down, Huebsch." But quite evidently his interest had kindled in the Georgios who was now doubtlessly doffing his apron and brushing his moustachios. . . . I shook my head.

"He did it with no hope or desire that the communist revolution would follow these activities. The manager's failure to appreciate music was the cause."

"Music ?"

"Here is Georgios himself. He speaks French."

Simon piloted his cousin amid the tables to the place where we sat. He was perhaps five feet in height—or should I say shortness ?—with the large head and serious eyes, no apron, and verily the great sweep of moustache fresh brushed and glistening. He might have been forty years of age. He bowed, sweepingly, astoundingly, favouring me with a quick, commendatory smile. I looked a gravity I did not altogether feel.

"Georgios, these gentlemen are archaeologists. They and I are going out to Abu Zabal to dig in the earth for ancient instruments. We want you to come as cook—providing you will relate to MM. les Americains your exact reasons for assaulting the manager of the Avallaire."

"Messieurs, he insulted my art !"

"Your cooking ?" Marrot, ever the quicker, questioned with eyebrows and clipped French. Simon's cousin made a contemptuous gesture.

"Cooking ! I could cook M'sieu's hat and the note-book of Colonel Saloney into a mess that the three of you would devour with cries of delight. Cooking—M'sieu', I am the best cook in Cairo and would long ago have been recognized as such but for the jealousy and hatred of my skill among the

clown-like of the hotels. But my art—M'sieu', I
play upon the silver bugle."

He paused, looking at us not at all like a cook
seeking a situation, but like the great musician he
believed himself. I think all three of us kept grave
faces. He nodded again.

"The silver bugle, Messieurs. Music—it is my art,
my passion, my life. In every moment that is mine
I retreat to my room and seek to find the sum of
beauty in the long sweetness of some single note. So
I did at the Avallaire, and they listened, astounded
and respectful, saying nothing. . . . Till the coming
of the new manager."

"And what did he do ?" inquired Marrot.

"M'sieu', he burst into my room the second day
he came, saying that I raised a hideous noise like to
crack the walls. When I understood I laid aside my
little bugle and answered that perhaps his head would
achieve the result more quickly. Then I took him
by the ears, Messieurs, and beat his head against the
wall, and beat it upon the floor, and might have
beaten in his empty skull but for the fact that his
screams brought him rescuers. Then I left the
Avallaire, I and my little bugle."

He stopped. I looked at Marrot. Marrot, lighting
a cigarette, looked at Huebsch. The great Jew, it
was plain, was slowly and justly working out the
matter in all its details.

"Now, Georgios, we want a cook," he said at
last, carefully, "and Colonel Saloney here recom-
mends you. We'll pay you a decent wage, but you

must understand that we're going out to a place that
is practically a desert, so there will have to be certain
restrictions—even, I'm mighty sorry to say, on your
activities as a musician."

The little Greek stiffened absurdly.   Huebsch
nodded, ponderously.

"Now, I'm not like the manager of the Avallaire.
I don't resent music. It's just that I know nothing
about it. To be frank, Georgios, I'm so ignorant
in the matter that I would probably know no difference between a boy tootling on a tin whistle and the
exquisite sounds which I don't doubt you produce
on your bugle."

The haughtiness was smoothed away from
Georgios' face. He nodded commiseratingly.

"I understand, M'sieu'. There are such men—
and it is no fault of theirs."

"Exactly. Now, I can't answer for Colonel Saloney,
but my colleague here is exactly the same. Completely unmusical. So, when we go to our camp at
Abu Zabal, and you find the time and inclination to
practise your art, you understand that it'll have to
be done at some distance from the camp. Both in
our interests and in yours. We'd have no appreciation and would merely be distracted from our
researches ; while you yourself, if you practised in
our vicinity, would be constantly vexed by the
thought that you were wasting your genius on ears
both dull and indifferent."

Georgios saw that. "M'sieu', I thank you, and
will certainly comply with that condition. M'sieu'

may be no musician, but he has the understanding heart."

"Well, well. Then I guess Colonel Saloney'll fix you up about pay and so forth later. We start in two days' time."

The Khalig was alive with hasting lights. Night had come. The doorway of Simon's café cast us a dark, humorous wink as the form of the entering Georgios blotted out its radiance a moment. Marrot's acid chuckle suddenly smote the air as we rose to our feet to leave.

"You never know ; a player on the silver bugle —he might be useful in an allied capacity."

"Eh ? . . . How ?"

"Why, when we find the Lost Trumpet."

CHAPTER THE FIFTH

'South we went towards Abu Zabal, past deserted
Helmieh and its lost block-houses in the sands, into
that quiet, pale country.'

Subchapter i

FANTASTIC as might be the nature of the search
on which we were setting forth, neither Huebsch
nor Marrot displayed impracticability. From morning till night I was in constant activity here, there
and the many other places all over Cairo. They had
sold or otherwise disposed of their archaeological
equipment in the Jordan Valley, and fresh tools in
abundance had to be procured—spades, levels, sieves
and filters, casket-like crates wherein to bestow the
treasures buried so long ago by the renegade Levite
or other weak-brained ancient. With Marrot for
adviser I also engaged the native labourers and
purchased provisions.

There were ten labourers—Egyptian fellaheen, all
of them, immigrant countrymen who had found
the life of Cairo no great improvement on the
immemorial slavery of Nile-bank's little fields. Marrot
would have offered them double the current rate of
wages, but I restrained him.

"That is far above the normal rate."

"But how the devil can they live?" he protested.

"It is a low wage. Yet they will consider it good —at least, until the communist revolution."

He nodded. "When I hope they'll cut the throats of all such parasites as ourselves."

"I shall be pleased to watch Mr. Marrot approving of having his throat cut for political reasons."

So we would spar, yet we grew to a certain degree of friendliness. With Huebsch it was otherwise; to me it seemed impossible that anyone could fail to admire that immense, unswerving, unhesitating devotion to clarity and justice and good sense that was his. But Marrot added his footnote.

"The worst of Huebsch," he remarked, while we stood watching the Jew discussing with a salesman the hire of a suitable lorry, "is that he's got no sane and believable purpose in the world—and knows it."

"No purpose?"

"He'd give his life to know what the hell he's alive for."

Subchapter ii

We set out for Abu Zabal at nine o'clock on the Wednesday morning and arrived near eight at night. Setting forth this record I am struck again by that sad lack of the unexpected in Egyptian weather. All mornings of those months are cloudless; ours of that day no less. In front of us, piloted by a labourer who had affirmed to a knowledge of lorries, the hired Leyland wobbled unchancily from the Abbassieh yard. It was loaded with much gear and stores, the nine other labourers, and, perched high above all other burdens, Georgios Papadrapoul-nakophitos, clutching in one hand two indignant chickens in a coop and in the other a case that I guessed to contain his silver bugle.

Our aged Darracq Marrot drove on this occasion, Huebsch sitting greatly and placidly beside me in the back seat. He drove with one hand, did the thin, sardonic Marrot, and with that single hand performed those prodigies of skilful steering and retarding that is the genius of the born motorist.

Through Abbassieh, into the radiance of the sunlight coming down the road from Heliopolis. The morning freshness had not yet quite gone. In the air through which our Darracq sped, chasing its own shadow, there was still the tang of night coolness. Bugles were blowing in the English barracks. A train of donkeys; a squad of native soldiers, with thin, pipe-stem legs absurdly enwrapped in those puttees imitated from the English; a hospital matron on a motor-cycle; three camels swaying in line, the little bell of their leader tinkling down the road. . . . We were following that route that Pelagueya and her lover had taken two years before. And the day brightened, and the sun climbed the sky, and in front of us the lorry, emulating an inebriated snake, curvetted Abu Zabal-wards.

But a little beyond Heliopolis, on the Helmieh road, it came abruptly to a standstill, almost jerking the little Georgios from his perch. His caged fowls screeched. So did Georgios. Leaning down, clinging to an out-jutting leg of furniture, he cursed the driver resourcefully. We drove up and stopped.

"What is wrong?" I asked the driver, a labourer who bore the heroic name of Kalaun. He had dismounted and was peering under the bonnet of the Leyland. He grinned sheepishly, looking sideways at the other two labourers who had occupied the seat with him. There was silence until Georgios, craning perilously over the front of the vehicle, explained scornfully:

"Messieurs, the man is a fool, as were doubtlessly his parents—if ever he had any. They brought—he and the others—the pail of tea with them, and to keep it warm placed it inside the bonnet. Now it is spilled and the engine refuses to function."

"Is this the case?" I asked Kalaun. He grinned again, exasperatingly. Huebsch, Marrot and I descended and inspected the damage. I had certainly seen a cleaner engine. Huebsch looked at it carefully, looked consideringly at Kalaun, opened his lips to speak, and was at once forestalled by Marrot.

"No, you don't, Huebsch. Cut it out. He didn't know any better. How the hell can you expect him to? Pay him starvation wages and expect expert mechanical skill—!" He snorted angrily and took off his jacket. "Damn nonsense."

Huebsch shook his head. "Well, well, I wasn't going to slate the boy, so what's the fuss?"

Marrot had turned his back on us. Huebsch considered that back carefully, and, as it seemed to me, compassionately. Mystified, I went to the assistance of Marrot.

At length, after much expenditure of rags and much sluicing with ill-to-be-spared water, we had the engine cleansed and restarted. Kalaun and his sheepish companions resumed their seats. We did the same in the Darracq. The lorry jerked forward, paused consideringly in a fashion that was somehow reminiscent of Huebsch himself, and then, gathering speed, fled in advance of us at such rate as caused Georgios and his chickens to oscillate wildly. Huebsch chuckled.

"Better get down to it, Marrot. Else we'll not be in time even to hear the dying wishes of your protégé."

The Darracq fled in pursuit. I turned to Huebsch.

"This incident—Kalaun and his fellow tea-drinkers. What did Mr. Marrot fear? It would have been well for Kalaun to be rated in the matter."

The great Jew beside me sighed ponderously, settling himself in a greater comfort. "I know. Done the boy a power of good. But Marrot won't hear of that kind of thing—not even though it was to save his own life five minutes later. You see, he's obsessed with the cruelty of employers to employed. He had some pretty shocking experiences of it himself in the war—he enlisted as a private in the army. And he's never forgotten that thin time. I've seen him look murder at a man speaking sharply to a waiter. And up in Transjordan he punched the head of a British sub who had hit an orderly. . . . And I must say the orderly was only getting what was coming to him."

I followed out this circumlocution, but it lessened the puzzle of Marrot but little. I had not associated such passionate humanitarianism with his cold, sardonic being. "Surely this is no part of the orthodox Marxian creed?"

"Communism? Oh, he's a communist more from sentiment than economics, I guess. Best archaeologist in the Near East—if only he'd give himself to the job in hand. His failing is that he lacks a purpose."

"Eh?"

"A purpose, Colonel. If he could see through the fogs of time and circumstance the real purpose he's intent on he'd make it bald-headed though it cost him his life."

Subchapter iii

South we went towards Abu Zabal, past deserted Helmieh and its lost block-houses in the sand, into that quiet, pale country on the desert fringe, flat and sad and steaming a little, with its squares of fields vanishing to right and left in the haze, and the mud-walled villages creeping up from each horizon in a glitter of white mosque and dovecote. Near 'Ain the lorry stopped to provide leisure for the labourers to descend and lunch. We saw the halted dot two

miles and more off before we came up with it. A
mile away we did more than see—we heard. And it
was horrible—like the screaming of a lost soul in a
Sivaistic purgatory, I thought. Huebsch started
from sleep as though he had been knifed.

"What in hell's that row?"

And then I had it. "That, if I mistake not, is the
good Georgios making music at the lunch-halt."

Nor was I mistaken. There he was, a little apart
from the canal-ford and the lorry, his absurd little
figure drawn up pursily, the coop with the chickens
at his feet, the silver bugle at his lips wailing in
dreadful anguish. Marrot stopped the Darracq and
appealed to him.

"For God's sake fight fair, Georgios. Remember
your bargain with us."

Our cook ceased from mortal metal strife, regarding Marrot with a chill hauteur. "*In* the camp,
M'sieu', there are certain conditions. But not before."

"Quite right. But as a favour——?"

The little man polished the mouth of his ornate
instrument and returned it to its case, regretfully.
"I shall always be happy to oblige M'sieu'."

Huebsch levered himself from the Darracq.
"Could you oblige us with a bite of tiffin, then?"

"It is ready, M'sieu'."

And there, miraculously, at the other side of the
ford, under the dusty drooping of a solitary
eucalyptus tree, was spread the small table-cloth,
flanked by three camp-stools. Napery and plates
gleamed. Cold chicken and freshly boiled eggs were

ready. Coffee steamed. There was a fine salad.
Georgios served us with skill and impressiveness.
We, the two Americans and I, sat and marvelled
humbly and ate greatly. Marrot said :

"Georgios, I have no soul for music, but I don't
doubt after this meal that you are as great a musician
as a cook. No man with a soul lkie yours could make
a poor show at anything he tried."

The little Greek beamed upon him. "M'sieu' will
have more coffee ?"

We lay beneath the shade of the eucalyptus and
spread maps, considering Abu Zabal and its features.
To the left of the road was the village, as I knew.
To the right a track wound down through a semi-
cultivated tundra waste to that Turkish house on the
desert fringe where Oliver Gault and Pelagueya
Bourrin had consummated their sad, mad love-
saga. Of other features in the district I was uncertain. Nor did I alone own to uncertainty, for the
maps seemed equally vague. But Huebsch and Marrot
had already the lie of the excavations plotted in their
minds.

"We'll take this road turning down to the right.
We're then in the lands of Selim Hanna, who has
given us permission to dig up where we will," said
Huebsch.

"So he damn well might, considering what we've
paid him."

"Well, well, down to the right. We can't be
sure of the most likely digging spots until we get
there and attempt to synchronize the details of the

old MS and the modern contours of the land. Now this house here, I'm told, belongs to the mistress of an Englishman, Gault, who was killed in Sahara eighteen months ago——"

"Is the harlot in residence?" inquired Marrot.

"M'sieu', the lady is a Russian princess—and my friend."

Both stared at me. Huebsch rubbed his chins consideringly. Marrot said:

"Glad of it. But I seem to have offended you. Why?"

"Does that need explaining?"

"Should think so. I said: Is the harlot in residence? Just as I'd have said: Is the plumber in residence? or: Is the married woman in residence? Just as I'd refer to any of them by their professions if I didn't know their names."

"Your references are too glib. The Princess Bourrin is not a harlot. She and Gault were lovers, free and equal, in that sense which you communists are supposed to approve very highly."

"Then I *am* sorry. I hope I'll meet her." He looked at me disgustedly. "And what the hell did you mean by referring to her as a lady, then? If she's acted and lived like that she's a *woman*."

I shrugged away from that ambiguous rating. It was not a case in which I cared to argue matters of nomenclature. It was not a case I had ever hoped to discuss again.

Huebsch poised his pencil above the map. "And *is* the Princess at the house just now, Colonel?"

"She has been gone these last nine months."

"Well, well, that's a pity. But it can't be helped. She might have given us permission to dig over her land as well, in case Hanna's doesn't cover the complete area we'll have to excavate. Still, if she's away and the place locked up——"

"We'll do the digging without asking," said Marrot, turning his pale, cold eyes on me questioningly. I shrugged again.

"I cannot imagine that she would object," I said. Nor could I. A picture of her, in that poise of amused, indifferent insolence, arose before me and I stared at it wearily, and through the bright stillness of the day by the 'Ain ford-bank heard again the chirping of the grasshopper. . . . Huebsch's voice:

"Well, well. Then we'll try her house for drinking water anyway, and camp over about here"—his pencil came to smudgy halt in the midst of a little field about a quarter of a mile from the Gault house —"if it's at all suitable. To-morrow you and the Colonel can push out with the theodolite and make preliminary surveys, Marrot. I'll set the labourers to digging up our camp."

"Will that be necessary?" I inquired.

"Absolutely. Once knew a young man up near Damascus who prospected a site for close on five months and then had a fine Roman pavement found him by his cook—while the latter was baking a chicken in the earth." He looked over his shoulder towards Georgios with massive affability. "And we

don't want our follower here to dig up the Lost
Trumpet by accident and startle us some morning
with its strains !"

Subchapter iv

Abu Zabal rose on the horizon half an hour
before sunset, still in the pale land, though there
were deeper shades of brown here from the stubble
of the fields. Windless country we found it, very
quiet but for the unending calling of doves from
distant cotes. The Leyland had halted uncertainly
by the branching of the roads, and we called to
Kalaun to turn to the right. He had better control
of the lorry by then and wheeled into the narrower
track without mishap. So before us lay the country
for our exploration and excavation.

In front, half a mile away, was the deserted Turkish
castle of Oliver Gault, a hideous thing of Parisian
baroque and gimcrack imitativeness that the wester-
ing sun was tinting in unexpected austerity of line.
Left of us, the autumnal village lands, cut in their
narrow plots. To the right the three great fields of
Selim Hanna, intersected by a half-dried canal. Remote
beyond fields and house a blur, a brown metallic
shimmer that was the desert.

It had memories bitter enough for me, this region,
as I watched the house jut to view and vanish again
in the swayings of the frontward lorry. There Gault
and Pelagueya and I had listened to the tinkling of
that camel's bell that had lured him to his death ;

there I had made fantastic journey to speak to my
princess, and left with my speech unspoken ; there,
for the first time in my life, I had truly envisaged the
reality of the romantic middle-aged tourist-tout, had
known myself cursed with such clarity of intro-
spection as no romantic dreamings might ever serve
to veil. . . . So Pelagueya had vanished from Abu
Zabal and my life and wandered brilliant and
unresting—where ? Italy, perhaps, or the gay French
coasts. And how much or ever did she remember
of me or that Gault whom a raiding band of Tuareg
had killed and mutilated in the mountain-passes of
Mesheen ?

Oh, these old, unhappy, far off things !

Now, some quarter of a mile distant from the
house, Kalaun's lorry halted again, as he had been
bidden to halt it, and then, brown and golden, like
an ancient dragon in the evening light, swung right
again, into the waste, moist fields of Selim Hanna.
Moist we in the Darracq knew them to be even
before we came on them ; the Leyland wallowed
like a dinosaur distressed. But in the distance of some
ten yards or so it attained to a track of fair firmness
that ran by the brink of the neglected canal and in
this track we followed, the while the darkness, coming
over the shoulder of the village of Abu Zabal, waited
for us impatiently. And at length Huebsch, elevating
himself from beside me with startling creakings,
sent his immense shout down the still air.

"That'll do, Kalaun ! Camp her there for the
night."

The lorry halted. We squdged forward and halted beside it. In a babel of sound the labourers set to unloading stores, gear and Georgios. Our cook, bearing chicken-coop and bugle-case, waddled stiffly forward.

"In a quarter of an hour, Messieurs, I will have dinner prepared."

"You're a miracle, Georgios," said Marrot ; and added, generously, "We shan't mind though it's twenty minutes."

A little to the east of the canal was a slight elevation—a natural one, said the archaeologists, both intently aprowl—firmer and less green than the surrounding flatness. To this our three tents were transported and erected. Below, near the Leyland, Kalaun and his men set up their marquee and Georgios the store-tent. We plunged into the activities of camp-making with some zest, Huebsch, ponderous, a man of Heidelberg against the sunset, carrying great loads from lorry and car to the tents, Marrot beating in pegs with cheerful staccato blows that echoed across the flat tundra lands to the desert edge and returned, like flashing birds, and zoomed overhead to the dark cluster of Abu Zabal. . . . We had camped. To-morrow our work would begin, and——

And I had a sudden irrelevant thought, accosting Huebsch midway the little eminence.

"This Lost Trumpet—if it were found and blown —would it——?"

Huebsch breathed greatly, lowering a miscellaneous burden of implements, considering me with his

slow smile. "Would it act as in the days of Joshua ?
Haven't a notion, Colonel. But you'd better not
sound Marrot on the matter else he'll preach you to
death on the materialist conception of history—
Joshua no more than a desert bandit and his Trumpet,
if found, a moderately interesting antique horn."
He stretched himself, greatly. "Fine sky there."

It was a very fine sky. Now the darkness, giving
us up as impossible loiterers, had passed over our
heads, and the dusk came after it as a fine lace veil
trailed in the hands of that darkness. But still in the
east the sunset colours shone for a moment, very
gay and insouciant, like the lights of a palace ball
with revolutionists at the gates. . . . Huebsch
spoke again, musingly. "You never know. That
wall there"—he pointed to the bending sheet of the
horizon rim besieged by darkness—"The Lost
Trumpet might bring it crashing about our ears !"

That I found amusing. " 'And the heavens shall
roll up like a scroll—'. . . . The good Georgios
appears to be vexed."

Gesticulating, he was ascending towards us from
amid the magical array of stoves and cooking impedimenta that had shaped to swift being in the lee of the
lorry. "Messieurs !"

"Well, well," said Huebsch, "you surely haven't
served dinner already ?"

"But no." Georgios almost wrung his hands. "I
had forgotten—this I had not anticipated. The
canal water is undrinkable, and there is no other."

"That," I said, "can be remedied easily. Send one

of the labourers to me with buckets and we can go
and fill them at the deserted house at the end of the
road."

Georgios heaved a sigh of relief and turned away
nimbly. "Very well, mon colonel." Then paused
and pointed. "Deserted? It does not appear so."

Lights were shining at us across the dusk from the
upper rooms of Gault's Turkish castle.

CHAPTER THE SIXTH

'I knew that voice. I had half-expected to hear it,
yet disbelieved I would ever hear it again.'

Subchapter i

THEY shone steadily, no chance glimmer from
the lamp of a raiding burglar, as the labourer
and I stumbled along the roadway in the dusk.
Drawing near, we saw the light streaming from
below a door in the courtyard. We crossed to that
door and I beat on it until we heard the sound of
approaching footsteps along a stone-flagged passage.
They were quick, light footsteps. A voice said in
French : "Who is it ?"

I knew that voice. I had half-expected to hear it,
yet disbelieved I would ever hear it again. I leant
against the wall and the labourer, bemused, stared
at me and clinked the handles of the buckets. The
question was repeated, impatiently, and then the
door opened.

So, after nine months, I saw Pelagueya again, in
silhouette, backgrounded by the light of the corridor,
tall and slight, with burnished, blue-black hair and
her face in shadow ; and, as ever, her gown seeming
to drape in over-affectionate admiration the lines of
beauty of her long, swift body. A scent of lilac came

out to the two of us, looking up at her. The burnished
head bent towards us. Unalarmed, half-impatient,
half-amused, she said again : "Who is it ?"

Now at that I took off my hat and stepped forward
into the radiance of the corridor light. There was a
moment's silence, and then, without cry or greeting,
her arms were around my neck.

"Anton Kyrilovitch !" And I felt my heart almost
cease from beating at sound of the sweet Russian
syllables. "Oh, Anton, I thought Cairo had lost and
mislaid you ! Wherever have you been and how did
you know I came back to-day ?"

I found I was holding her in my arms, as I had
never done, and the burnished hair was a miracle of
fine metallic weavings against my cheek, and I was
dizzy with the smell of lilac, and the reluctant gown
had yielded to me, as if happily, and with a sigh of
content, that curving beauty of breast and limb that
was Pelagueya. So, while she jerked out the questions,
we stood a moment, looking at each other mistily.
Then I had dropped my arms and Pelagueya hers.
She drew back a step. She laughed.

"Still the same Anton ! And do come in. Who's
that with you ?"

I looked over my shoulder at the labourer.
Foolishly :

"He wants water."

She gave a characteristic gurgle of laughter. "He
may have wine if he chooses, I'm so glad to see you."
She called aloud : "Ibrahim !" and a native servant
came hurrying down the corridor. She motioned

towards my labourer. "Give this man food and drink. And now you'll come with me, Anton."

But I was emerging from my daze. "I should love nothing better, but my employers are awaiting their dinner. We have come for water to make it."

She stared, with that haughty tilt of head and brows that I knew so well. " 'Employers?' Oh, then you are in that party of the automobile and lorry that has camped in Hanna's field?"

I nodded.

She frowned; her decisions were as quick as ever. "Your man will go back with the water. But I myself haven't yet dined. So you must stay with me."

"I——"

She put her hand on my arm, shaking me a little. "Anton! Pelagueya Bourrin or your employers?"

Subchapter ii

Book-cases of light native wood-work lined the walls of the room. Two hacking knives of the Tuareg, grisly things that it seemed to me Pelagueya might have spared herself, hung crossed above a stuffed ostrich head and neck. The paper was peeling from the walls. The service was of silver . . .

Gault's house! Still half of Gault—those straying, yellow-backed Tauchnitz editions that heaped the dusty cases, those relics and trophies in tasteless jumbles, those lumps of quartz and rock-crystal crowding the glass-doored shelves. . . . We sat

at dinner, his mistress and I, eating cooling and
cold and execrably-cooked viands, and looked at
each other, and talked unnaturally about unimportant
things—Pelagueya and her wanderings on the
French Riviera, in Italy, in America; Pelagueya
and her letters I had never received or answered
because of a changed address; Pelagueya bored with
wandering, wandering back to this desert house of
Gault's——

"But in a little while again you will be very bored,"
I said. She shrugged impatiently.

"Of course I will. But what else am I to do? Oh,
living alone can never satisfy anyone, I think. Living
with too much money. I want to work and argue and
talk—politics and industry and the state. Lovely
and exciting things. I'd love to work in the minutest
sub-department of some government ministry. But
how can I?   How can any of us White Russians
except in our own country?"

"And why not there?"

"What—with the animals who killed my brother
in control?"

Pelagueya's face clearer to me now than at that
mazed doorway encounter. Unlined still, and fresh,
with that curl of lip that was like the curling of a
finely-moulded petal, and her eyes, great and dark
and gay and—as always they had seemed to me after
Gault's death—haunted eyes. Nor had that haunted-
ness yet gone from them, whatever the scenes and
encounters of the past nine months. The scents of
the tangled wreckage that was the garden came in

to us as we sat at meat, and towards Abu Zabal I saw a little stir of fires and a steady radiance from the camp I had so unwarrantably deserted. Now Pelagueya, with that burnished mop of hers bent low in thought, raised it and looked at me, and opened her lips to speak when there happened a thing that I had waited for ever since the lorry and car made camp.

Far up the Abu Zabal road there came the tinkling of a camel's bell. Pelagueya's lips closed and her eyes widened. She put her hand across the table. "Anton! Does it still bring you as bad memories as that?"

I thought of that mutilated body long ago stripped by vultures in the passes of Mesheen. "And you?"

"Poor Oliver! Unforgettable for ever." She looked through the window and then back at me. "And not a man at all in my memory, Anton. Hardly even a lover known in a dream. I think we were just two wild, pitying desires that met and loved and parted." She laughed a little, but I saw her hand tremble and her head was bent again. "And you think I'm heartless?"

"I think women can forget."

"Can't men? Can't you, Anton?"

And I knew the meaning of that question, and suddenly the elaborate pretences we had kept up since she had opened the door for me an hour before shivered away. This was something we had never talked of, but I found myself talking of it at last.

"Pelagueya, do you remember those days in Kazan?"

She nodded, her dear face mantling a little flush across the clear pallor of her cheeks, under those smooth cheek-bones. I heard myself go on, clear and unincoherent at last in this business that had haunted my life.

"I loved you then. You lived in my memory and I loved you through thirteen long years, Pelagueya. Why? Because of your beauty, of course. Because you have hair as you have it, and the way you smile, and because even the loveliest clothes upon you seem to me sacrilege, for the loveliness that they alone know was surely meant for gladdening all the world——"

Still that blue-black halo to my gaze, but her voice very low and untremulous. "You might have it to gladden you at least, if it would make you glad, Anton, my dear."

I flinched a little perhaps then, but it was my moment and I held to it. "And the play of your mind that seems to me a thing of beauty, because even when I do not think as you yet I can understand your thoughts. And the fearlessness you have, and the oh! stupendous ignorances, and the sweet way your lips curl back, and the breath-taking thing it would be if you were the mother of a child of mine. . . . All these things I could remember in those twelve or thirteen years. They came out of the darkness and lighted my saddest moments, a fairy-tale and a fairy-princess remembered. And then we met in that room at Shepherd's while we waited for Gault, and you told me you were Gault's mistress."

"And because of that——?"

"Do you think that would matter if I had still the faith to put my dreams to the test of reality— and come to you and ask for their fulfilment? You are more dear and adorable than ever you were— but, oh, I've grown old! Twelve years, Princess. Thirteen now. And I have seen so much in those thirteen years. Beauty hunted and dreamt of and followed; achieved at last. And then—satiety or smirching. . . . So I may sit and love you here, or when you are nowhere to be seen or heard, and you are mine as never you'd be if I came round this table and held you in my arms."

She laughed, playing with a little pyramid of brown bread-crumbs upon her plate. " 'The Apologia of Colonel Saloney.' " Then raised her head and looked at me again. "And me, Anton? Suppose that I do not believe a dream can be smirched because it is realized? Supposing I believe this creed of yours is a coward's creed?"

"Even with that supposition," I said, and halted and stammered and then some anger came on me. "Pelagueya, you have played with life all your life, and it has given you prizes easily and readily. Me you can forgo without heart-break. Queen Cophetua and the Beggar-Man! Do you think I would live on Gault's money?"

"That is vile, Anton Kyrilovitch!"

CHAPTER THE SEVENTH

'Aslaug Simonssen. I did not doubt her for a moment, nor she me. With that name this could be no one but Aslaug Simonssen.'

Subchapter i

WE were awakened in our tents at dawn by the crowing of the diminutive rooster Georgios had brought from Cairo. It crowed not only piercingly, but with a shrill, petulant insistence there was no denying. I heard the sound of hasty movement in the tent of Marrot, which was nearest to me, and glanced out. Poising a boot, the noted Egyptologist scrambled through the cords of his tent. The projectile hurtled through the air. There came a loud thwack, a startled giggle from the hen cooped up with the rooster, and the rooster's crowings crescendoing into an outraged chirawk. Marrot stood cursing unemotionally, yawned, turned about and caught my eye.

"Hello! So you did come back. Thought we'd mislaid you among your desert friends."

I had been uneasy about that unwarranted absence. "The Princess Pelagueya is an old friend of mine," I explained, and stared at Marrot, forgetting him. *Is?* That white-faced Pelagueya who had called me vile and had not moved as I left her table and house? . . . I shook off the memory. What did it matter to the middle-aged dragoman-employee haunted by the chirping of the grasshopper of futility? This little man was my master, awaiting explanations. "I should have secured the permission of Mr. Huebsch or yourself before I made such a lengthy absence."

"Permission!" He snorted and stared at me contemptuously. "Good God! Need *you* be slavish as well?"

With that he disappeared back into his tent. Oppressed and weary though I was I turned to dress with a wry smile. I had made a faux pas. In the ideal world of Mr. Marrot employees periodically insulted their employers and lectured them on the materialist concept of history . . .

The morning was unaware of all concepts economic or religious ever fathered by men on nature. Far in the dunness of the sands a bird was crying, and there was a dimness-shielded flapping of wings. Dawn came liquid, a soft flow and froth across the still, pale lands. The house of Gault stood black against it, then changed into a fairy tower of beaten gold with its crazy arches and mountings the battlements of a fairy palace. Across the neglected fields of Selim Hanna came flowing the light, spun in spume amidst the impedimenta of our encampment, shimmered and surged and overflowed the banks of the disreputable canal, poured in a mounting tide westwards upon the village of

Abu Zabal. . . . Kalaun, yawning, crept from beneath the marquee of the labourers. The others followed him. Monotonously, mechanically, they knelt and genuflected. Georgios, emerging from the store-tent, regarded them with a pitying contempt, twirled his immense moustaches, and made a dive towards the coop where the chickens were. There arose a terrified squawk. The rooster was without his mate and our evening's dinner was assured.

Going down to the canal, I encountered Huebsch returning from it, a great bucket of water in either hand.

"Well, well. Morning, Colonel. Going for a sluice ? Guess there's enough here for both of us. I'm told the Princess Bourrin has come back ?"

"That was the reason why I did not return in the evening," I said. "I trust you were not inconvenienced ?"

"Not a bit of it." He chuckled. "And for God's sake don't apologize in Marrot's presence. He was greatly pleased over your absence last night. He thought it was a deliberate flouting of us and has high hopes of you in consequence."

I affixed myself to the handle of one of the buckets. We laboured tent-wards in company. "Surely this viewpoint of Mr. Marrot's has occasional drawbacks ? Have not other employees taken advantage of it before this time ?"

The great ovoid head was shaken very decidedly. "Not one. You see, Marrot's always at them about

sticking up for their rights and to hell with capital-
ists and employers—in the case in question, of
course, always himself. And they're generally so
staggered that they treat him and their work with
scrupulous respect. Or they're so enthusiastic at
finding themselves regarded as human beings that
they insist on working overtime—and vexing Marrot
into a frenzy. Well, well, it's a mixed world."

Georgios spread our breakfast on a camp table
unearthed from the lorry. It was crisp and fresh
and admirably cooked, as though he must have
arisen at two o'clock in the morning to set about
the work. Yet he had done no such thing. Huebsch,
eating immensely, rumbled forth, as if absent-
mindedly, a revealing remark.

"Fine breakfast, Georgios. How you managed
both to attend to it and carry Mr. Marrot an early
cup of tea is beyond me."

Georgios retired in confusion. Marrot himself
coloured a trifle. Already, as I was to find, he was
hopelessly popular with labourers and cook alike.
He spread out the map towards Huebsch and myself,
brusquely.

"I'll take an observation and then Saloney and
I'll do the survey while you dig up the camp,
Huebsch. I've ringed round the probable area in
pencil." He raised inquiring brows towards me.
"Can you sketch?"

"I was once the Maps Officer of General Deniken."

"Oh, were you? The brigand who raided the
soviets in South Russia?"

I shrugged.   Huebsch interposed, immensely.
"Never mind the brigands.   I was reading up that
MS last night and I'm almost sure that the area we'll
have to tackle ultimately lies over there"—and he
pointed to the extreme Hanna field that verged on
the lands of the Gault house.

"Why ?" asked Marrot.

"Look for yourself.   The land, I guess, is thinnest
there.   There's a shadow of a rock-ridge below the
top-dressing of soil."

"But how does that make it a more likely place ?"
I asked.

"This was desert when the renegade Levite stole
out at night and buried the treasure from the Temple.
Or partly desert.   Now, most of the land has been
dug and cultivated to extremes since then.   Except
perhaps along that ridge, where I guess they were
never able to go very deep. . . .   So I calculate
the treasure must be somewhere in the lee of the
ridge, else it would have been found before this
time."

I checked a remark that the finding might well
have taken place long ago.   Huebsch would twinkle
immensely and retort that that was impossible,
otherwise the Lost Trumpet would have been found
and blown. . . .   How much of that fantastic tale
did he himself believe ?

By noon Marrot and I had narrowed the possible
area of excavation to the ridge, the land east of the
canal-bank—there were perhaps two acres of it—
and the camp-site.   This last portion was already being

put to the question, for as we returned for lunch
we saw a great criss-cross of black earth uprising
throughout the heart of the encampment.   Two
trenches, intersecting at right angles near where the
lorry stood, had been scored through the soil under
the direction of Huebsch.   The great Jew himself,
sweat-exuding, a Syrian Baal in the flesh, sat under
the shadow of his tent awaiting our arrival.

"Nothing doing here, though, of course, the
trenches aren't absolutely confirmatory." He searched
amid a pile of letters on the table. "Mail just out from
Cairo. One for you, Colonel."

I looked at the unfamiliar, staccato lettering on
the envelope, broke it open, unfolded the single
sheet it contained, and read :

                                    Alexandria.

'DEAR COLONEL SALONEY,

'Roger and Dawn Mantell told me to write
to you as soon as I landed in Egypt.   They
themselves were to send you a letter telling
you why I am here.   I hope you've received
it and that you won't think it too much trouble
to see me.

'I shall be in Cairo about three o'clock the
day after to-morrow, and I'll put up at Shepheard's if you shouldn't be able to meet me at
the Station.

           'Yours sincerely,

                    'ASLAUG SIMONSSEN.'

Subchapter ii

By half-past twelve I was on the road to Cairo in the aged Darracq. Huebsch had assented with disinterested kindliness to my request for an afternoon's freedom, Marrot with scornful objurgations. I had felt no great gladness either in making the request or in accepting the permission. For the truth was that I had forgotten Aslaug Simonssen and her mission very completely and entirely, and now drove to meet her with nothing to urge me but the ghostly memory of a far-off friendship.

But I found the Darracq ran sweetly enough after the first mile or so, when it had ceased to wonder why the quick, nervous hands of Marrot were not at its controls. We settled down into good partership and at half-past two I was going past Helmieh in the fine cloud of dust. At ten minutes to three I left the car near a little open-air café in the Esbekieh Gardens, and hasted on foot to the station.

It was only as I stood at the end of the platform watching the Alexandrian train steam in that I realized this girl and I had no method of mutual identification. Nor had I Roger Mantell's letter at hand to assist me—if any assistance it contained, which I could not remember. There was nothing to do but trust to a remote and unchancy chance.

Steam and clatter and a profound expiration of breath from the engine, squatting somnolent and exhausted upon the rails. Much banging of carriage-doors and now the forward stream of passengers into

Cairo Station. I stood a little aside and considered them. Three Jews—Egyptian Jews, not of the Huebsch variety, with thin, Syrian faces and quick eyes, and each a mistress hanging lymphatic upon his arm. An English Army officer, his soldier-servant panting dustily and with much sweat, baggage-laden, at his heels, following his master's quick, irritated stridings through the crowds with moist, respectful eyes. How came it that the Anglo-Saxon, the originator of so many things democratic, was in the servant class of all nations the most abject and easily cowed? Now, a Russian servant of the old days would have hailed his master: "O Alexander Petrovitch," or "O Anton Kyrilovitch," and declared himself dead-beat, and asked that master to carry part of the baggage. And the master would have cursed him and done so, in a manner matter-of-fact. While of the new order in Russia——

But I had to make concentration again on the train passengers. Two American women with husbands greatly be-spectacled and cigarred and blasé—mid-aged, mid-prosperous exports of the Middle West. A chattering mob of fellaheen. A Greek. Another Jew, with a canary on his wrist, like a falcon on the wrist of an old-time hunter. Two French boys, with collars absurdly starched, like small, dyspeptic calves agape above white-painted gates, the herdswoman a governess. . . . Aslaug Simonssen.

I did not doubt her for a moment, nor she me. With that name this could be no one but Aslaug

Simonssen. A porter followed her with two suit-
cases. She herself walked unladen and untrammelled. She held out her hand.

"Colonel Saloney ?" She smiled correctly, politely.

"Miss Simonssen ?" I also bared my teeth.

"Yes."

She put her hand on my arm. I piloted her through
the throngs, outside the station, into the clamorous
greetings of taxi-drivers and gharry-men innumerable. A gigantic Negro backed away in front of us,
genuflecting, his rear pointing invitation to his
vehicle. Aslaug Simonssen halted and gazed at the
scene capably, collectedly, a little heavily. It was
unbelievable that she was only eighteen or nineteen
years old.

"Which shall we take ?" I asked. "An arabiyeh or
a taxi ?"

"Are these arabiyehs ?" She scrutinized them
without enthusiasm. "Oh, I think we'll take a taxi.
Much quicker. To Shepheard's ?"

"How long are you to be in Cairo ?" I asked.

But that she could not say, as I knew. "I think
it will be simpler if at first you put up at some pension,
then."

"Very well, Colonel Saloney. Do you know of
one ?"

I took her to the Avallaire and engaged a room
for her. Then I said :

"Now we must go and talk. Shall we have a
discreet and comfortable English tea—or go into
the real Cairo and talk there ?"

She hesitated. It was obvious that an English tea and not too much dust and smell was what she wanted. But it was also obvious that she had heard of me from the Mantells, and had been properly brought up, and knew that it was the correct thing to please me.

"I would like you to show me some of Cairo, please, and some place where I can have something cool to drink."

She had spoken to me, slowly and distinctly, since we had met, articulating carefully each English word, as to an idiot. In some little amusement I attempted to put her at ease.

"I understand English quite well, Miss Simonssen. I was once a professor of English Literature. And I still keep my diary in that language."

"Oh," she said, stiffly. "I didn't know."

I hailed another taxi. So presently we entered the Khalig-el-Masri, Aslaug Simonssen looking out at afternoon Cairo with pale, attentive, incurious eyes.

I have said that none who had heard the name would fail to fit her with it. She was Scandinavian in traditional style—almost, indeed, as though the style had slightly bleached. Almost five feet ten in height and built in proportion, not clumsily, you understand, but indeed with a kind of gracious heaviness that was not heavy, that for some reason made me think of an active peasant woman ploughing a hillside, her husband dead and the little farm her care, and the cold streamers of the unsetting

Northern sun behind her. . . . Cool, with pale,
clear blue eyes, very fair hair and brows, a comely,
cleanly-moulded face with a rounded, barbarian
Viking jaw, a long mouth, even-toothed, small
hands and feet. And that heavy coolness. . . . It
plagued me and piqued me. It is permissible for
any woman to look like a Valkyr. But no god or
code that ever existed has given authority for a
Valkyr to gaze and speak like a young woman of
the epoch Mid-Victorian, her mind a stubble field
stacked with dun and grainless clichés . . .

"And what do you think of Egypt ?" I asked in
some desperation, for I had been accustomed to other
types than this. She turned her strong-jawed face
upon me questioningly.

"Very nice. But the streets are very filthy, aren't
they ? And the smell . . ."

Which was Egypt to the eyes of Aslaug Simonssen.
Cool and unsmiling of body and face and soul,
and fantastically woolly-minded, I appraised her
as we sat and ate the good Simon's honey-cakes.
And there was something else about her, something
in those eyes unhealthy when matched with that
magnificent body——

Looking straight in front of her, I found she was
beginning to tell me about the murder of her brother
Carl.

"——if he had been killed as people are killed
in fights with natives we'd have known exactly
what happened. But it wasn't that way, and I've
come to find out about it."

"It was at Rashida that the tragedy took place?"
I inquired.

"Yes. Carl had a house there, and two or three
servants. One of them, I think, wasn't a servant. She
was his mistress."

Saying this, she turned away her face from me.
The blood welled in dark patches below her high
cheek-bones. I also looked away, pitying and a
little amused. She had done better to stay among
the frigid folk of Edinburgh if such a word could
make her blush.

"She was mentioned in the papers of the court of
inquiry—the Egyptian Government sent us copies
of those papers. She was blind."

"Blind?" I felt a sudden, sick distaste for the dead
Carl Simonssen.

"Yes." That part of the matter did not appear
to shock her. "And they said that Carl had no
special enemies, even though he lived so wrongly.
But he was found one morning by one of his servants
—not the blind woman—with his throat cut from
ear to ear."

She said it with no special emotion, that unfathom-
able look still in her eyes. And then I saw that it was
no look at all; it was as though her eyes were thinly
and trimly glazed. Not, I commented to myself,
that they lacked health; they merely lacked indi-
viduality.

I roused myself to speak about this matter of
her brother's murder. "Perhaps he committed
suicide."

"No, he didn't. Why should he, he was not mad? And besides, the knife was not found near him."

"That certainly rules out the suicide supposition."

"Then why did the Egyptian Government not proceed with the case? They did nothing. The police officers were plainly in league with the murderer. They never seem to have attempted to seek out the blind woman—and I *know* that she was the cause of his death."

"Then what are you going to do?"

The cool, glazed eyes of the Victorian Valkyr regarded me unwaveringly. "I am going to the Ministry of the Interior to tell them I am here and to ask their co-operation for me to go down to Rashida and make inquiries on my own."

I thought for a little while. "I can help you there," I said. "I know one of the officials of the Interior."

I called for ink and a pen from Simon, who brought a great Chian quill and a bird-decorated Chian bottle. I wrote a short note to Peters, and passed it across the table.

She read it. "Thanks very much." She smiled politely and stood up. "Would you mind taking me back now, please? I'm very tired."

I also rose. Did she know what she was doing? "You know what will happen to your brother's murderess if they succeed in tracking her down?"

"Yes. They will hang her."

Subchapter iii

Leaving Aslaug Simonssen at the Pension
Avallaire, I went down to Esbekieh to seek the
Darracq. And there, at one of the little tables of the
open-air café, sat Adrian, absorbed in a self-game of
dominoes. He looked up, unsurprised at my touch
upon his shoulder, and then swept aside the dominoes.

"Hello, Saloney. Thought I recognized the
Darracq during my stroll. Beer?"

We sat and consumed its bitter coolness through
long stalks of Syrian wheat. "Found the Lost
Trumpet yet?"

"Not yet," I said. "Only the lost princess."

"Eh?"

"The Princess Bourrin returned to her house in
Abu Zabal yesterday morning."

"Splendid! She is well?"

"So I think."

He looked at me with his head characteristically
cocked to one side. He shrugged. "What a romantic
you are, Saloney! If you don't marry what the devil
are you to do? You can't remain a dragoman for
ever—not even the most handsome guide in Cairo,
as the dear tourist-ladies of the Continental call you.
For one thing, you'll soon be too old."

"I shall set up a booth near the Pyramids and
dispose of antiques from Birmingham."

"Quite. And tell every possible purchaser that
they *were* from Birmingham. . . . What's wrong,
of course, Colonel, is that you're an anachronism.

Out of date. Mediaeval and damned. This outlook
of yours on Pelagueya Bourrin—by the by, do you
realize I've never met her ?—and life generally ; it
used to be called chastity——"

"But the good Freud would doubtlessly say that
my mind-garden is choked with inhibitions ?"

Adrian chuckled at that. He is no Freudian.
"Ascribe it all to the fact that you weren't allowed
to bite your father in the ankle at the age of three,
I've no doubt. Romantic turned inside out, Freud
—and shiveringly concerned with the messy appearance of his inside. . . .   No, the thing's much
plainer than that."

"Is it an explanation all-embodying enough to
account for a normal young woman having the
glazed eyes of a heifer over-fed and the mind of a
surly hangman ?"   And I told him about Aslaug
Simonssen.

"Even for that."   He waved to a waiter that our
glasses might be refilled.   "Ever heard of the Diffusionists ?"

I shook my head.

"I've been reading them lately. New school of
historians and archaeologists. They say that all
this"— he motioned towards the streets beyond—
"and your reluctances and hesitations over Pelagueya
Bourrin, and Al Azhar mosque there, and enjoyment
of cruelty and throat-cutting—all these things are
incidental and accidental."

"They are mystics ?" I inquired politely.

"Lord, no.   This is the point they make : that

none of these things—civilization and its viler acces-
sories—are innate in human nature. You and I and
everyone else, owing to an accident here in Egypt
six thousand years ago when agriculture originated
civilization, go about with superimposed on our
minds and bodies a hideous swathing and garbing
of ideas and clothes that are quite unnatural to the
human animal—who is fundamentally a sane and
decent and plain-thinking animal."

"It is a fantasy. Man was originally a slavering
beast of the jungles."

I had stood up. Adrian reassembled his dominoes.
"Not a scrap of proof that he was ever any such thing.
Mere theory. And scores of proofs to the contrary,
that he was once a kindly, golden-skinned hunter of
the Golden Age. . . . Keep that in mind, Saloney,
as I'm doing, and see how it works out explaining
yourself and other people. This girl you've met at
the station—try it on her."

CHAPTER THE EIGHTH

'I think they will live with me always, those days.'

Subchapter i

BUT the next morning banished Aslaug Simonssen from my mind as completely as it banished the grasshopper. So in the days that followed. I came to know and share in the toils and perplexities and the heart-breaking exactitudes of research with which the archaeologist afflicts himself. Abu Zabal's mosque, a small blue dome brooding in the west ; Pelagueya's house, affronting the eastern sky with the crazy uplift of its baroque towers—these were the only permanent objects on my horizon, seen mostly, as it seemed to me, from betwixt my own legs as I stooped over this or that or the next trench ; or impinging themselves on my eyes with a sudden ache because of their sun-radiance at the same time as I would unbend and another ache bite sharply and efficiently between my shoulders.

For the rest, it was a world of flux. We moved the camp further along the canal-bank ; dug ; discovered nothing ; moved it back again. We went out on more mensuration with a theodolite. Of nights, dead weary, we made tracings of suspected drainages on our sketch-maps ; sometimes we were so weary that we did but scant justice to the excellent food of the little Georgios. There was no time or inclination, I found, to brood on the great Twin Insects. For even though all things were a weariness under the sun, yet now it was a physical weariness, bringing a cheering glow of well-being to my body, long pent in the soft airs and colours of Cairo.

I think they will live with me always, those days. The heat and flare of the sun across the parched lands of Selim Hanna—land that under our probings and questionings steadily betook to itself the appearance of a hard-fought trench-sector on the Western Front in the European War; the gang-chanting of the labourers, bent double as they trotted with bags of earth up and away and down again in this or that excavation now growing the deeper; the booming of Huebsch's immense, considering voice; sudden view of his great ovoid head over a bank of earth, with its stare of purple-blue eyes, the great red lips slowly shaping to propound a new proposal or demanding to know of the size and no-being of our luck; Marrot, energetic, tireless, yet at every possible chance adjuring the labourers, Georgios and myself to remember we were dupes of the capitalist system and go slow, for the love of God, and act like men, not helots; Georgios——

Georgios wailed the comic chorus of each day in a nullah far to the east. It must have been twenty minutes walk there, yet religiously every evening, having served us our dinner, he set forth to practise, an absurd little, proud little figure offset by a drooping

immensity of moustache. We would watch him go,
clambering and threading the wrinkled agonies of
the field, then growing to a dot. And presently,
remote from that direction which he had taken,
would arise a sound that seemed to me like the soul
of a stuck pig wailing its immemorial griefs by the
side of some porcine Styx. Marrot, with objurgations
inelegant but justifiable, would cover his ears.

"If only he'd be sick and have done with it !"

The great Huebsch would listen with his head
slightly leant towards one shoulder. "There's a kind
of rhythm in it, though. Listen : So : Oh—ahee—
oo—ah——"

"For the love of Sabaios and all the other gods of
Jewry, give it a rest, Huebsch ! Georgios is bad
enough on his own, but an interpreter as well——"

"Well, well, well." The huge Jew would continue to listen with unabated seriousness. The dead
pig was being beaten over the head by Charon ; it
was in flight ; it had fallen into the brimstone lake ;
it was being flayed alive ; it had lapsed into uncon-
sciousness—blessedly re-dead ? ; revived again ;
remembering its wife and children——

I would rise. "I think I shall take a short walk.
I cannot abide this post-mortem torture of a useful
and harmless animal."

"Pretty bad, pretty bad," Huebsch would agree,
and would turn his great eyes, that were on occasion
so oddly restless, upon me. "Which way are you
walking, Colonel ?"

I would gesture towards Abu Zabal, conscious

that both of them were looking at me. Marrot would
put the question :

"Why not the other way ? Have you quarrelled
with the woman ?" And Huebsch add : "The lady
may be pretty useful to us, Colonel, if after all we've
to tackle that hog-back on her land."

But the word hog-back would be too much in
conjunction with the distant wailings of Georgios'
silver bugle. "I have quarrelled with no one. And I
walk towards Abu Zabal to put the better distance
between myself and the ghost of the pig which
Georgios knew and slew and laments over."

And I would walk away with Huebsch's great,
slow boom of laughter following me, for he was
childlike in his appreciation of broad and open jests.
But walking the road to the village I would have less
certainty upon myself that this direction I took was
justified solely by the desire to escape from Georgios
and his pig. . . . And I would sigh, and hit at inoffen-
sive bushes with my stick, and begin the hasty singing
of scraps of song, as a man does when he has no
wish to think or come face to face with that other
self who propounds alarming questions and refuses
lies for answers. So to Abu Zabal, walking in the
polychromatic flaunting of the many night-garments
with which the heavens beguiled the sun to rest.
There I would generally halt, and listen to the
unending coo of doves, and then, with darkness
treading at my heels, turn back and reach the camp
to find Georgios snoring in his tent and no one
about but the great Huebsch, smoking immensely

his pipe, with about his head great cloudings of
smoke as incense about the head of an ancient god,
his eyes fixed on the horizon.

And then I would remember that jest of his—
his threat to the horizon-walls when we had excavated
and blown the Lost Trumpet. The horizon! There
were walls in our hearts that towered to infinity—
and ah, what things of horror or loveliness might
burst upon the world if those walls fell at the blast
of some magic trumpet!

Subchapter ii

Whatever the Lost Trumpet might have accom-
plished in bygone ages it appeared on the fifth night
that Georgios' un-lost bugle had already consequences in Abu Zabal. First, we gathered from
Kalaun, who had a sly sense of humour, that it was
popularly believed in the village that an afreet had
taken up its habitation in the desert nullahs and there
nightly devoured the souls of the unwary and the
straying. He told us this, newly-returned himself
from Abu Zabal, the while Georgios' bugle brayed
faintly—on another note, it seemed to me, as though
his researches had been transferred from the porcine
to the asinine. Hardly had Kalaun finished when
Marrot, sprawling in some weariness in a deck-chair,
indicated the track that led from the Abu Zabal road.

"We're having a visitor."

We looked in that direction and saw a figure
which had turned, unhasting, into the fields of Selim

Hanna and now approached us in the soft evening light along the bank of the canal. "Probably a delegate sent to ask our co-operation in hunting the afreet," hazarded Marrot.

Huebsch took his pipe from betwixt his thick, curling lips. "It's a woman."

Thereat I looked again. It was Pelagueya. She had seen the three of us sitting on the little incline, and evidently recognized me, or made chance of the recognition. She waved her hand. We stood up and I went towards her. She was in an evening gown and cloak, with a froth of silk about her ankles. The cloak was lined with scarlet and gold, and her head, like the head of some dark flower, came out of that colourful sheath.

"Anton, what *is* that shocking noise over in the desert ?"

"That," I said, taking her hand, "is our cook."

"Cook ?"

"He is also a musician."

"He is a horror," said Pelagueya. "Every evening. To-night I got out my revolver. But I have no cartridges. So I came to borrow some."

She glanced round interestedly at the camp, the revolver dangling from her fingers ; then up at Huebsch and Marrot, standing politely not looking at us.

"It *is* a shocking noise. But really, Anton Kyrilovitch, I came because I was very bored, and wanted to be friends with you again, and to meet your employers. . . . Shall I say 'sir' to them ?"

This was a sneer at myself. But I was too happy seeing her to heed it greatly. "You may say what you choose—looking as you do."

"That is very sweet." We climbed up towards the archaeologists. "And have you found a lot of treasure ?"

"None," I said. Then : "Messieurs—the Princess Pelagueya Bourrin. Princess, Messieurs Huebsch and Marrot."

"The noted performing illusionists," added Marrot, obscurely. Huebsch, bowing immensely, consideringly dragged forward a deck-chair. Pelagueya, very sweet and slim and wonderful, sat herself in it. Marrot looked down at her.

"Princess—exactly what of ?"

She looked at him amusedly. "Of myself, at least."

"Then we are all princes ?"

"Not at all. Some are kings."

He grunted. Huebsch intervened, immensely conciliatory. "We're very glad to meet you, Princess. For yourself, of course, and also because it seems we'll have to get your permission to dig on that hog-back over there."

Pelagueya brought out a little case. I shook my head. So did Marrot. But Huebsch, laying aside his pipe, accepted a cigarette, and lighted hers, and smoked his own to uselessness in perhaps the half-dozen puffs. She said :

"Well, I think you can. So long as it doesn't mean your cook comes and serenades the servants. . . . It is really very dreadful."

Georgios was wailing the after-death sorrows of all unlovable beasts again in the nullah hidden in the east. Pelagueya listened. "But—I've noticed it before—there is a kind of rhythm in the awful sounds. As though he might do better if a miracle happened —quite suddenly."

"Or the Lost Trumpet was discovered," I said, and then halted, reflecting that I had had no permission to speak of that. Pelagueya said: *"What* trumpet ?" and looked from one to the other of us.

Huebsch explained. The night came close. So, a hasting dot across the furrows of our excavations, did Georgios. Catching sight of our visitor, he halted at a distance and bowed with impressiveness.

"Would messieurs—and madame—like some coffee ?"

Huebsch nodded. "We'd be greatly obliged, Georgios. You'll have some, Princess ?"

"I'd love some. . . . So that's the Jewish relic you've come in search of ? The Lost Trumpet! What would it do—supposing you did find it and it could be blown ?"

"It might bring down the horizon walls," I said.

Pelagueya laughed. "That would be amusing. . . . I'm going to Cairo to-morrow. Can I borrow Colonel Saloney for the day ?"

Huebsch said: "Why, sure." Marrot, who had lain back in his chair unspeaking, staring upward at the sky, sat up.

"Don't be so sure, Huebsch. Who's Saloney that we can lend him ? It's up to the man himself."

Pelagueya raised bewildered eyebrows at him. I said : "I shall be very pleased to escort the Princess."

Marrot, thwarted in his designs to up-stir the proletariat, sank back again. Georgios brought us our coffee—coffee of marvellous goodness, served with the suave skill of a Cairene hotel, not a camp in the desert. Pelagueya thanked him with that cheerfulness that has always made of her the poor aristocrat. Georgios shrugged.

"The coffee—the cooking—it is work that any man can do, madame." He sighed. "It is my ambition to do other things."

Pelagueya with charming heroism maintained a grave face. "But of course. Your music."

He stood beside the three of us, his small face absurdly serious. "My music, madame. Every night I practise—there. Perhaps you have heard me ?"

"I think I have."

He sighed again. "And every night it escapes me. I search for the chord that will give voice to the beauty I know I can sound for the world—but it is a search unavailing. Thus far."

There was an uncomfortable silence. Marrot, surprisingly, broke it. "We all, in our ways, search for that chord, Georgios," he said.

Subchapter iii

"Anton ! Tell me a story."

"What kind of story ?"

Behind us the lights of the camp ; in front, the

lights of Gault's Turkish castle; overhead, neither
darkness nor light, the sky awaiting moon-rise. We
sat on a bank of turf by the side of the road. It was
very silent, the night world. Pelagueya turned a dim
face towards me. Her voice seemed to come from
very far away.

"Oh—any kind. . . . A fairy-story. . . . Something no one else can believe and you believe."

I lighted my pipe. A fairy-story to suit the whim
of a moment—the whim of a princess. I went
searching back to my childhood. And then, slowly
up through the years of my own life, I saw a story
unfold. I heard myself begin to speak.

"This is the story of the Three Brothers. You
will not be cold?"

There was a little laugh. "I hope I shall be
warmed."

"Once upon a time, long ago, they set out on
their journey. But from where I do not know. Nor
in their lineage has the story any interest. They
were brothers, triplets, I think, but unakin, and with
no great respect for one another, as is the habit with
brothers. Setting forth, they went not together.
They travelled separately and apart.

"And the first of the brothers, as in all good
fairy tales, was the tallest and strongest, with a
handsome nose and proud, and garments gay and
costly upon his back. Round his middle he carried
slung a great purse—all the Brothers bore purses—
which fact is the central point of the story, and
which, like the ancient story-tellers, I give away

regardless of the surprise-losses to the plot. But this Brother's was the greatest purse : seemly, strong and well-embroidered, with the seals and cunning locks, I think. And greatly, like the belly of a stout man, did it bulge. For within it this Brother had laid up for the journey all things that were needful to travel in comfort. And being a man with the much luck and the gross appetite—albeit he was a kindly soul enough when no footpads came near—these purse-storings were many. For within those embroidered folds he carried food and wealth, and honour and fame and pride and achievement, sleep and lust and laughter. In a sardonic moment—such as is allowable in no real fairy-story—I have even imagined him carrying therein a commissar-ship under the good soviets. . . . At the least, everything needful was there, even—though how this came about I do not know—tenderness and the love of women and a little pity.

"And he walked clear-eyed, if a little over-proud, with a fine swing of his shoulders and, I think, a mole on his left cheek. And on that journey much he spent and acquired of appetites and satieties. Till presently, climbing a mountain-pass, he rounded a corner and saw in his path a giant figure, fronting him as Apollyon fronts Christian in the pages of the English Bunyan. And this figure was the figure of a Robber—a Robber coarse and without much brains and the no-respect, and a bored eye. And, with but the briefest preliminary survey, and ere ever the First Brother had cleared his eyes of dazement, the

Robber uplifted his club and smote the Brother to the ground, and slew him, and pounded the contents of his purse into shining drift-motes of dust.

"And then—for so he had done to many travellers, and he was a very old and unprincipled Robber— he yawned."

"Go on."

"And, by the different routes and by-paths indeed, yet straight to that same mountain-pass where his Brother lay slain, went on the Second Brother. He walked hastily, and with jerking shoulders, and frequently—for he had developed the corns soft and painful—he stopped and rubbed his feet and cursed, glancing about him with a wary, jaundiced eye. His garments were not so gay as those of the First Brother, though yet serviceable and respectable. Nor was his purse of so great a bulge ; and this was to him continually an anxiety and a vexation.

"For this purse had become not his servant, but he its. Its condition had grown a continual source of anger and confusion and astonishment. His was the continual fear of lurking footpads—or rather, the apprehension, for I think he did not lack courage. Continually he would hasten forward to the next city to refill the purse with this or that necessity, only to find himself forestalled by some traveller who had journeyed ahead. Or he would find that the purse had developed a leak and strewn much of honour or strength or satisfaction by the way. And once he stopped and looked at the purse—at the time well and comfortably filled—and made inventory of its

contents. And these contents seemed but the sum
of a grey nothingness because of the one article that
was missing. It had been crushed out, dropped by
the wayside, or forgotten long before. It was love.

"He sat down by a wayside pool and laid his head
in his hands in a surly dissatisfaction, knowing that.
But the journey had still to be continued. So, clutching his purse, glancing right and left in search of footpads, he went on. He walked limpingly, and choleric
because of his corns and the hot weather, and so
walking, rounded a corner—and there, in front of
him, like Apollyon in Bunyan, he glimpsed for a
fleeting moment the giant Robber. And the Robber
yawned, and surveyed him, and lifted his club, and
pounded him, him and his purse, into little fragments indistinguishable from the little fragments of
his elder Brother."

Far out in the desert the rim of the moon had
uprisen, and there, a mere rim, seemed to halt, as
though the earth had ceased to rotate and the satellite
gazed down on a world as tideless and immovable
as itself. Pelagueya touched my arm.

"There was a Third Brother."

"Ah, yes. Now, by yet another route—if route it
could be called—came on the Third Brother. Through
no such carefully mapped and planned country as
his brothers did this third one come. For long he
wandered in a land of flowering bogs with the gay
yellow of the poison flower a startling colour amidst
the tufts of green, and the calling of strange birds
heard across stagnant meres. Sometimes by moun-

tain slopes he had wandered and watched sunrises
and sunsets unearthly. Once, on the shore of a name-
less sea, he had watched for weeks the rise and fall
on the horizon of a fairy island. And for a space of
years he had turned aside into the clamour and call
of city ways, into lives and loves and enthusiasms
innumerable. But now he was growing old.

"And, however had strayed his feet on this route
unplanned, straight towards that mountain pass at last
he walked. His clothes were the soiled vestiges of
ancient finery. His face had a hanging jowl after all
that journeying, and heavy pouches under the eyes.
But still in those eyes was a curiosity almost child-
like. And, as he walked he sang, in a voice a little
cracked, a gay chanson of the road.

"About him was slung his purse—a purse fantastic
of shape, weather-beaten and be-patched. All the
journey, however he had used of its contents, he had
walked almost unconscious of the possession of that
purse. But now, sitting down to rest a brief while,
it flapped against his leg and he picked it up and
opened it—he, the roué-child, the rather stout figure
who sat and pursed his lips to the whistle of the
little chanson.

"And within the purse—was left of honour and
fame, wealth and food, pride and achievement, not
one little atom. Neither was love there; he had
spent it long ago—or sold it for a dream. He forgot
which. Long ago. And the dream——?

"Surely it was there? But he was very tired by
then, and besides he had grown short-sighted. And

if indeed it lurked amidst the folds and crinkles of the purse he could see of it no trace. And suddenly he yawned, cavernously, displaying the teeth he had had stopped with gold in the days of his wealth. And he got upon his feet and climbed up the mountain-pass where the air, as he noticed, grew chill— perhaps because of the great height.

"Upon his thigh flapped the gaudy, empty purse. But it seemed to him that perhaps, somewhere, somehow—some debt there was that he would yet collect. He had never counted the contents. Beyond the hills—perhaps some long-forgotten debtor awaited him there.

"And at this thought, cheered, he began to sing again, albeit puffily, for his breath was short and the path long. Singing, he rounded a corner, and there in front of him, like Apollyon in Bunyan, burly and broad and bestial, stood the Robber. Alone of the travellers, before that last moment, did the Third Brother glimpse face and yawn and club. And terror gripped his heart and then passed; and with a shaking voice he stood and sang."

"And—?" Pelagueya, tight-wrapped in her cloak, was standing beside me.

"And that, of course, is the end."

"Oh, Anton—a fairy-story and not one of them lived happily ever after!"

I stood up beside her. "Assuredly one did—The Robber."

CHAPTER THE NINTH

' "Only, wonderful to be alive and see and smell.
And to touch you." '

Subchapter i

IT was hardly dawn the next day when Georgios
came beating anxiously at the flap of my tent.

"Mon colonel !"

Dressing, I drew aside the flap. He thrust a hasty
cup of tea in my hand.

"Madame la princesse—she is waiting for you.
Twice she has made the hoot-hoot."

And there, at the junction of Pelagueya's road and
the track that led to ours, was verily a small automobile. As I drank the tea it hooted again, urgently.
The air was crisp and cold and clear, but with already
a shadowy warmth. Against the far desert rim the
cypress trees of Gault's castle stood as if caught to
a dark silence by the coming of the morning—
peering into the west, perhaps, to hear the wind that
sang their owner dead in far Mesheen. One leg
very much tucked up, an ibis stood straight and
stiff above its nest near the canal. A flight of cranes
passed overhead towards Abu Zabal. The klaxon
of Pelagueya's automobile broke into a lunatic
yammer.

I dropped the tea-cup into Georgios' willing hands, struggled into my jacket, and made haste from the camp towards that quivering automobiline impatience. Pelagueya I discerned ensconced at the wheel and her laugh met me.

"Well run, Anton!"

She seemed very much amused. I leant, panting, against the tonneau.

"What is wrong?"

She opened the door for me. "Nothing. What would be? You promised to come up to Cairo with me to-day."

"But at this hour? And with all this wild bleating on your horn I had imagined——"

She laughed again. She moved restlessly. "Oh, do come in and sit down. Sorry if I disturbed your middle-aged slumbers. . . . But you're always half-asleep anyhow, aren't you? . . . And you can have a nap as I drive."

I had seen this mood once or twice before. I sat beside her and snicked the door of the automobile. "I think I had better drive."

"Not if I know it." Hatless, she glanced aside at me, with a jerk of her head flinging back the cluster of hair from her forehead. "We'll all be in our hearse-processions soon enough without acting as though we were in them while alive. Hold tight."

The dim morning cluster of Abu Zabal jerked towards us in crazy bounds, attained momentum, charged upon the car like a running panther, swerved to the right, missed us by a hair's-breadth, vanished from the scenery. The Cairo road opened and closed, opened and closed with the glister and screech of a fast-run film. The browns and faint greens of the land to either side were a blur of racing no-colour. "Do hope these goats are active-minded," said Pelagueya.

A straying dunness upon the road careered towards us, swayed, broke, departed on either side with a wild bleat and one elongated screech from a human throat. I looked back. A doll with toy animals in its charge waved miniature arms and vanished down the edge of the horizon. I brought out a cigar and lighted it and leaned back, turning my head and shoulders so that I might look at Pelagueya, not at the foolish antics of the landscape. And I forgot the landscape, so looking at her, bending in that Nike Apteros intensity of motion and purpose, with those fine Greek arms of hers curving upon the wheel and her hair back-blown in the rush of the wind, and a spray of fine blood below her cheek-bones, and a little vein beating in the pallor of her throat. And I seemed to see then things of a breath-taking beauty and wonder with which, foolishly, I had never made myself acquainted. That little curve of nostril—a second curve just where nostril met with cheek: that was a wonderful thing. And a fine down—a tracery that was Spanish—along that curved upper lip. My God, I had never noticed it before! Nor the miracle of uptilted breasts beneath a thin dress——

I became aware of a gale that had ceased, of a landscape that crawled, of Pelagueya, very white, swaying at the wheel. I caught it from her in time

and steered the automobile to the side of the road.
So we slowed down and stopped. It was still the
mere beginning of the morning. The car coughed.
I turned off the engine. Pelagueya leant her face in
her hands. I said nothing. Straight and blue, little
pencillings of smoke arose from a village far down
the Cairo-wards horizon. Pelagueya took her hands
from her face.

"Do you know what I intended to do, Anton ?"

I did not look at her. "You wished to make a
great speed, and did so."

"I intended to wreck the car and kill both of us."

I nodded. There was no point in pretending the
lie that I did not know that. "And why did you not ?"

She laughed shakily. "Because of that look of
yours. Anton—hadn't you ever seen me before until
you realized . . .? That look, there was nothing else
could have stopped me. . . . Oh, God !"

She took herself from my arms after a little,
staring up at me. "Anton !"

I think it was I who was trembling then. I said :

"But even so I can still remember and believe
what I said at dinner a week ago, what I told in that
parable last night. . . . And *I* am going to drive
now."

She laughed. "You can remember and believe
and drive what you will, Anton Kyrilovitch." We
changed seats. I did it with elaborate rigidity. She
sank down in the place I had vacated, and ran her
long, slender fingers through the metallic miracle
that was her hair, and touched her flushed forehead.

"I feel much better now. Don't start up yet, Anton. I shan't ask you to make love to me—I'd never violate your dear scruples so. . . . Only, wonderful to be alive and see and smell. And to touch you. . . . Don't let's talk."

Nor did we, sitting there in that increase of the day. In a little all that tumult that had arisen in me had died down into a foolish, unreasonable glow of gladness, and that into perhaps as pringling an awareness as Pelagueya's of the wonder of this day in which we found ourselves alive—instead——

Perhaps neither of us would have been killed, would have lain smashed and in quivering agony in the wreckage of the automobile. Or died very fully and quickly, going into that which, spite all my romantic dreamings, I still knew for an end and no beginning ; have seen never again the miracle of that soft tracery of down upon Pelagucya's lip, or the breathing swell, like quickening buds, of a woman's breasts . . .

I came away from that thought, moving sharply, starting up the automobile, and starting Pelagueya from a dream that seemed as deep as my own, if of other content. "Already ?"

"We will now," I said, "have neither a hearse-procession nor a procession in quest of a hearse. And why are we going to Cairo ? Or——"

"Or did I plan my suicide and your murder yesterday ? Oh, no. It was an impulse that came on me ; slept badly on top of that abominable fairy-story of yours, I think. I wanted to smash up the world this morning, Anton. But yesterday I wanted a holiday only—in this world, not out of it. And I remembered I'd never seen Cairo."

I maintained an interrogative silence the while the still landscape, sane again, moved past us. "No, of course I never have—the Cairo of which you've talked. Only Shepheard's, and the places about Esbekieh. I want you to take me to the Warrens, and your Khalig, and the unmentionable places that men snigger over when they believe themselves alone. No need to drive so fast, Anton! Hateful if anything happened after—after the way you looked at me."

But I had brought the automobile to fifty and left it there. I said : "Nothing will happen. And I will show you Cairo."

Subchapter ii

Great houses, their fronts dimly uplighted even at midday, and shadowed now, reared themselves to right and left. From a side-valley came the monotonous beat of music to the obscene posturings of some hidden dancer. The air had a charnel-house smell. And, unempty, there was no true being or sound in that place : it was a place of fetid ghosts.

"This," I said, "is the Wagh el Berka, the Street of Prostitutes."

Pelagueya nodded. She was very white by then, but still carried her head erect. She looked round now with lips that trembled, but yet voiced no surrender. "I see," she said.

That was in the late afternoon, and not until then, looking at her in that moment, did I realize that I also had been mad, that I had shown her things that might scar her memory for ever.

Cairo—real Cairo without the colours and the drapings. This she had demanded and this I had given her! Cairo in horror and Cairo in loveliness—lanes and lost cul-de-sacs of the festering Warrens that are cloven through the heart by the bright sword of the Sharia Mohammed Ali, places where men and women and children lived hideous lives far sunk in such abyss of poverty and disease as no European has ever experienced; places where children had run after us with unclean demands and invitations; places no tourist had ever penetrated, dank, lost courtyarded houses emitting screams of pain as we passed; houses and dens where the harem-rule remained intact and slaves were beaten with heavy whips. . . . These, and the blaze of colour and beauty unescapable in the wide khans of the metal-smiths and the leather-workers and the place of the fine mushrabiyeh work. . . . Food in a native restaurant, behind the Tentmaker's Bazaar, with the cracked Mosque of Merdani blue and hot through the sun haze and the strange, repulsive food barely passing Pelagueya's lips. But—she had eaten it, only asking:

"Can I have some water? And is there any more sight-seeing?"

I had said, without dramatics: "We have hardly begun the sight-seeing yet."

Nor had we. I took her down through the Bab el
Zuweiya into that wilderness of abandoned khans
where strange trades, ancient and evil as the East
itself, are still plied ; where the scum of Europe's
dance-halls carry on in secret, lamplit rooms unclean
entertainment for the smuggled audiences. We had
passed through shrouded doors and down twisting
corridors and so through other doors, after the
making of passwords and signs, into one of those
lamplit theatres ; we had sat side by side watching
the Gomorrhan horrors enacted in the sweating
silence, with the light so low that others also present
—and we seemed the only white people there—were
dim and faceless. Twice Pelagueya had leaned forward to cry out ; then stayed herself. Once she
had covered her face with her hands and then dropped
those hands again, for not to look would have been
to fail the bargain she had made with me. Perhaps
she was the only white woman who had ever seen that
vileness. . . . They led the woman and animal—
both bewildered, dull-eyed automata—off through the
musk-stenching curtains at last, and I rose to my
feet, and Pelagueya walked out beside me, the colour
drained from her cheeks, her eyes feverish.

"Anything more ?"

"But plenty."

Yet I need give no record of that plenty here.
It had seemed to me that at last Pelagueya might
know something of the horror and terror of that
life she had but touched with tentative, amused hands
for so many years—that underpinning of cruelty

and blind hopelessness on which the gay lives of such as herself were built, that refutation undying of the ethical claims of modern civilization. Perhaps there was cruelty enough in my uncovering of that dark world ; sadism even. But I could not forget that bright road from Abu Zabal and the careless pet in which she had been prepared to risk and end both her life and mine—our lives which were sweet and clean and pleasant things in comparison to these tenebrous existences. So, under its dull, crumbling balconies, past the bulky English military policeman on guard, into the most shameful street in Cairo—almost deserted at that hour, for the traffic is a night-time one ; yet with here and there soft-stepping couples of little Greeks on holiday or the saunter of the tall, raw-boned American youth, looking incompletely detached and tourist. The smell of the street was almost a visible miasma. . . . And Pelagueya looking round it—I shall not readily forget my princess there ! I said, soberly :

"Once I had a friend who said this was the ultimate reality, this street. This is the place, Princess, where the essential fact is that you are a woman and I am a man, where the essential fact between all men and all women is a thing without disguise. . . . It is a humorous place, the Wagh-el-Berka, and they say it chuckles very loudly at night."

She looked at me then, wide-eyed. "What about ?"

"At love, and Dante's 'Vita Nuova', and tenderness, and the emancipation of women ; and at the love of children and the women who weep their unreturning lovers ; at that little vein in your throat, Princess, and the sweet down upon your lip, and your memories of Gault and your kindliness to me ; at me—at the thing I did this morning. . . . At all and every one of those pitiful veils whereneath we guise the essential fact——"

"Anton—I know I deserve all this : for the foolish things I said and did in the car near Abu Zabal. And I haven't complained. . . . I've said to myself that I wouldn't be a nuisance, that I'd wait till I got home again and then kill myself, quietly without fuss, after those horrors you've shown me. . . . But I won't now." She laughed. I stared at the colours returning to her cheeks. She put her hand on my arm. "Oh, Anton, my dear—*you* to pose as champion of this shoddy 'realism' !"

She looked round her, almost gaily. "And do take me further into this place if you want to. Only —it won't trouble me too much now. Pitiful and dreadful. But—oh, Anton ! the romantic illusions of all your life—if they are unreal, *this* is a lie also. . . . I've never lived in the gutter but I know that."

So did I, with a twinge of shame. "You need not bother to forgive me," I said—"all the things of this afternoon. Some are unforgivable. But let me take you out of this, back to Esbekieh."

"Do, and we'll have tea there."

"Then——"

"My dear, what is there to forgive ?—unless it is making me make love to you in the street of prostitutes ? . . . Ugh !"

Subchapter iii

I had pulled her aside, barely in the nick of time, as the three figures, fighting and clawing, rolled out of the doorway near which we stood, hit the street with considerable impact, and in the gutter continued the dispute with unabated vigour. Pelagueya I pushed away and made for the combative trio as I saw the flash of a knife. The point of my shoe and a wrist came in sharp contact. A yell rent the air of the Wagh el Berka. Encouraged, I applied the shoe again, to call forth similar appreciation. The triumvirate split apart, Crassus, an old woman, catspitting and half-clad, her grey hair in a tangle about her face, bolted back into the doorway of the house ; Pompey, fat, a bloated Egyptian in a fez, abandoned armaments and followed his fellow-triumvir precipitately. Was left Caesar, sitting upright, touching the side of his head with tentative fingers.

"B'God, it's still whole !"

"What is ?" I inquired, staring at him half-rememberingly.

"My skull, you fool." He stood up, swayingly, and set to beat from his clothes a cloud of dust. Pelagueya I found by my side. I suddenly recognized the evicted triumvir. It was the young man who had informed Huebsch, Marrot and myself on the authentic character of Solomon that night at Simon's.

"I see," I said, "that you have been emulating the good Solomon."

"Eh ?" He stood upright. He reeked of brandy.

His young haggard face jerked from me to Pelagueya. "Solomon ? That one of his tarts you have with you ?"

My nerves were not at their best after the mixed experiences of the day. . . . Pelagueya gasped. I knelt down beside him. He had hit the ground like a pole-axed heifer. There came the sound of running feet. I looked up at the English Military Policeman, burly, be-belted, a prideful hand upon his revolver.

"'Ere, wot's all this about ?" he inquired, without politeness.

The triumvir sat erect, slowly. I stood up. Pelagueya, with something like a giggle, lighted a cigarette. The boy in the gutter sought to rise, failed, grasped at the policeman's leg, and slowly levered himself upright.

"Damn good hit. Knew it was going to happen. Happen," he added vaguely, and then caught my look. His glazed young eyes brightened. "I'd like to jam you up against a wall and eviscerate you— just to see what you're made of. . . . And what the devil is *this* ?"

He had turned his astounded attention upon the policeman. The latter coloured richly.

"Never you mind 'oo I am. I'm the military policeman in charge 'ere, that's 'oo I am."

"Good God, thus spake Zarathustra. Take it away. Cremate it—else it'll smell." He put his hands to his eyes, forgetting all of us. "Oh, God, my head, my head !"

The policeman grinned. But to me it was obvious

that the boy was in agony. He had been drinking himself to death, I guessed, in the brothels of the Wagh el Berka. Knowing the hopelessness of the attempt, I could yet do no more than make it, with Pelagueya standing there wide-eyed.

"Leave Cairo. Go away from this place. Otherwise you are finished."

He staggered, shaking off my hand from his shoulder. He stared at me glassily. "Go away? Go where?"

"Anywhere out of Cairo. Go out to the desert. Go a walking tour by Abu Zabal," I added at random. The boy dropped his hands from his head.

"Walking-tour. Out to the desert. Right. Sheik. I'll be a sheik. Right."

And, catching every now and then at the street-wall as he went, he turned and swayed away down the Wagh el Berka. The policeman made a movement to follow, thought better of it, walked away in the opposite direction. I turned to Pelagueya. She was looking past me.

"He's coming back."

"Out to the desert. Right. I'm damn drunk, else I'd like to know you. Both of you. Look as though you had guts. Both of you. Here, read this. Book of mine that'll make you sick. Write care of my publishers and tell me how sick you feel. Right. Out to the desert."

CHAPTER THE TENTH

' "What can a modern of the twentieth century do, then, to reach his essential self, and be that self?" '

Subchapter i

"IT seems," said Pelagueya, "almost as insanitary as our afternoon's tour."

"The first few lines had told me that," I agreed.

We sat at tea in the Esbekieh Gardens, with the unauthentically cheerful hum of the tourist life about us, and the greenery of the Garden, a little tarnished by the late sun, still a cool and refreshing panache. And in front of Pelagueya, propped up against the water-jug, was the book the mad triumvir had thrust upon me in the Wagh el Berka. I had read a little of it and then had had it abstracted by Pelagueya, who ate crisp cakes with coconut in them and drank a cup of the horrid Cairene tea and inquired into the outlook of Esdras Quaritch upon the world.

"You know, I've heard of him before."

I nodded to that, recalling readings in belated literary journals that had found their way from Europe. "So have I, though this is the first book of his I have met. And it, you will note, though in English is printed in Italy. Another of his books was banned in England, and for America the boy appears to have a very bitter regard indeed"—and I related the incident of his encounter with Huebsch, Marrot and myself.

Pelagueya read on, a very lovely figure. I sat and smoked and watched the tamed and clipped and much bescrubbed Cairene scene—this part of the life Cairene that for me has no attraction, this impingement of the shoddy Western pleasure-seeker upon the shoddy, imitative East. Pelagueya closed the book and searched for cigarettes, and I made haste to offer mine—the cheap native ones I had once found so sickly and sweet. She made a comic moue at them, shaking her head, and then reached for one resolutely.

"Why shouldn't I, I suppose? They smoke worse things in the Warrens—when they can afford to smoke at all. . . . Anton."

"Princess!"

"Strange how I love you to say that. . . . But something else. You know that Oliver left me all his money?"

"I did not know it was all."

"Every piastre—though I had to go to England to settle some things. I'm a millionaire twice over; so they told me."

She fell into a muse, dark head down-bent, as she told me that. And I also mused—on the twists of chance. The money that the elder Gault had made as a war-time profiteer in England—his son had passed it by with a savage sneer on his dark, twisted face, passed it by and gone restlessly and perhaps

knowingly to his death, though this money had given
him all that he had passionately longed for in one
month—freedom and ease and Pelagueya. And the
Princess Pelagueya Bourrin, descendant of boyars
from the low lands of Kazan, was sole controller
and inheritor, as Gault's mistress, of the money
wrung from a feverish war-time English Government. . . . Pelagueya was talking to me.

"It will haunt me—oh, horribly! and especially
at nights—all that you've shown me to-day. Anton,
will you help me? We'll organize some Central
Charity for the Warrens. I'll endow a big fund—I'll
give it a million—and we'll place it in the hands of
some trustworthy native committee. People of the
Wafd, perhaps. And it will be for relieving destitu-
tion—with no questions asked as to how any destitute came to be so. *That* for the essential condition
in endowing the Fund. No one has any right to
question the destitute—I never realized before the
horror of that . . . We can save thousands yearly
in the lanes behind those khans. You will help
me?"

It was a difficult thing to do, with her eager face
cupped in her hands, awaiting my consent. But I
did it. I thought of the starving miners in the English
coalfields and the long queues of the unemployed
there; the serfs on England's green and pleasant
land. And were not the Gault monies invested
in France?—France, with its rat-like peasant
life, its bitter strugglings as of rats in a sewer. And
no money in investments was static, these days of

International Banks of Settlements. In German
chemical works—who knew ?—there were pallid
young folk accruing dividends on that money of
hers ; on tramps at sea, with guano from the
Peruvian islands ; in Italy, with its comic State
ferocities and its hunger-line industrial workers.
. . . I saw these things, in picture after picture, and
Pelagueya lowered her head again, listening. And
suddenly she said something of which indeed I had
not thought.

"So in every country—except our own !—this
stuff that gives me pretty clothes and the memory of
Oliver and Colonel Anton Saloney for my escort on
pleasure-jaunts—it is the surplus of folk who live
on a hunger-line only a little above that of the
Warrens ?"

"That is so," I said, and Pelagueya, with almost
the same gesture as the drunken boy in the Wagh el
Berka, put her hands to her head.

"Then there's nothing I can do. Is there ? And
after all—even the making of my pretty dresses and
the taking of me on pleasure-jaunts : they provide
work, do they not ? I spend only the smallest fraction
of the Gault income. It is reinvested to make work
for more people. So——"

She looked at me, bright-eyed with hope, with
that horrific memory of the cheated of the sunlight
fading behind the easy, protective veils the mind can
self-drape at such moments. I said :

"There is nothing you can do, but even that does
not absolve you. Nor any of us. We have made of

civilization and life a cruel and bestial thing. In a
sane world this money of yours—this property of
yours—it would be controlled for the good of the
community by the responsible and efficient."

"Am I neither ?"

"You are a Princess, and beautiful. And there is
no voice so lovely in the world, I think, as a Russian
woman's. And your mind is ruthless and eager.
But it is no industrialist's : it is the mind of a dream-
ridden Slav politician."

"Oh, I know !" She flung aside Esdras Quaritch
—so impatiently that the book fell on the ground
and I had to stoop and retrieve it. "I am Russian to
the core, Anton. Lovely voices—think of all the
other lovely things they have ! Remember the Volga
and the roofs of Kazan in winter——"

"And the music, and the *live*, kind faces," I said,
and she rekindled her torch at mine.

"—and the talk, so good and fine and understanding and desperately silly and desperately splendid.
And the selflessness—and the Asiatic fanatic and saint
in the most stupid face—and someone reciting
Lermontov——"

We stared at each other, white-faced Pelagueya
as I think I was, and sick with nostalgia. Russia !
Around us the green and brown babble of Cairo.
If we took the road to a ship and Suez—to Istambul
—through the Black Sea . . . some morning the
quays and towers of Odessa would rise, kindly and
grey, and those beloved, foolish voices ring in our
ears again. . . . Pelagueya was laughing whitely,

gathering together the little impedimenta of her handbag.

"We've forgotten the communists, Anton—no more of that talk now, nor the pleasant socialist pleasantly preparing to bring about Utopia. Instead —a Georgian peasant in the Kremlin, trampling underfoot everything clean and sweet, the clown in the palace of the Tsars——"

"I cannot imagine that the palace will know much difference," I said. "And at least it is not dynastic, the clownishness that rules now."

"Anton—you're a communist."

Pelagueya was angry at last. And I could not but smile at that *emigré* anger. I said: "I have ceased holding to any 'ism', Princess."

She stood up, still angry. "You have almost ceased to hold to life!"

I stood up also, Esdras Quaritch's book falling open in my hand at a great freakish blob of illustration. It caught Pelagueya's attention also. She craned over my shoulder, angry but curious, to see it.

I think I have forgotten to say that the book was not only written by the drunken boy of the Wagh el Berka, but illustrated as well. And a certain eager vividness and power of the macabre he certainly did possess. Across the page sprawled a blind and horrifying and proliferating object, something in shape between a three months' human embryo and such monster as might have crept from a jar of Paracelsus. Multilimbed, mindless, blind, this Thing climbed with a dim suggestion of angry purpose amid the blue and scarlet of a nightmare mountain-range.

Below it was a scrawled inscription. Pelagueya bent to read. "*What* is it ?"

"*Life*," I read, staring with some repulsion at the filthy thing portrayed.

Then I raised my head. Our eyes met. The anger went from Pelagueya's. Twin armies with torches and banners came dancing there. And suddenly our laughter went echoing across the Esbekieh Gardens, startling the neat tourists at their tables ; Pelagueya clung to my shoulder and laughed, and the horrific book of Esdras Quaritch slipped from my hand and hit the ground again with a petulant, youthful spite.

Subchapter ii

"Life was never quite so silly or unclean as that —in its entirety." Pelagueya had reclaimed the book again ; she was going to use it as a bed-book, she said. She stood beside me at the Gardens' entrance, and gurgled again at memory of the illustration we had just surveyed. "Poor boy—too horrifying to be anything but funny. Anton !"

"Princess !"

"Still that ? My dear, you showed me all the horror the world contained this afternoon. Real horror—but even at its worst there were other things ; memories of them only, perhaps, but these

things had been. . . .   That woman and that
beast——"

I put my hand on hers. "I am sorry I took you
to that."

"*I* am not." But the laughter had gone from her
voice; she quivered. "That woman—Anton, once
she must have been the loveliest baby. People loved
her. She was a girl. She ate nice things—oh, once in
a while, sometime. Once—if only once, one night
and one kiss—she had a lover who was a hero and
unbelievable and splendid. . . . That beast—it was
once a foolish, braying colt, and people rubbed its
ears. . . . This book of the boy might have made
me sick if I hadn't seen the reality. But I had. And
now—" she was wistful—"I know I don't deserve
it, but can't I see that other side—here in Cairo?"

"It is easy to find the hideous and the dreadful.
But beauty is as incidental as happiness. Sight-
seeing? There might still be time to see the Citadel
in sunset——"

She shook her head at that. "I want to know
something of the essentials in human nature, not in
architecture. You have begun my education; and
Anton, you must go on with it."

Now, some phrase of hers fitted with a little click,
as if it dovetailed in another I had once heard. And
suddenly I remembered that other—spoken to me
by Adrian the last time I had seen him. . . . I waved
to a passing taxi.

"Now where?" asked Pelagueya, as we sat
together and the taxi turned towards Shoubra,

avoiding with narrowness the slaughter of a vendor who attempted to sell us packets of indecent post-cards, an umbrella, and a box of Turkish delight. I leant back and looked at my watch, and then at Pelagueya.

"To a physician. You have heard me talk of him —Dr. Adrian, the gynaecologist."

The armies with torches came hurrying in the deeps of her sweet eyes again. "A gynaecologist? My dear, you don't think I'm a suitable patient? . . . Oh, Anton Kyrilovitch!"

I made hasty disclaimer of that. "It is not his gynaecology but his philosophy that is of interest. If we can find him at home I will have him expound it to you."

He was at home. He was in his garden, deserted of the sun now and over-brooded by the thought of evening. He sat at that little table where I had first made the acquaintance of Huebsch and Marrot, and as the Greek servant showed us down the path he looked up irritatedly.

"Didn't I tell you I couldn't see a soul to-night, Trikoupi? . . . Oh, it's you, Saloney." He caught sight of Pelagueya by my side and stood up, with a regretful frown towards the manuscripts that strewed the little table.

"Dr. Adrian: The Princess Pelagueya Bourrin."

My little Adrian's eyes lighted. "I am very pleased to see you at last, Princess." He flapped dust urgently from the two chairs where my employers had once sat. Pelagueya nodded and sat down and took off her hat and ruffled her hair, sitting with that long, drooping line of figure and limb that the Attic sculptors remembered, carving their Victories and their Heras. Adrian scowled at her inquiringly and she smiled at him.

"We're neither of us visitors, Dr. Adrian. We are patients."

She speaks English more faultless than mine, because more colloquial, but has still that slight difficulty of the Slav when confronted with the English "w". But she made of it a musical difficulty, so that the "ooe" for "we" was a lovely mispronunciation—or so I thought, and sighed at that reflection upon myself, for I found Pelagueya lovely even at her most stupid and reckless. But Adrian was regarding her incredulously, having no fine appreciations in phonetics.

"Patients? Neither of you look so."

I said: "But we are. And our disease is serious, my good Adrian. So if you will abandon the so-urgent manuscript of 'Fifty Years a Physician in Cairo' we will relate to you the symptoms."

He coloured a little, pushing aside the papers in front of him. "Only some notes. . . ." He became the physician, glancing from one to the other of us. "Go ahead."

"Our trouble is this little matter of human nature."

"Eh?"

"What we want to know is: Is there anything on earth that will act as a measure of the Good Life, and how may we find it?"

Pelagueya capped this : "And, providing there is a Good Life, and it may be attained—why anyone should want to attain it, or go on living it once attained ?"

He looked, justifiably, considerably surprised. We sat and regarded him with some amusement. "Sure you haven't both been out in the sun ?"

"Both of us have been," said Pelagueya. "At least, such times as we weren't underground—" and she proceeded to relate, with unswerving fidelity to detail, her eyes on the quietened expectation of the garden, the horror-sights I had shown her that day. Adrian, after the first few sentences, had sat rigid. As her recital went on he relaxed, and as she stopped he grinned sardonically, and then, looking at neither of us, began to answer, apparently at random :

"Seven thousand years ago, say the Diffusionist anthropologists, man was a sane and happy animal. There were no gods, no magics, no mystic hates or hopes ; no patriotisms, no clothes, no communists —no princesses and no Saloneys. There were no savages and no pacifists, no tabus, no culture and no cruelty." He waved his hand over the garden-wall. "And then an accident away to the south there brought about the beginnings of agriculture and the beginnings of civilization ; an accident, mind you, no innate urge in human nature. From that accidental starting point it spread abroad the planet and has ever since spread and grown and bloated, fungoid

rash upon rash. . . . Now, if the Diffusionists have
divined the truth, *that* is your cure, Princess, and
yours, Saloney." He paused and grinned at us. "I'm
about to have dinner. Join with me?"

Pelagueya nodded, her eyes twinkling to his. "I
love fairy-tales; Colonel Saloney tells them. . . .
And supper. But please——"

"Yes?"

"What is the *That* in the fairy-tale that can cure
Colonel Saloney and myself?"

He had stood up. He walked half-way up the
garden-path and summoned Trikoupi and gave him
orders, and then turned about and came back to us,
his hands clasped behind his head.

"The cure in diffusionism—well, it is very simple:
Be your essential self."

Now, I have learned a little of history and anthro-
pology also, and this fantastic resurrection of
Rousseau which Adrian had lately achieved sounded
to me as so much out-dated nonsense.

" 'Essential self'—but, my dear Adrian, that would
not do at all. The world would fall to pieces about
our ears."

He grinned at me, sidelong, still standing and
considering the two of us.

"Not the world would fall, but something else
might."

"It would mean anarchy, murder, bloodshed, the
loosening of the beast in men—if each were his
essential self."

"But if man were never a raving beast—except

the beast that civilization has made of him—how
could acceptance of his essential self loosen that
imaginary monster ?"

I shrugged aside the question. "We have discussed
this before. All the evidences of history point to
the slow evolution of man, by means of laws and
tabus, from a lawless savage."

He was very cheerful. "Not them. Not a single
evidence. Like everyone else, you've been misled
by the theorizings of the evolutionists. Theories
aren't evidence. . . . Think, Colonel ! *Does* the
essential Saloney want to batter in my jaw, and
creep up behind Trikoupi and cut his throat for the
sake of smelling blood, and—you'll forgive the
illustration, Princess—rape the Princess Pelagueya
Bourrin ?"

They both looked at me then. Pelagueya, her head
a little on one side, said :

"I at least feel very safe."

Somehow that angered me—me who had here
heard the grasshopper but such a short time before !
"Yours is the least reason for composure—in a choice
of the three eventualities."

Adrian said : "Even if that is the case, even if
you wanted to do all three, they're not necessarily
acts of desire of your essential self. They're prompt-
ings, not of the inhibitions of the beast but of the
repressions of the tortured human animal—once a
kindly animal."

Pelagueya had turned her attention from me after
that one feline stroke. But now, sitting very still,

clasping her hands about her knees in that attitude that was characteristic, she said :

"Doctor—if these historians you talk about are right, and their cure is the one to aim for—what can a modern of the twentieth century do to carry out that cure, to reach to his essential self, and be that self ? What can I do ?"

"There you have me. There is no magic way."

"But——"

Adrian laughed. "Dinner is ready. I see Trikoupi signalling. . . . Princess, I'm sorry. I can diagnose your complaint with the aid of the Diffusionists : I can diagnose the complaint of the world. But how to effect the cure. . . . The trumpet-voice of human sanity was stilled long ago. It is the great Lost Trumpet of history."

CHAPTER THE ELEVENTH

'Sweet to dance to violins.'

Subchapter i

WE came out from Adrian's into a Cairene
darkness made of velvet, hung with little red
jewels that were the street-lights, and very quiet
except for the whoom and clatter of the distant street-
cars that held towards Esbekieh. I looked for a taxi,
but none was to be found, and we walked the rutty
streets towards the garage by Bab el Hadid where
Pelagueya had left her automobile. But less than a
score of yards from Adrian's door Pelagueya took
my arm and said: "Listen!"

And then, remote to our left through the night, we
heard the distance-softened clamour of dance-music.
A violin dominated the sound and sank and rose
again. A ball was in progress in some place.
Pelagueya's face was a dim red-ochred silhouette.

"I'd love to dance. Where is it, Anton?"

In a moment I was sure. "No public place, I am
afraid. It is the Pension Avallaire. The ball of the
season for residents. Why——!"

I had suddenly recollected Aslaug Simonssen.
Pelagueya threw away her cigarette.

"A girl you know there? Then she'll take us in. Let's go."

"These are sad hours for a middle-aged drago-man."

She laughed mockingly. "I will find you a nice basket-chair to sit in at the Avallaire."

Now the glitter of lights begilding the usually sombre frontage of the Pension burst upon us. Another dance was in progress. I said:

"The good Oscar Wilde, you will remember from my English classes in Kazan, was a favourite of mine."

"Who?"

"Wilde. A not-so-clean little English genius. And a verse of his says:

> " ' 'Tis sweet to dance to violins
>   When love and life are fair,
>   To dance to lutes, to dance to flutes,
>   Is delicate and rare,
>   But it is not sweet with dangling feet
>   To dance upon the air!' "

"But I don't want to dance upon the air!"

"Nor are you in any risk, Princess. But I was only a moment ago. . . . For no doubt I should have had the decency to go and hang myself had I accepted your challenge at Adrian's and put it in practice in that dark street we have just left."

"Why, Anton Kyrilovitch!" She stopped and put her hands on my shoulders. We stood so, ludicrously, and it was well it was night and not day, for even

Cairo would have gaped its astonishment at us. I
saw the white gleam of teeth from the sweetly parted
lips, and I bit my own at thought of that adorable
face so close to mine in the cord-velvet of the dark.
"If that is true—there might be no need for
violence."

"You mistake me," I said. "The thing that walked
with me in that alley-way we have just left was
neither love nor lust : it was merely that sporadic,
mindless cruelty essential in a man's nature—or one
of civilization's creations, if Adrian would have it
so."

"Cruel, that, Anton."

So I realized as she released my shoulders. I
turned cold looking at her shadowy, averted head,
and for once that supreme honesty in which we
had been wont to deal one with the other shook
and quivered like a crazy bridge of reeds spanning
a dark torrent. "Princess !"

She said, subduedly : "Nothing, Anton. Oh, I
understand."

The music drifted out to us. So did a waft of
such perfume as never rose from terrestrial flower.
Abruptly Pelagueya giggled. "The Brazilians are
there—I was once a nursery maid among them and
I can smell them miles off. Come along, Anton !"

In we went, then, dusty and un-festa-like, both
of us. The haughty French manager accosted us with
suspicion. I presented to him my card, asking for
Miss Simonssen, and in a little the folding doors
through which seeped the music swung apart and

through them, a brooding Valkyr, came also Aslaug Simonssen. She halted and looked at Pelagueya and myself, and then recognized me, coolly and slowly.

"Why, it's Colonel Saloney. Sorry I didn't write you, but I've just got back from Rashida."

I bowed. "Miss Simonssen: The Princess Pelagueya Bourrin."

They touched hands, Aslaug Simonssen reservedly, Pelagueya consideringly, lightedly, and I looked at them and though I was more than a little weary with all the upsets and downsets of the day, enjoyed the contrasts and points of resemblance they offered—Pelagueya's dark flame of beauty, sheathed in dark red, her face a Slavic pallor with encarmined lips; and Aslaug Simonssen's blond Norse sandiness and freshness and dazed youth. And then to my surprise, and evidently to Aslaug's, the two kissed, and released each other, and the girl blushed slowly, her polite gaze kindling a little.

"I am pleased to meet you, Princess. Will you both come up to my sitting-room?"

I looked at Pelagueya ruefully. But her eyes were bright and her face turned towards the sound of the music.

"I would with pleasure," I said, "but the Princess insisted that we should come here and attempt to filch from you invitations to the dance."

She looked a little surprised. "Why, of course," she said, woodenly. She turned towards the ball-room. "Do come."

But before we had gained the door the haughty

manager had insinuated himself between that desirable entrance and the three of us. He bowed profoundly to Aslaug Simonssen.

"Mademoiselle, but one guest is allowed at the ball, as you know."

He was for some reason malevolent. Suddenly I remembered. This was the man on whose chest our cook Georgios had sat, and whose head he had used so vilely to maltreat a wall. I said : "Do you know a cook and musician, one Georgios Papadrapoulna-kophitos ?"

The haughty Frenchman quite blanched. "But certainly."

I regarded him gravely. "He is of our party, and is out in the night there with his bugle. If he knew of any strict enforcement of rules I do not doubt but that he would be pleased enough to stand just inside the door and aid your orchestra."

"The good God forbid ! Entrez, mesdames ; entre, M'sieu' !" He flung open the door, casting the while a terrified look towards the main entrance. As we passed through we heard his voice shrill out an order that the outer door should be closed immediately. Aslaug and Pelagueya regarded me with surprise as we stood in the glare of the ball-room and the per-spiring, unauthentic musicians beat and brayed with their instruments, and, in a variety of dress, the habitues of the Avallaire and their guests sailed to and fro in the cataleptic measures of the fox-trot. I explained.

The girl Aslaug smiled politely and unintelli-

gently. The glow had faded from her face and eyes.
Pelagueya's laughter was the chipping of a hundred
little hammers at the flood-gates of mirth, and the
falling of the gates and the coming of the dancing
flood. . . . No laughter so sweet as that.

"Oh, Anton !" And then grew serious. "But,
you know, in a way I'm disappointed."

"But why ?"

"Because I don't think I ever heard you tell a lie
before."

"Nor did I this time."

"Why, didn't you say Georgios was outside with
his bugle, ready to fall on the Avallaire ?"

"Not at all. I said he was of our party. So, at
Abu Zabal, and I trust in bed, he is. He is therefore
out in the night with his bugle. And assuredly if
he had known of the manager's reluctance he would
have come to our assistance."

Pelagueya shuddered. "Thank goodness there's
no chance of that. I think he was one of the principal
reasons why I wanted a holiday from Abu Zabal."
She looked round the room inquiringly. "They
don't seem very enthusiastic about asking us to
dance."

Aslaug Simonssen flushed at that. "You see, I
don't know them." Pelagueya twinkled at her,
mischief kindling in her eyes. I looked away. Now I
saw that the dancers were indeed of somewhat
different quality from those who usually frequent the
modern ball. True that they swooped and curvetted
and jigged like inebriated chickens ; true that the

male clasped the woman of the moment in attitude
of such intimacy as mankind has hitherto left to
discreeter moments ; true there was neither rhyme,
reason nor restraint in each blared-out tune. But the
dancers, so far as was possible in these measures,
danced with a certain frigid restraint. Pelagueya had
noticed this.

"Most of them look as though they couldn't forget
that death ooaits for each and all," she said in her
easy English. "Ooat is wrong ?"

Aslaug explained. The Avallaire at the moment
was almost entirely filled by a party which had come
from Alexandria for a week and was rejoining its
steamer at Port Suez—a party of the United Churchfolks' Social Guild which was touring the world.

"Poor planet," said Pelagueya. And her eyes,
which had grown disappointed, suddenly brightened
again. She glanced at Aslaug again with that secret
flash of mischief. "I know ! And we're quite justified. Will you dance with me ?"

I made to intervene and then refrained. It was
plain that Aslaug, though doubtful because of its
unconventionality, saw nothing shocking in the
proposal. Pelagueya said : "I'll play cavalier,"
and flashed a smile at me as I stood back, and
so in a moment they were in the measure of the
dance.

For a little their irruption went un-noticed. But
presently I saw a craning of necks above the dutiful
prance and undulation of bodies. Near the bandstand
two couples detached themselves from the dance.

And, as a surge reached towards where I stood, another couple came to halt within a yard of me.

The man, who had the look of an over-eager plaice, said : "Say, guess we should see the management."

The woman, possessed of puffy eyes and an unfortunate dewlap, said : "Disgusting."

And, with myself, they watched Pelagueya and Aslaug pass.

Pelagueya had entered the dance I think still with the devil upon her. Aslaug's face had assumed a slow flush of surprise and pleasure as, held in those lithe Russian arms, her feet caught the beat of the tune and Pelagueya's white, mischievous face bent over hers. The churchgoing social plaice beside me cleared his throat. "Guess they're professional dancers."

"Guess they're women off the streets," said the churchly female bloodhound, and at that moment the dance ceased. Looking across the ebb of disengaging and engaging partners for the next number— for the most of the social churchfolks were but small in stature—I saw Pelagueya and Aslaug surrounded in a twinkle, saw Aslaug flushingly consider a number of suitors and accept a great raw-boned boy. But Pelagueya shook her head and made her way through the halted groups. The plaice and the bloodhound backed a little towards the door, the bloodhound whispering hoarsely : "Gene, you're *not* to go with her."

"Next one with me, Anton ?"

I bowed. "Charmed, Princess," and had the mean

twinge of satisfaction at hearing a mingled canine and piscine gasp from behind me. Then the band struck up again a Negroid air to which it appeared an alcoholic addict arrested at the cretin stage of mental development had set words in pseudo-English, and Pelagueya and I were dancing to the strains of "A Night with You."

She said: "Well, Anton?"

I said: "Not well at all. If you were not a princess and I not a dragoman, but two negroes in a forest of the Congo, with a moon above us instead of that lard-like face that conducts the orchestra——"

"Fun it would be! Anton, I know! Let us go there—to the Congo. Equip a caravan and set out through the Sahara. Go south till we strike Timbuctoo and then down that River——"

"All so that we may dance in the Congo?"

"It would be great fun. You dance very well still, if a little like a Negro who has been at a missionary school . . ."

She stopped in that remark, for her words and the tom-tom beat that underlay the frills and adornments of the foolish music had made me for a moment forget my self-admired composure. She looked up in such fashion as I do not care to write of.

"Oh, Anton—sometimes you forget the mission school!"

And at her words I instantly remembered it, seeing the curious glances cast on us. We jogged and dipped and stamped and slithered with decorous seemliness. Pelagueya sighed, sweetly, whimsically.

"So there is to be no Congo. Anton, do you think Miss Simonssen is comfortable here?"

"She seems not greatly enamoured of the place."

"I myself don't think she is. Poor thing. . . . Do you remember a horrible little English picture with a legend: ' Where the brook and river meet?' "

"I think so. Why?"

"It is time this girl was pushed head first into the river. Why? Oh, don't be so simple, Anton! . . . I'm going to ask her to come and stay with me at Abu Zabal."

I said I doubted if Aslaug would do ,that, and as we passed round the room again I told her of the reason of her coming to Egypt, and how she had journeyed down to Rashida to seek out clues regarding her brother's murderer.

"So that is it. Transferred interest. . . . That glazed look— Oh, a horrible shame!"

I was justifiably bewildered. "Shame?"

"Of course, this obsession of hers, cultivated by her surroundings in England. A diseased thing. All people who cannot forget deaths and wrongs are diseased."

"Then most of us White Russians are that."

She said, absently: "No communist propaganda now, Anton. I want to cultivate the Simonssen girl. You must help me to persuade her. There she is. Come along."

Aslaug turned a comely, momentarily-transformed face upon us. The raw-boned youth dithered undecidedly near her, with a mingled look of exhaustion and not over-clean desire upon his unhealthy face. Pelagueya said :

"Let us all go and have ices."

Aslaug nodded, and turned with Juno-like deliberation towards a far door. The pallid youth made a step to follow her, and then, with a peculiar gurgle, refrained. We left him and sat beside a small table in the Avallaire courtyard and ate the moistly-warm ices Pelagueya ordered.

Now, here we were lost from the full beat of the dancing. It was a remote inharmonic noise. And presently we heard something clearer and cleaner. No doubt it came from some gardener's outhouse of the Avallaire—a man twanging on a single stringed instrument and a voice uplifted in the strains of an old, old Arab song. Down the dim night it came to us, sitting in darkness and caught to attention :

> *' Ya aziz uu-u-uu eyni, w'ana biddi aruh,*
> *Beledi !*
> *Beledi, uu-uu beledi, w'ana biddi aruh*
> *Beledi :*
> *Yazmar !'*

It was very penetrating and eerie and sad. I heard a whisper : "What is it, Anton ?"

> *' Marmar zamani, ya zamani marmar !*
> *Tebla eynunu illi ma yehibbak*
> *Yazmar !'*

"*Oh Love, sing low of the homeland, sing!* . . . It is some lost tribesman remembering the tents of Kedar, Princess."

"As we do—so often."

Aslaug said, very slowly and looking at us, I knew puzzledly : "You mean Russia ?"

I nodded. The dull voice went on : "It must be awful—your country in the hands of those murdering Bolsheviks and criminals. I read it was just like the people escaped from the lunatic asylums and prisons in charge of a country."

I waited, knowing what to expect. Never yet had I heard the much-detested communists abused by an alien in Pelagueya's presence but she sprang to their defence.

"You read—oh, my dear schoolgirl ! What nonsense then you have read ! The Bolsheviks like that ? Instead—instead—you fought them, Anton. Tell us what they are like."

"Titans storming heaven with hammer and sickle, Miss Simonssen—Titans a little crude in method and purpose, and unforgiving either the cruelties or the beauties of the gods. But the good Marrot could no doubt tell you more about the communists than I —though I doubt if his communism is orthodox."

"Marrot ?"

"He is one of the American archæologists employing Colonel Saloney near my place at Abu Zabal." Pelagueya had remembered her intention. "I think you must be very bored here, Miss Simonssen. Why not come out to Abu Zabal for a fortnight or so— unless you are absolutely bound to Cairo ?"

There was a moment's hesitation. "I should like to, only—" The blonde head was turned towards me. "I went to Rashida, you know, Colonel Saloney, to find out about Carl's murder."

"And you found out——?"

"I think more than the Egyptian officials wanted me to. I found out that all the evidence points to the woman Huth Rizq as the murderess, and that she was allowed to slip through the fingers of the police. She disappeared—or so they said. But I followed up things, and I know she came to Cairo."

"And you have informed the police here?"

"I spent all to-day at the Ministry of the Interior. They're going to comb the native quarters for her."

That was a bigger task, I thought, than probably either the police or this girl realized. How much did this murderess-hunting mean to her? Strangely, Pelagueya must have been following the same train of thought, for she spoke my question.

"And even if she's caught and proved to have murdered your brother—will it help him much?"

"But—she must be punished. You can't allow murderers to go unpunished."

"Are you a Christian?"

I think she winced away from that question and then pulled herself together, remembering that it was a foreigner who spoke, one possibly ignorant of the fact that in Edinburgh God and Christianity were impolite topics. She said: "Yes, I think so."

"Then you ought to forgive the murderess. But I don't suppose you will—yet. Sometime—forgiveness is such complete and obvious commonsense! . . . But will you come to Abu Zabal?"

Again a hesitation. The native singing had ceased.
The sound of the band was louder. Then :

"Yes, thank you. They can easily let me know
from the Ministry when they've found the woman.
But, Colonel Saloney——"

"Yes ?"

"I think you're an awfully good dancer. I saw
you with the Princess. Can we have one before I go
and pack ?"

Subchapter ii

Twenty minutes later Pelagueya and I found ourselves again in the dark streets outside the Pension
Avallaire. She took my arm.

"It is nearly midnight. We'll have to hurry and
bring my automobile if we hope to get back to Abu
Zabal before morning. . . . What is it, Anton ?"

"Nothing," I said.

Pelagueya laughed. "Miss Simonssen, of course.
Were you shocked, Anton ?"

"I was a little surprised."

"You would be. Oh, all men are fools. But I—
I knew as soon as I looked at her that no one had
danced with her as she should be danced with. So I
set to awakening her."

We stumbled in Cairene pit-holes. A dog growled
at us from the shadows. Cairo dreamed under a
great splendour of stars. I thought of Aslaug
Simonssen in my arms, in a fierce, shy abandon and

wistful terror that had amazed me. "There is danger in some awakenings."

"What ?—while she was with *you*, Anton ?"

"I can let that sneer go by, Princess. But I am not the only dancing partner she had—or is likely to have. I understand now the hog-like gogglings of the raw-boned youth."

"Pfuu ! Loosen his inhibitions as well—and he'll be able to get them tied up nicely for five dollars or so as soon as he gets back to America and consults a respectable psychoanalyst. . . .   Anton, what's that ?"

I had thought it a dog—mutilated as I have seen· many Cairene dogs mutilated, with the tendons of the hind legs cut and trying to crawl out of the street into some corner in which to die. Lighting a match, I looked down on something that made Palagueya shiver. Then the match-glow flickered out. The thing mouthed at us in the darkness.

"It was a woman." Pelagueya's voice was the voice of one sickened as we went on.

"It *had* been a woman," I said. "And perhaps she had over-indulged in the loosening of inhibitions."

"Anton, you are puzzling me nowadays. Especially to-day. Something is happening to you."

"What ?"

She sounded troubled and impatient. "Oh, I don't know. Satisfactory change—and sometimes horribly the reverse. . . . What a day it has been ! And I'm tired."

"I'll drive back to Abu Zabal."

"But no, you most certainly will not. To-morrow you have work to do." She looked up at the stars. "Or is it to-day?"

"To-day, I think. It is after midnight."

It was after one when we brought Pelagueya's automobile to rest in front of the Avallaire. The disharmonic clamour of the dance-music was loud as ever. Aslaug Simonssen stood on the Pension steps beside a neat stacking of suit-cases. With the aid of a Pension servant I had bestowed that luggage about the exterior of the automobile in a moment or so, bestowed its owner in the back seat, and stood motioning to Pelagueya to descend from her place at the wheel.

"But why? I told you I'd drive."

Her face came into the lamplight, peering at me rebelliously. I still held the door open.

"Hurry, Princess."

She sat for a little looking at me, and I suppose Aslaug Simonssen, uncomprehending either our looks or our barbaric Russian speech, wondered. Then Pelagueya put out her hand, caught mine, followed the hand, and swung into the back seat with the pivoting of a single small foot.

"Comfortable, Miss Simonssen? We'll let Colonel Saloney drive. He's afraid I may go mad again and attempt to kill us all—as I did this morning driving into Cairo."

"Did you have an accident, then?"

I closed the door and sat at the wheel, but heard

Pelagueya's voice answer, clear and composed and casual.

"Oh, no. I tried to kill Colonel Saloney and myself."

"But why ?"—in a slow crudescence of horror.

"I was very tired of things this morning. It seemed the best way out."

"And you tried to *kill* yourself ?"

"Yes. And Colonel Saloney. But he looked at me so nicely I couldn't do it. . . . Just a moment. I have two pillows under here. And there's a rug in that corner. So. And here's a book you may like to read, because I never talk on journeys."

"Oh, thank you. . . . Esdras Quaritch ? Is it a novel ?"

"Yes. Nice and old-fashioned. Comfortable ?"

Kasr-el-Nil and the River below, dark and warm in its northward sweep. The roads were deserted and Cairo slept dreamlessly but for the purr of the engine. Northwards, over that age-old flowing of the Nile, Sirius crept down the sky, the Dog Star, the hunter of the morning. . . . In front the scud of the road. Behind the Nile.

How many men in the velvet dark of this and that night had looked at and brooded on River and Star ! From what drowsiness of bed-dreams had heads lifted from pillows and looked north and east, waiting for the coming of the morning and the Dog Star loping on its trail ?

From more than pillows—before the world had dreamt of pillows. Dark men of the Old Stone Age had seen these midnights and sky and waters—six thousand years before the birth of Christ perhaps some hunter had walked this very track, naked, spear-gripping, his kill upon his shoulder, back to the reedy hut where his woman slept. And looked out and up and wondered a little and thought that these things would still be there when he and his woman and all he knew were nothing. . . . Adrian's men of the Golden Age, before in Upper Egypt they tamed the first growths of corn . . .

Helmieh by then. Into the rays of the headlights shot a lurching figure, plodding southwards. Some peasant—some labourer, rather, in that rag-tag of European clothing. . . . Buildings uprising and fading to right and left. . . . The open road.

Had Man indeed once walked free and unhampered of any laws—and been no raving brute of the nights and dawns, but that child of whom the poets had dreamt and sung ? Was this world of the last six thousand years no more than a world diseased, a torture and enslavement of the human spirit through the chance of an accident ? And what remedy was there if that were the case ?

Mile on mile of featureless road. The waning glory of the stars. Silence behind me, though Pelagueya, leaning forward to look at some object, had forgotten to lean back, and remained there still, her hand upon my shoulder, her finger-tips touching my neck. And I dreamt on with the purr of the engine in front and the smooth glide of the wheel in my fingers. How ? *How ?*

Find our essential selves ? But could that ever be done—even if I and Pelagueya and Marrot and Huebsch possessed those essential egos ? To dig down below the layers of prejudice and habit and superficial like and hate and distaste and lust—to find the essential human being and live with him and be him——

Oh, God, if one could !

CHAPTER THE TWELFTH

' "It is . . . a Levite ornament. We're close on the track of the Lost Trumpet." '

Subchapter i

IT seemed to me I had slept a bare hour. Yet I awoke with the sunlight streaming in upon my face ; and, lying in the disorder of my tent, knew that I had very grievously overslept. For that beam of sunlight was not due to make entrance until at least ten o'clock in the morning.

This came of gadding around the Cairene scene in company with an *emigré* princess and an anachronistic sagawoman !

We had reached Gault's castle at five in the morning. There, having seen to the awakening and decanting of Pelagueya and Aslaug Simonssen, I had betaken myself, stumblingly, for sleep was almost upon me, across the dimness of the Egyptian night, on my way narrowly escaping a fall and a broken neck from a new and unexpected traverse the archæologists had cut in my absence. The speculations and queries of the journey from Cairo trailed after me like footsore phantoms. But wherever yet were the philosophical agonies which over-

due sleep could not put to rout in one short, sharp
bout ? . . .

I got out of bed and looked from my tent-opening.
All the camp seemed engrossed on the tasks attend-
ant the digging of the new traverse.   There was
Huebsch himself, an archaic figure out of Semitic
history, a Shophet of Punic days in a stetson hat and
large boots, a-lean above the toiling back of Kalaun.
Marrot was at the remote end of the traverse : the
body of the labourers worked midway.   From the
cook-tent a little stream of smoke, blue and shot
with silver, rose up and quivered questioningly on
the ghost of some breeze of the upper reaches.
Ascending the incline, laden tray in hand, eyes
protuberant and benevolent behind the luxuriant
foliage of his moustache, was Georgios himself.

"M'sieu' has slept well ?   It was the order of
M. Huebsch that he should not be disturbed."

I made way for the tray.   "I had thought such
order to be more in accord with the principles of
M. Marrot."

Georgios chuckled.   "But he is the slave-driver,
that one ! With the bitter kindness and the preach-
ings of revolt does he drive ! . . .   I trust M'sieu'
had an amusing day ?"

"Killing, Georgios," I assured him in that con-
temporary Romaic which has filled the City of the
Violet Crown with clamorous acceptance of the
latest in American colloquialisms. His small, absurd
figure padded away down the hill. I turned and sat
down to the fragrant invitation of the tray's contents.

Sleep and food. Food and sleep and sex. How good they were and how much of our lives they devoured!

Sleep—a third; food—its eating only—a sixth; food—its gathering—a third; sex, and all its consequences—another sixth. The sum total of man's activities. Yet somehow, in the corners and string-knots of this mathematical mesh, he raped from time those scared, idle moments in which to stare at the stars and dream of fate and life and God and death and the coming of the millennium and the cheese-greenness of the moon . . . till the clamour of his belly or his children or his sleep-weighted head jerked him back to the concrete realities of concrete desire!

If man had had a digestive system that preyed not on his nerve-centres for drugging rest! No sleep; and a third of his life saved. If he had but followed some wise and seemly line of biological evolution and remained heterosexual and self-satisfying, budding off his children from his body as the trees bud new branches—yet another third saved. And with those two-thirds——

But my musings had not arrived at the point where I could begin to catalogue the glories of talk and smoking and wine-drinking and high adventure in which men might indulge but for distractions of sleep and sex—when I heard a hurried step come up to the tent-door and the small, dark face of Marrot was thrust into the opening.

"Hello, colonel! Sleep well?"

"Too well," I said, and offered him a cup of

coffee. He accepted it hurriedly, standing and drinking as if the work at the traverse still claimed his
urgent attention. He banged down the cup and prepared to leave.

"I'd turn in again, Colonel, if I were you. No
need to start until the afternoon."

"I am coming down with you now," I said, rising.

"Why the devil should you ? You'll get no more
thanks for it. . . . Right, then. Bring your geodeter,
will you ? You can take the middle section of the
new traverse and start two new side-cuttings from it."

We had reached the day-old traverse by then.
The Punic Shophet straightened in the distance to
wave me greeting ; then re-bent to his work. Marrot,
admonishing me to go back to my tent and sleep
if I felt drowsy, departed in short, sharp strides
towards his section of the excavations. I myself,
with a smile after him and a moment's wonder
whether or not his skill in making all of us so toil-
desirous were conscious or unconscious, paced out
two likely side-cuttings and set a labourer to each of
them ; and found a spade and went to work myself.

The sun climbed. The sweat dripped down our
foreheads. There was no other sound than the
crunch of iron in soft, black loam and sandy shale.
One of the labourers, a great dark-pigmented fellah
from upper Egypt, dug beside me with the precision
and unintelligence of a machine, his eyes dull, his body
exuding that peculiar odour that seems the heritage
of all Asiatics, bathed or unbathed. He had a brutal,
prognathous jaw and his eyes when they glanced

towards me were shifty and hard and of no great pleasantness. The other labourer, digging a side-cutting on his own, seemed small and oppressed and overworked, for he panted and shovelled with a desperate earnestness and his dirty trousers hung slantwise and unimpressive from his meagre hips. . . . Descendants of the Golden Men of the Golden Age !

It was plaguing me again, that question. I cut and hewed and kept a sharp regard upon the ground, knowing that was my business. But mere mechanical labour has never had power to prevent me thinking of something widely different from the task in hand. And surely here, in these two Egyptians, were question-marks gigantic enough to set up against the fine romance of Adrian's theory. Men, kindly and brave, splendid and free—and these their descendants ! Had civilization made that low, brutal brow—that weak, foolish face and sagging body ? Surely not !

And then I saw a side-twist to the argument. Surely yes ! For without the resources of food-cultivation the weak would certainly have died off early in life. So perhaps also the brutal, who indeed could seldom have made any success of the sim-plicities of existence. Brutality flourished on com-plexities. Two marks scored up for Adrian !

"Colonel !"

I looked up and saw Marrot, waving to me from the far end of the traverse. Abandoning my two labourers—who promptly dropped their shovels and impacted their buttocks upon the earth—I went towards the mound where the archæologist-communist squatted under the gigantic shadow of the sitting Huebsch. Beside them, tray-laden again, a Ganymede of the desert, was Georgios. As I approached Huebsch held up something for my inspection.

"Ever seen the like of this, Colonel ?"

I cupped my hand to enclose it with as much care as he put it there. It was a golden brooch, two inches by two and a half; so Marrot measured it later. I knew it gold in spite of its earth-incrustations. And I stared without much comprehension at the intersecting triangles. Valuable, perhaps, but certainly not Ancient Egyptian.

"What is it ?" I asked.

The Punic Shophet gave a great sigh and affixed his rich lips to the edge of a tumbler handed him by Georgios.

"It is the Shield of David; a Levite ornament. We're close on the track of the Lost Trumpet."

Subchapter ii

Kalaun had found it. I went and examined the spot. There was nothing else. It had lain beneath the black cultivation loam, on top of the sand-levels. And for three feet around the sand and loam had been gathered and riddled and sieved. I returned to the two Americans.

"If there is nothing else——"

Huebsch shook his great head. "I didn't expect anything else after the first few minutes. What happened must have been this: The Levite in his hurry dropped the brooch from his tunic or else spilt it from the container holding the Lost Trumpet and other treasures. It's a clue to the fact that we're on no wild-goose-chase, as Marrot here had begun to think. The Trumpet itself may lie within a foot of us. Or maybe it's a thousand yards. But it's here somewhere."

Marrot seemed to take the discovery coolly enough. He stood up and yawned. "Exchange sectors with you, Huebsch?"

The immense ovoid head was moved negatively. "I've a weakness for finding Levite treasures myself." He smiled slowly, gigantically, remotely. "Keep a sharp look-out, both of you, and don't damage the Lost Trumpet with a spade-thrust."

"If you hear me shout for Georgios you'll know I've found the thing and want him to blow it," retorted Marrot, flippantly, and we went back to our traverse-sections. The news had spread from Kalaun among the other labourers. The apparently lunatic activities of the Yahudi and the Don't-Worker had borne a measure of reward. And Kalaun would probably be rewarded. . . . My giant and pygmy were sending the earth showering in the fashion of dogs at the mouth of a rabbit warren as I approached them. I restrained their enthusiasm a little and resumed with my own spade. The loam Huebsch had said we might now disregard. But every shovel-

ful of the shale-sand might be with advantage sieved
and riddled.

This trebled the labour. I sent the pygmy for a
sieve and bade him abandon his side-cutting and
take to sieving the labours of the giant and myself.
Upwards climbed the sun. New Zealand-ward
descended our trench. And the smell of the earth,
upturned for the first time in many hundred years,
grew so pungent that at moments I had to rest and
breathe unchoked the hot air of the Egyptian midday. No further word of success came from either
Huebsch or Marrot, but, unbending once, I was
hailed by Georgios, crossing the riven lands yet
again towards the traverse.

"A letter from the Princess, mon colonel."

So it was—a miniature, faintly-scented envelope
to which the grime on my hands added no attractive-
ness. I broke it open and stood and read the contents ;
then handed the letter back to Georgios.

"Show it to M. Huebsch and then to M.
Marrot."

Two minutes later Huebsch's great voice boomed
down the windless air to me.

"Colonel !"

He stood with Pelagueya's missive elevated in
his hand. I shouted back on a note of less
volume.

"Well ?"

"Eh ?"

I decided this was absurd and made towards
him.

"Can't read Russian, Colonel. So what's the good of sending this to me?"

He considered the missive, head on one side. "But it's a very fine and pretty note. And what's it all about?"

"The Princess Bourrin would like the three of us to drink tea with her to-morrow."

"Well, well, that's fine. I'm honoured."

"You will go?"

"Sure, I certainly will."

I sent the anxious Georgios—who imagined he smelt an overturned saucepan—back to his cook-tent, conveyed the note to Marrot myself, heard his hurried acceptance, and then wrote our triune accept-ance on the back of Pelagueya's sheet of paper. Her messenger—Gault's house-boy of olden days—took it, grinned at the condition of the paper; and departed. I returned to my traverse, expedited on the way by a hail from my giant.

"There is something here, khawaga! Metal! My spade has struck against it!"

The others heard the hail and collected around us. Huebsch came, huge and earth-shaking as the beasts of Pyrrhus, Marrot at a swift, perspiring run. We cut and excavated with care. The find was certainly of metal, cylinder-shaped, encrusted. I lifted it, shook it free from its coatings of earth, stood para-lysed a moment, and then handed it to Huebsch.

"Unless the good Levite included a Ford car among his possessions——"

It was a petrol can.

Subchapter iii

We retired to lunch and siesta after that. But the memorable events of the day had not ended with the finding of the petrol container which Gault, perhaps, had used to fill the tank of the great racer in which he and Pelagueya had toured this desert fringe.

I went and lay down on my bed and read for a little in *L'Ile des Pengouins*. But I had read it too often. Amongst my luggage was a worn Lermontov and with him, till I fell asleep, I found greater kinship, that Scots-descended Russian Learmont who somehow never sang the Russia he loved, but a Scotland that a Russian might have created.

At three Huebsch's whistle roused us and we trooped back to work again. It was still a day of blazing heat. The corn had ripened about the lowlands north of Abu Zabal and the radiance of the harvest-quiet fields lay against the azure sky like the light from a copper bowl. I looked towards Gault's castle and saw two women stroll from a doorway down towards the nightingale garden—Gault's mistress who had tried to kill me, and Aslaug Simonssen who seemed to dream of nothing but the killing of her brother's murderer. . . . Huebsch was calling instructions.

"And if that boy of yours digs up any more gascans, Colonel, tell him he can keep 'em."

"Less levity and more Levite, in fact," supplemented Marrot, and went off, whistling, followed by the slow, wide grin of the Jew.

So we held at it again. About four in the afternoon I stopped and climbed out of the trench and
was lighting my pipe for a moment's blessed conso-
lation when I saw a figure crossing the land from
the road that led towards Abu Zabal. I stared at it
a moment, speculating what villager was approaching with a fresh complaint—I have forgotten to
tell how there had been scores of these, though our
activities infringed hardly at all upon the village and
its rights and dignities. Then I saw that it was no
villager. It was European, fantastically garbed. It
was——

It was, in fact, no other than the drunken boy-
novelist of the Wagh el Berka.

CHAPTER THE THIRTEENTH

' "Look, I'm a wandering intestinal worm trying to find out the truth of things." '

Subchapter i

NO other. He had a rucksack slung across his back. Hugely-sombreroed, slim-hipped, with wide trousers and slouching shoulders he came drifting across the field. He came in my direction and, glancing along the line of excavation, I could see the reason for that. Mine was the only back that had unbent.

"Hello, it's you. Thought it'd be you. Told me in the village something like you was here. So'm I now. In the desert. Right."

He had halted, swaying a little as he regarded me. I saw then that his boy's face had an almost corpse-like pallor. His eyes smouldered like dull coals. He nodded, vaguely.

"D.T.'s—just on the verge. And sleeplessness. . . . Would you mind keeping still so that I can be sure whether there's one or three of you ? Right. What are you doing here ?"

"We are excavating," I said.

"Oh." He sat down. His rucksack slipped from his shoulders. He leant back against it ; yawned cavernously, stretched himself widely and freely, turned his cheek against the rucksack, and in a moment was asleep.

All of which had happened so quickly that I had remained standing still, staring astounded. But the final movement of this surprising avatar I found too much. I bent over the boy and shook him.

"You cannot sleep here. You are in the open sunlight."

He might have been one of the Seven Sleepers of Ephesus. His body shook leadenly under my hand. I shrugged and desisted, but uneasily. Ridiculously and needlessly, I felt in some measure responsible for this drunken youth whom Pelagueya and I had seen being kicked from a door in the Street of Prostitutes.

My two labourers had grown aware of him by this time, had unbent their backs and were leaning on their shovels. I set them to their task again. Esdras Quaritch slept on, unmoving, scarcely breathing it seemed to me. I took a shovel and flung a few fills into the shape of a little mound beside his head, so drowning his face and shoulders in shadow. Then I resumed work, and grew interested in that, and drew some distance away from the sleeper, and forgot him.

But half an hour later the voice of Marrot was upraised nearby.

"What the devil's this?"

He had crossed from his sector and was standing by the recumbent novelist. Quaritch had opened his eyes, but made no attempt to get up. Instead, he replied in his quick, high-pitched voice :

"And what the devil has it to do with you ?"

The syllables lurched less intoxicatedly from his lips after that brief nap. Marrot stood arms akimbo, looking down at him. "My name's Marrot, I'm an archæologist, and you're lying about on land we're excavating."

The boy turned over on his shoulder. "Excavate till it blisters your soul," he advised. "But don't come and afflict me with your ghastly accentuations. Else I'll strangle you with your own entrails."

His eyes closed. Marrot pushed at him with his foot. The novelist remained unperturbed. I walked over and examined him myself. He was again asleep. The American pulled at his lip.

"Who is he, Colonel ? Friend of yours ? I seem to have seen him before."

I reminded him of the incident in the Khalig and told him of the previous day's happenings. As we stood regarding the camp's recumbent and uninvited guest, Huebsch came across to us.

"Well, well, given it up for the day, both of you ? Think I will as well. . . . Hello, who's the boy ?"

"The fat boy in Pickwick, by the way he sleeps," said Marrot. "But the Colonel here says he's a novelist and pimp from a licensed street in Cairo."

"Well, well. Let him be. We'll have a dish of tea now, I think."

We broke off for the day and went back to the tents. Georgios was just setting the tea for us in the usual place, outside Huebsch's tent, when a voice spoke startlingly near my shoulder.

"The flesh-pots of Egypt, b'God! Jews in front of them, too. . . . Can I, sir?"

With that, a hand swept over my shoulder, snatched up the cup I had been about to take, and was rapidly withdrawn. I turned to see Esdras Quaritch, deathlier than ever of appearance, lowering the cup from his lips.

"Damned sorry to pig it like that, but I've a couple of blast-furnaces below my breast-bone." The cup dropped from his hand. That hand shot convulsively to his brow. "Oh, hell, my head!"

Huebsch and Marrot, who had been bending over a plan together, stared their astonishment. Huebsch said: "Better sit down, young man. You're the authority on Solomon's domestic affairs, aren't you? I seem to remember you lecturing me about them."

Quaritch sank into a deck-chair, still holding his head. "Quite likely. I've lectured all kinds of fools in my time. Quite unavailingly, too. . . . Sorry, that was damn rude. Still, I've no doubt you deserved it. . . ." His hand clutched out towards me. "*Do* pour me another cup, sir."

I poured a fresh cup. We sat and looked at him drink it, I at least idly etching on my mind the outlines of his portrait. Wild and young, with inexplicable shynesses and unexpected courtesies of word and demeanour emerging from a general flow of speech and act that went unrestricted by any canon of taste or decency. Drunken: Sure of himself, inso-

lent, a satyr, lewd and amusing enough. Half-sober:
Now like a pitiable boy, now an undergraduate,
now swaggering like a street lout. Sober—I had yet
to meet him that——

And all these within the compass (I guessed) of
some twenty-four or twenty-five years !

He put down the cup and surveyed the two across
the table with aching, defiant eyes.

"I want to sleep in your camp to-night. Any
objection ?"

Huebsch considered the matter, immensely, benevolently. "Even if we did object, we could hardly throw
you out. Though you'll get no bed. Why, yes,
sleep here if you like."

"You—any objection ?" This, sharply, was to
Marrot, whose eyes had returned to the map in front
of him. He glanced up an acid, contemptuous
moment.

"You may sleep all over the damned place if you
feel that way."

"Nor have *I* any objections, Mr. Quaritch," I
forestalled him.

"Thank you, sir." He nodded to me, glazedly,
slung his rucksack again over his shoulder, rose, and
turned to go. Then he paused and regarded me over
his shoulder, shyly.

"Read that book of mine, yet ? You or the lady ?"

I smiled at him. "You must forgive us.
Neither of us has had any training in assimilating
garbage."

He blushed, vividly. "That's damn unkind."

And, spite memory of portrayed and penned indecencies in that book of his, I felt ashamed of myself. Unkind I *had* been. He looked away, the boy, the colour slowly draining from his cheeks, and then flung up his head with a boyish sneer. "Though I suppose it's to be expected in the company of Jews."

"Well, well, an anti-Semite. And what's wrong with the Jews, young man ?"

He slewed round still further, nearly overbalanced, and regarded Huebsch's great figure with a loathing that startled me.

"Wrong ? Their noses, their circumcised genitals, their prophets, their God, their Temple, their greed, their swinish lack of imagination, their treatment of the Greeks, their crucifying of Christ, their ghastly tabernacle, their fouling of every clean and sweet thing in the world. . . . Not that there are any such things. . . . Jews ! History vomits upon their name." He steadied himself. "Thanks for the tea, you men. I'm—I'm going to sleep again."

Subchapter ii

I had sat with my Lermontov two hours perhaps, Huebsch and Marrot had gone to their tents, report and letter-writing to the Chicagoan Institute which financed them. The Egyptian night hesitated on the fringe of the desert, waving dull, flame-shot wings, pecking and uncertain, preening its eagle head now this way, now that ; and the lights in the heavens flamed and fell and rose again as the great bird of darkness waited there. Georgios had disappeared to his bugle-practice, but I heard no sounds this evening. From the camp-fire of the labourers, however, arose thin shrieks of unwonted merriment. I put down my Lermontov and sat and smoked and watched the fire grow brighter and the surrounding landscape duller; and once turned to look at the house of Gault, pin-pricked in window-radiance there against the hesitating darkness. With that turning I became aware of the figure of Georgios hurrying kitchenwards and realized with some satisfaction that supper-time was near.

For we had abolished dinner.

I must have fallen into a doze then, for the noise of the arrival of the hunger-urged Huebsch and Marrot was what aroused me. Georgios was laying places and dishes, deftly, napkin draped across his arm, neat and trig and trim. Huebsch, benevolently expectant, levered himself into his seat.

"Well, Georgios, what is it to-night?"

"Fish, M'sieu'. Omelette. Coffee."

"Guess you're a blessing right from Olympus, Georgios. . . . Well, well, our boys are very bright to-night."

Another burst of laughter had arisen from about the labourers' camp-fire. Georgios, laying the final dish and standing back with a flourish, shrugged apologetically.

"It is the mad gentleman conversing with the natives."

"Eh ?"

"He is seated at the fire with them, eating their food and smoking their cigarettes. When I questioned him as to his right to be in the camp he threatened to break my neck and then said he had your permission. He is now drinking arrack provided by the foolish Kalaun."

"That's bad. Ask him to come up and have supper with us."

Georgios departed. Marrot stared after him in the direction of the camp-fire. "Strange tastes this young fool has."

I could not resist a thrust here. "Perhaps he is a practical equalitarian, Mr. Marrot, and immersed in study of the noble proletarian nature."

"Not it. If either of you knew the elements of communist philosophy you'd be aware that the communist's only interest in the proletariat is its abolition. . . . H'm. Here's Georgios ; on his own, too."

The little Greek bowed to Huebsch. "M'sieu' at the camp-fire thanks you and says he has already eaten."

Our Jewish leader considered the diplomat tolerantly. "Were those his exact words ?"

Georgios' gigantic moustaches lifted and fell in a smile as he turned away. We gathered that those had not been the exact words of our uninvited guest's refusal of an invitation.

I went to bed with some speculation as to whether the erratic youth would be either in camp or alive next morning.

Subchapter iii

But he was both, as I discovered coming out of
my tent for breakfast. He sat at the open-air dining-
table, his tousled, youthful head glistening wet, his
face less pale than on the previous day though his
eyes were dark-ringed and bloodshot enough.
Huebsch emerged from his tent at the same moment
as I emerged from mine.

"Morning, Colonel. Morning, young man."

"Morning. I like your camp. I want to stay here
and dig. . . . Morning, sir."

I returned his greeting, and sat down. Huebsch,
engaged in placid consideration of the boy's request,
also lowered himself upon a chair. "Well, you
can."

The tousled head nodded curtly. "Same wages as
the rest of your labourers ?"

The great Jew raised his brows. "Well, well.
You're serious, then ?"

"Of course."

It struck me he was more subdued this morning.
The arrack either had had some dulling effect, or he
was slowly recovering from the complete sum of
his potations. He sat with slouched, slim shoulders,
jerking out questions and replies, and staring over
the desert lands to the west. Huebsch stroked his
beard.

"Maybe you'd better tell us something about
yourself so that we can decide."

"What is there to tell ?"

"The Colonel here told me you were a novelist."

"So I am. . . . Mind if I go and be sick for a minute ?"

This was surprising enough. But he was back in less than a minute. He sat down. Huebsch shook his head.

"Guess you're in a pretty bad way. I suppose you want to go in for this digging for—'copy', isn't it ?"

"Not a bit of it. I want to work because it'll tire me, because I want to have my back and shoulders ache like hell, because I want the sweat of clean tiredness on my face. If I put that in a novel later it has nothing to do with the job—except as a by-product. . . . Sorry I'll have to be sick again. Sorry, sir. . . . All writing, all art, is merely the excreta of physical emotion."

"Well, well, you seem to have been pretty emotional lately." Huebsch waved to Georgios, who had been standing by disapprovingly, to serve breakfast. "Like some food ?"

The answer was curt. "I'll breakfast with the other labourers."

He rose and left us at that. Marrot came out and we told him of the new addition to our staff. He lighted up at hearing of the fact.

"Excellent. Now perhaps he'll put some guts in them."

I thought this an unwarranted aspersion. "But surely they are good workers, all of them, as it is ?"

He snorted. "Of course they are—from our point
of view. Damned serfs. He'll perhaps stir them up
to get shorter hours and more pay and look after
themselves a bit. . . . What the devil are you
laughing about ?"

Our laughter had indeed echoed down the clear,
tonic air so that Quaritch himself must have heard
it. Marrot ate his porridge, glared at us, drank hasty
coffee and caught up a tape-measure. Huebsch
protested.

"Quarter of an hour before the first shift yet."

"Nothing to do with any of you. I'm off on my
own."

We watched the result amusedly. No sooner had
he reached the traverse than we observed the
labourers trailing after him from the direction of their
marquee. Huebsch chuckled.

"Well, well, if that's how they work the Five
Years' Plan in your Russia, Colonel—good luck to
them !"

So I myself thought, going down the hill to
measure out fresh side-cuttings from the traverse.
A multitude of these cuttings had been plotted on
the previous evening, so that presently the new
traverse would look like a herring-bone, with a fringe
of questioning excavationettes outsprayed on either
side. My giant labourer I found already at work.
But the little man stood aside, for his place had been
usurped by Quaritch, who was wielding his spade with
mathematical regularity. I called to him.

"Enough of that cutting. We are to make new

ones all along either fringe. You know what we are in search of ?"

"Metal implements, isn't it, sir ? So those chaps have told me."

"Metal implements or any other archæological finds. . . . And why do you address me as 'sir' ?"

"Because I want to, I suppose, sir."

I shrugged and turned away. It was doubtlessly my antique appearance that was the reason. Marrot came along half an hour later and stopped to watch, without approval, the flying spadefuls of loam. "Seems to imagine he's a dredger," he remarked to me. I nodded.

"But I think he is dredging something other than earth."

The sweat was streaming down the face of the young Englishman. His coarse shirt clung damply to shoulders and chest. His long hair swept over his face at every downwards bend, swept regularly up again as he straightened to hurl aside each excavated spadeful. Marrot rubbed his chin. "Keep an eye on him, Colonel."

"But why ?"

"Keep an eye on him. You'll see."

See I did very shortly indeed. A cry from the little labourer drew my attention to Quaritch. He had fallen into the trench and lay there in a dead faint.

I pulled him out, laid him flat, and sent the little man for water. That dashed over him, the boy slowly opened his eyes and put me aside and sat up.

"Good Lord, did I go off ?"

"You did, very thoroughly."

"Arrack on top of a touch of Greek brandy delirium tremens. . . . Very fin-de-siècle; infernally Beardsleyish. . . . What's your name, sir ?"

"Saloney."

He knit his brows at me. "Not English, are you ?"

"I am a Russian."

"*Emigré ?*"

I found this catechism faintly amusing. "Like yourself, I have left my country for my country's good. . . . When you are able to walk, you had best go and ask Georgios for some coffee."

"Right. Thanks. I will."

I left him lying there and with my depleted staff resumed operations. The work was beginning to have more than a deadening monotony about it. There were no more Levite brooches ; no more petrol-cans, even. At eleven o'clock Huebsch, as usual, came to inspect progress. He puffed disappointedly.

"Nothing to report, Colonel ?"

"Not on this front. And yours ?"

"Two sheeps' briskets and what looks like a fossilized pumpkin. Well, well, and what's become of the writer boy ?"

I looked round. Quaritch was no longer there. Huebsch stood mopping his forehead the while I told of my new assistant's fainting-fit.

"Boy's been on the ramshazzle a long while, I suppose. Better not let him back at the work."

Subchapter iv

At noon I passed the labourers' marquee, and,
seeing Quaritch lying there, told him of Huebsch's
fiat. The boy lay flat on the ground in the shadow of
the canvas, with a stubby pencil in one hand and
an immense pad of paper, no doubt drawn from his
voluminous rucksack, under his wrist. His face was
still pale, but some of the marks of dissipation had
gone from about his eyes. He stared at me blankly,
coming out of far depths of thought.

"Resume ? I've no desire to. Thanks all the
same. I'm in search of realism, not sham romanticism
disguised as archæology. . . ." His glance grew
remoter. "Decent of you to direct me to this place,
sir. Just what I wanted for a spot of Nature splurge."

I said I was glad, and turned and went up the
incline to where lunch and the archæologists awaited
me. Climbing towards them, I was conscious that
almost a fortnight's fruitless search had passed in
this riven tract of ground. Had there ever been a
Levite ? Or a Lost Trumpet ? Or the burial of one
by the other ?

I voiced my doubts as we sat eating of that fare,
unfailing in excellence, provided by Georgios. Marrot
nodded, avoiding Huebsch's slow, considering eye.

"Begin to think so myself. We've been led on a
wild-goose-chase from Transjordan."

We awaited Huebsch. He showed no emotion.
"And the Levite brooch ?"

Marrot answered for that. "I saw you drop the

thing in the ground a minute or two before Kalaun found it."

"What ?" I cried.

The two Americans went on with their lunch. Huebsch glanced at me with great, smiling lips twisted a little wryly. His slow boom was as even-toned as ever.

"A process known as 'salting', Colonel. I believe they practise it extensively in dud gold mines."

I was still befogged. "But why in this case ?"

"Because Marrot here was fairly plainly beginning to believe the search a dud one also. I dropped the brooch—old and genuine enough, by the way ; it comes from Hebron—to encourage him. Seems to have had no great shakes of a success, though." He turned to his colleague. "How'd you know ?"

Marrot shrugged. "I know you of old. Remembered other places you'd salted—the Hittite camp especially. Just at the end of the first fortnight it's come to be in the regular order of things. Yesterday I had a hunch the usual dope was due. So I kept my Zeiss on you at intervals."

"Why didn't you expose the fraud at once ?" I asked, and had no answer to that, for all three of us paused to hear the outbreak of a loud squabbling by the marquee of the labourers. It rose into an agitated chatter. Abruptly there was the sound of a scuffle and then a loud scream.

We had jumped to our feet, Huebsch and I, and Marrot was a third of the way down the incline when we saw the figure of Quaritch ascending towards us. He was walking slowly, looking at something in his hand. He came and halted beside Huebsch.

"Sorry to interrupt. One of your men had this thing—dug it up and intended to take it into Cairo and sell it. I thought you might have a better use for it."

Marrot had resumed his seat. Quaritch, his pale boy's face composed and indeed contemptuous as he glanced at the two Americans, flung the "find" on the table and turned away. I smiled. Marrot gave a snort of disgust. The great Jew stared down at the thing passively.

It was a Shield of David : a Levite brooch.

Subchapter v

"So that's the object of the expedition ? Shouldn't have thought a Jew capable of it. Of course there's no Lost Trumpet, nor does Huebsch believe there is one."

And the pale young face nodded to me, confidently.

"Then why is he so intent on this search ?" I sighed.

The boy with the pseudo-biblical name leant back against the side of my tent and blew a long clouding of silver-grey smoke from a short pipestem. "Probably gone mad as even a Jew is apt to do in this muck-heap we call a planet. He's like myself—in search of reality. Like all of us, in fact. And he's come to the conclusion in his conscious mind that

there's no reality—nothing but foam and fleeting.
He must have thought out the whole thing up there
in Transjordan. And then a lesion occurred in his
skull. His conscious mind went wonk. And a dusty
ghoul or so from the subconscious came to his aid,
denying the evidence of his senses and providing
for him a refuge in this fairy-tale of a maundering
Levite and Joshua's Trumpet. . . . A purely sym-
bolical trumpet, of course; Huebsch's Voice of
Reality. . . . Occasionally the fairy-tale wears thin
and then your Jew, assisted by the wreck of what
was once his conscious, comes to the aid of the
fable and patches it up by salting the excavations."

"An extract from the Gospel according to Dr.
Adler?"

He flushed at that, boyishly. "Oh, I'm young, sir.
But that's not a crime. Neither is Adler."

"But certainly not," I soothed.

It was stiflingly hot under the tent-walls; scorch-
ing without. The young Englishman had come to
borrow a pencil, and at my invitation had sat down
and heard the story of our quest. . . . Huebsch a
lunatic? I found that idea amusing. And yet——

"This is very interesting, Mr. Quaritch. Especially
the new light on my old friend Reality."

"Still leg-pulling, sir?"

"But certainly not," I soothed again, and lay
back in my chair and considered the canvas overhead. "Only curious. For thousands of years men
and women have been on this unfortunate and
malodorous planet of ours, Mr. Quaritch. They

have been born, they have grown up, they have
loved, they have mated, they have begotten their
kind, they have died—all without any great fuss as
to realities and non-realities, truth or no-truth.
. . . But nearly all of the young generations seem
to philosophize on these things nowadays. What is
the explanation ?"

"The thing's like my trick of blushing—obvious
but not easy to account for. . . . But I'll try. Suppose that by some freak of the chemic interplay a
liver-fluke acquired a reasoning mind—developed
an intelligentsia of liver-flukes who manufactured
satisfactory theories regarding the high destinies and
moral purpose of all intestinal worms and the beauty
of their abiding place. And the majority of the
flukes, busied in feeding on decayed foodstuffs,
accepted these theories with complacence. Good.
But something occurs inside the liver—a breath of
poisonous gas sweeps down on our colony of worms,
and they sway and gasp and vomit into a shocking
awareness of the fact that the theories on which
they've been fed are nonsensical. They abide in a
sty, a charnel-house. No great Super-Fluke awaits
them in the Beyond, across the dark blood-streams,
in a palace of meaty layers of ordure. The liver itself
is unaware of the flukes, except as a prickling,
poisonous annoyance. . . . Consternation among
the flukes—especially the young ones. Anarchy of
thought and immorality of deed, according to the
older theories of flukedom. Actually, a search for
reality."

The confidence and uncertain cruelty and the bright, shining rebelliousness of youth! I said:

"That is a very fine parallel, no doubt, with the Great War the poisonous gas of clarity. But, after all and though the poor flukes are unable to comprehend it, there *is* a meaning; as we know. The liver is part of a body, the body of some biological species, the species of some social group——"

He shook his head. "That isn't a meaning, it's merely a multiplication. Look, I'm still a wandering intestinal worm trying to find out the truth of things."

"And with what measure of success?"

He considered, pale face thoughtful; then smiled at me twistedly. "None, of course. Except to formulate some rules and beliefs for guidance on the quest."

"And what are these?"

"That I owe no duty to anything or anyone but myself. That all the creeds and codes are lies or mouldy rags and remnants. I don't believe there is a reality in man's nature; nor is there any possible voice to cry it. . . . Complete anarchy is the complete rule of life. Nothing else any thinking being can accept. . . . Sorry to be lecturing you, sir. You were made for better things. Not that there are any. . . . Dirty thing, Life. Dirty tyke, Man."

"And woman?"

He grinned, his face ageing, growing a satyr's and old and unpleasant, as can the face of the young in these days.

"I know *her* use and place, anyhow. In Cairo they call me the Little Brother of the Brothels——"

Subchapter vi

It was evident that Marrot had abandoned any real interest in the excavations. Throughout the afternoon I could see him stroll from beside the work of this labourer to the task of that, turning over mounds of sand with an indifferent foot. Occasionally he would stand, arms akimbo, staring Cairo-wards; and for long, at the passing of a southwards camel-train along the Abu Zabal road, followed the dust and tinkling of that train with his eyes and presumably his ears. . . . So I saw from an occasional glance in his direction.

Huebsch and his gang, on the other hand, seemed to be working as in a mighty fever, and I could not repress a smile at sight of that. After two bare-faced "saltings" it was hardly to be expected that the Jew's colleague would remain patient with the situation.

Nor, indeed, did that patience outlast the afternoon. Presently Marrot passed my sector, walking towards Huebsch with unswerving deliberation. The murmur of their voices came to me down the hot afternoon, Huebsch's a booming under-murmur, Marrot's like the crack of an irritably-wielded dog-whip. Then presently there came a hail to me from Huebsch.

I left my giant and pigmy to labour with slackened

muscles and went towards the Americans, finding
Huebsch seated on a mound above the excavations,
his great shirt rolled greatly upon his bulging fore-
arms, his head ovoid as an ostrich egg, his beard
jutting forth like the beard of an Assyrian bull-god.
But Marrot had taken no seat. He was walking to
and fro, irritatedly, with Huebsch's enormous,
benevolent gaze bent on him as one watching the
antics of a fretful but esteemed cockroach.

"Hello, Colonel." Huebsch slowly took his pipe
from between his red lips. "Thought you'd better
come over. Marrot here wants to break up the
expedition, and I'd like your opinion of the business."

Marrot snorted. The communist American had
evidently no great opinion of my opinion. I looked
from one to the other.

"My opinion is, I suppose, that of any other
employee who wishes to retain his employment. If
Mr. Marrot goes, do you stay?"

"Well, well, that doesn't come into it for the
moment. We want your opinion. Do you think we
should go on with the search for the Levite's Trumpet
—and with some hope of finding that Trumpet?"

"But I know nothing of the documentary evidence
on which you began the search."

"You heard an outline of the document's story.
We didn't keep anything back."

"Is it a question of money, then?"

"No, we're well enough supplied with Institute
funds for two more years' digging in the Near East
—detail of locality to suit ourselves."

"In that case, I think I should continue the search for at least another week."

"Why?" Marrot halted and shot this at me aggressively.

I had worked out the matter from a new angle. "Because, without some pressing certainty that there was the hope of a genuine find, I cannot conceive that Mr. Huebsch would have gone to the trouble to salt the ground so religiously for our edification."

"That's precisely the point." Marrot looked at his colleague acidly. "One salt is permissible. Two suggest things I won't speak about."

I was suddenly aware of an unusual tension between the two. Huebsch had resumed his smoking, but now, slowly revolving Marrot's remark in his mind, he again delivered the pipe-stem from bondage betwixt his great, even teeth.

"You think, in fact, that if we found the Lost Trumpet itself, it might prove to be another salt?"

"*You* have said it, anyway."

"Well, well. And how'd you take it if I told you that I'd never before set eyes on that second Levite's brooch—nor do I believe anyone else had since its original owner dropped it?"

"Eh?" Marrot had halted dead in his pacing. I myself, almost as electrified, stared at the Shophet bull-god. He stood up, and pulled on his jacket.

"Come over to my tent, the two of you, and look at the thing and compare it with the one I dropped in the excavations yesterday. You'll see No. 2 has never been cleaned and re-muddied. . . . Oh, we're on the track of the Levite all right, all right. The thing knocked me all sideways myself; and I had to save up the joke of it. Sorry, Marrot."

"So you damn well ought to be." But Marrot's eyes were blazing. "The Trumpet's hereabout without a doubt."

"Might be, might be. Meanwhile, when you've had a look at the brooch, I guess we'll want to clean up. We're going over to the house of the Colonel's Princess for tea, remember."

CHAPTER THE FOURTEENTH

' "What would each of us do—if we found the Lost Trumpet and it was as powerful as in the days of Joshua ?" '

Subchapter i

I BATHED inadequately in my tent and changed into clean drill and came out into the waning heat and sunshine of the afternoon and waited in readiness for Huebsch and Marrot. Below me the torn and gutted lands of our search; wider in encirclement of our camp the semi-desert lands that so grew on one's consciousness in a little space of time ; the labourers sprawling by their fire, awaiting the cooking of their evening meal ; in the shade of the cook-tent Esdras Quaritch, recumbent, chin in hand, staring blankly desertwards . . .

I had one of those slow impulses that have governed my life. I went down to him and he turned his head and looked up.

"Hello, sir. Thought you'd disowned me after finding my philosophy so unpalatable."

"Unpalatable ? But I made no attempt to swallow it. . . . You remember the lady who was with me when we met in the Wagh el Berka ?"

"Rose-flushed and warm from heaven's own heart she came."

"I beg your pardon?"

"A quotation from Swinburne—or what Swinburne would have written had he known her. . . . Of course I remember her, Colonel Saloney. You knocked me down because of her. In love with her, sir?"

"I am sorry I—knocked you down."

"I am sorry you thought I was knock-down-worthy."

"The lady was the Princess Pelagueya Bourrin. She lives at that house over there, and has invited Mr. Huebsch, Mr. Marrot and myself to drink tea with her. I think you would like to come also."

The boy shook his head. "After hearing my opinion of women's function? Too indiscreet, sir. My presence would profane any sacred love. . . . Besides, you told me to come out and soak my soul in the silences of the desert—not in the weak tea of a bun-fight."

"I believe even St. Simeon Stylites was wont to find the foot of his pillar surrounded with offerings of farm produce."

There are many types of laughter. The young Englishman's might have been a peal from the bell of Pelagueya's own mirth: the bell a little cracked. He jumped to his feet.

"So he did. And, my God, I'll bet he used to nip down to the pile often enough in the small hours! . . . Right, I'll come. Thanks awfully. . . . But

I've no small talk, you know, or any ability to conceal boredom when I develop it."

"I have no doubt the Princess will have cordial interest for both the fashion in which you wipe your boots on the tablecloth and the view of your back teeth when you yawn."

"Good bowling for a Russian, sir ! Wait for me a minute, then."

He disappeared into the labourers' marquee, dragged out his rucksack, shook out from it a heterogeneous pile, and made rapid selections therefrom. Then, incontinently, he began to undress in the open air.

"Guard my belongings from the proletariat, will you ?"

In a moment he was mother-naked in the sunshine, brown and golden and gleaming, narrow-hipped, Greek, and indeed beautiful. Kalaun and his colleagues turned shamed, grave faces from the sight, with that horror of a nude body in an adolescent which is so typically Eastern, and a product of the Eastern religions. The boy flung back his hair and grinned down at them sidelong.

"Hell, what minds !"

With that he went racing across the field, under the amazed glare of Georgios, reached the canal-bank, and vanished from our view. Presently there arose distant sounds suggesting one of the larger ungulates in a mud-wallow. Esdras Quaritch was cleansing from himself the dust of travel and travail.

"Ready, Colonel ?"

The Jew and the communist Gentile, both in very white and seemly ducks, Huebsch more Shophet-like than ever, were descending the incline. I indicated the pile of belongings at my feet.

"I am taking him with me. He may amuse a little."

"And where is he now ?"

"Denuding himself of half the soil of Egypt, by the sounds," and I pointed towards the canal above which was uprising the head of Quaritch.

In a moment it was more than head. He trotted across to where we stood, snatched up a crumpled towel, and was about to begin a vigorous berubbing of himself when he caught Huebsch's eye.

Thereat was magical transformation. He blushed, angrily, hotly, almost from head to heel. Bending down, he picked up various articles of attire and, with a mutter, and his face downcast, retreated into the labourers' marquee.

"Well, well," commented Huebsch, "and what's the boy all reddened up for ?"

"Maybe he was a sacrifice in a former incarnation," suggested Marrot, flippantly, "and your likeness to Baal is too much for him in this."

The marquee flap shot open. Esdras Quaritch, fully dressed in the not uncomely flannels, was beside us, knotting a colourful flare of tie. The great Jew considered him amiably, immensely.

"Guess you're the nearest thing to perpetual motion that's struck these parts so far."

An unpleasant sneer—a look of hate, almost, I

thought it—came on the boy's face.   He droned
through his nose in mimicry.

"Guy, you've said it." He turned his back on him.
"You can now lead me to the baked meats, sir."

Subchapter ii

"They are on the roof, khawaga," said Pelagueya's
butler, Ibrahim, as he admitted us.

"Then we will follow them there," I said, and
led the way up the stone staircase, and so out on
the broad roof, parapeted, where once Gault and
Pelagueya ——

Gault and Pelagueya—memory unescapable.   Even
though the years had trodden over it, and the thing
was long past, and there was Pelagueya herself,
garbed in green from head to heel, with her hair a
metallic net glittering in the sun, and, as always,
with power to unfocus my eyes for a little.   We
held hands, smiling at each other a little too long,
and I looked for that little hollow in her throat and
found it again with my refocused eyes, and she put
her hand up to it, still smiling. . . .   Then we
remembered, and she was smiling, not mistily at all,
but very cheerfully and competently.

"Welcome, messieurs," to Huebsch and Marrot.
And then with some doubt to Quaritch: "And
you, m'sieu'."

"You have met Mr. Quaritch before, you will
remember," I said. "And he gave us a copy of one
of his books to read,"

"Which neither of you did," murmured the boy.

"Why, neither we did." Pelagueya nodded to him apologetically. "We were awfully tired of being shocked that day."

He was of her own mental period, I thought, with a faint twinge of envy. "Some other time, perhaps?"

"Love to. Aslaug, this is Mr. Huebsch and Mr. Marrot. They are Colonel Saloney's employers. And this is Mr. Quaritch, who wrote that nice novel I loaned to you. Come and have tea. Anton, will you shout down the staircase for the kettle and muffins?"

By the time I had withdrawn my head from directing the ascent of Pelagueya's butler, the rest of the company was at the other end of the roof, admiring Pelagueya's view. At least, it was for that reason she had led them there. But they had fallen to three groupings when I crossed to them, threading a sprawling invitation of bright-cushioned basket-chairs. Marrot was standing looking back towards the camp; he had forgotten he had come to drink tea and was obviously considering the lie of the excavations afresh from this high elevation. Huebsch by the side of Pelagueya was turning his slow, immense interest upon the desert-view to which she was directing attention with that slim, long hand of hers from which the trailing sleeves of green fell away so reluctantly. Quaritch, white, with kindled eyes and hands clasped behind his head, was leaning against the parapet staring at Aslaug Simonssen, a blonde, puzzled sagawoman.

"You *are* Esdras Quaritch ?"

"Why, yes."

She was flushing with slow indignation, with shame. "I—I don't know how to talk to you. Or how it is you aren't in prison. That book of yours—I tried to read it——"

His stare did not relax. "You didn't like it ?"

"I thought—oh, one can't talk about it. It's the foulest thing I have ever read. Why do you write that kind of stuff ?"

The boy stared at her, fascinated. It seemed to me he spoke absent-mindedly. "Because it's the truth."

"Oh ! And those horrible pictures. . . . And that couldn't be true—that girl who died in hospital after that shocking time——"

"She was my own mistress."

But I was beside them then—Aslaug Simonssen, horrified, the large bonde deer in an outworn simile, Esdras Quaritch the snake. I said, with unnecessary loudness : "Ibrahim and the muffins, Princess."

Pelagueya turned round then. "Thank you, Anton. You will make a good muffin-man when you finish working for Mr. Huebsch. . . . Do sit down, all of you. Aslaug will pour it out."

She did, Huebsch and Marrot engaging her in small talk, the boy still staring at her unbelievingly. Pelagueya put up her hand and pulled me into the chair beside her.

"Sit down, Anton. And please don't look at me as if I were a fragile statuette."

"Statue you might be, but never in the diminutive."

"Am I so gargantuan, then ?"

Quaritch had sat beside us. He turned round eagerly, apparently having overheard the passage between us.

"Colonel Saloney's right, Princess. You've got a good skeleton."

Pelagueya stared at him a moment, brows upraised. For answer the boy surveyed her from head to foot, consideringly. Shook his head.

"Aphrodite mostly, of course. But too good skeletal structure for that. Puzzle a sculptor a bit if you were stripped. The Hera or Diana touch—I'm not sure which."

Pelagueya's eyes twinkled. She made him a mock curtsey from the depths of her chair.

"If ever I'm reduced to selling my skeleton, Mr. Quaritch——"

He coloured furiously, hurtly. "I was serious."

So he had been. Pelagueya's mockery lingered doubtfully about her lips. I said :

"Our young friend is a professional uncouth. When he enters heaven he will doubtlessly poke St. Peter in the ribs and tell him he keeps marvellously well-fleshed for an old man."

"Whereas Anton will never enter the gates at all, Mr. Quaritch. He will linger there with Peter, politely hazarding the opinion that no great profit would come from entering heaven and that, on the whole, he had best search out Nirvana in order that he may rest his poor, tired feet and have a long, long sleep."

All this she delivered sitting back in the depths of her chair, which had a red cushion to sit upon, but a green one at her shoulders—a green, I remember, that blended with the tint of her dress. In such wise was this that neck and head rose from and amid a sheathing of soft green, and again there fascinated me that likeness of hers to some strange hybrid bloom of fantasy and Shiraz—a rose out of Ferdusi, perhaps. She had looked at neither of us, speaking, but, finishing, her eyes peeped for a moment at me. I said:

"It is ill to stab an ally."

"But, Anton dear, you're such an uncertain one. Never more than the bearer of an entente cordiale."

Quaritch emptied his cup. "Then—though I hadn't thought it—your Colonel Saloney must be a fool, Princess."

Amazingly, Pelagueya flushed—that flush I knew so well, the flush of barbaric anger. "With a tithe of his folly, Mr. Quaritch, you might cease to crawl in your gutters and stand up as a man."

My clumsily-held cup caused considerable startlement as it hit the stone floor that was the castle roof and sprayed a rain of brittle pottery fragments about my feet. Fortunately, it had been empty. And the Gault millions would purchase many more. . . . As I bent to brush away the fragments Pelagueya's head came down a moment close to mine.

"Oh, my dear, do I require as much tactful handling as all that? Kick my ankle next time!"

Marrot had jumped like a criminal in the chair of humane America as the volts of American justice are propelled through the criminal body. He had ejaculated, "Hell!" with much sincerity and then had sought a cake from a stand in front of him. The delicate chalice of conversation upheld between the two others—I had overheard its mild grenadine trickle as comment on the changelessness of Egyptian weather—had fallen and smashed in sympathy with my cup. So Pelagueya observed.

"Food—Mr. Marrot? Mr. Huebsch? I have lots more of it, you know. How are the excavations? Have you unearthed anything yet?"

Huebsch consumed a cream-lathered sweetmeat with an immense skill that caught my respect. "One or two discoveries, Princess. Some fake and one, we believe, more or less authentic."

"What is the authentic discovery?"

"I've brought it here to show you."

It was the second of the Levite brooches, cleansed in acid now. Laid across Pelagueya's palm it glinted dully—a dark, unfriendly ornament of dark, unfriendly times. She turned it over and looked at the block of strange, un-Arab, un-Egyptian characters graved on the base of the upper triangle.

"Some writing here. Do you know what it means?"

Marrot interpreted. "'Jerusalem.'"

Huebsch amplified: "Most of such brooches had

that on them. Not that the 'Jerusalem' was a plain
reference to the city among the hills. It was more,
if you get me, an imaginary city——"

"It was, in fact, Blake's city," I said.

"Blake's ?" The great Jew had lived unacquainted
with the English mystic. Pelagueya also cocked her
head questioningly. I waved my hand to the three
remaining guests.

"The Anglo-Saxons know the verse. They will
recite you it."

Marrot shrugged away from the opportunity with
an acid smile. The novelist, staring at Aslaug raptly,
nodded to her.

"You do it."

She flushed, and, unexpectedly, complied. She
was standing at the moment, tall and straight against
the sunset colours of the Egyptian sky. She put
her hands behind her back, like a school-child, and
recited with a school-child's sing-song gravity :

> " 'I shall not cease from mortal strife,
>   Nor shall the sword sleep in my hand
> Till we have built Jerusalem
>   In England's green and pleasant land——'

"It's a hymn," she finished.

Pelagueya's lips twitched a little. So did Marrot's.
But Huebsch remained as grave, immense, and
ovoidly benevolent as ever. "Well, well, and a very
pleasant one, I guess, Miss Simonssen. Thank you.
Yes, so it would have been something like the
Jerusalem of this Englishman they meant when they
graved those letters twenty-five hundred years ago."

"Twenty-five hundred years ago!" Pelagueya turned the brooch over on her white palm, staring at its dark, earth-worn surface. "And all that time men have been dreaming of the same Jerusalem. And only a dream still." She shook herself and laughed and handed it back to Huebsch. "And who had left this behind? And when do you expect to come upon the rest of the treasure?"

"Treasure?" Aslaug Simonssen, pouring tea, regarded the Jew with polite interest: "Are you searching for treasure, Mr. Huebsch?"

He nodded. "Though not pieces of eight. You see, all the business began——"

Marrot groaned, turning with crooked lips to interrupt. But that proved unnecessary. We had sat there late at this tea-drinking. The land below us lay in still melancholy with the sun poised at the edge of the world. That to the west. But now from the east came that which smote all of us to silence.

It was a wailing like to that of a lost cat mourning its dead in a backyard of hell. Across a pain-wracked kaleidoscope of squawk it rose as the damned, opening their windows, hurled boots and earthen-ware vessels at the vocal ghost. It grew fainter and fainter; choked abruptly to silence. The cat had been caught and strangled with a barb-wire garotte——

In fact, Georgios, remote in his nullah, had attempted and ceased from an air on his silver bugle.

Pelagueya, withdrawing finger-tips from her ears, led the laughter.

"But, poor man, doesn't he realize how horrible it is?"

Huebsch, immense, boomed the answer: "Guess he hasn't the faintest, Princess. Else he'd stop it. Doesn't strike me as a naturally cruel boy."

"Sh!" said Aslaug Simonssen. "Is that him again?"

"Oh, Aslaug!"

Perhaps her ears were the slowest of any of us. Quaritch at the first sound made an angry gesture for silence, and crept to his feet and the edge of the roof-parapet, like a cat, without noise, and stood there, peering down. But presently the strain of his attitude relaxed. He was merely listening.

Huebsch cupped his great ovoid head in his hands and stared at the floor.

Marrot half-wheeled round in his chair, and so, in that twisted position, sat with his head flung back.

Aslaug Simonssen, puzzled, wondering, turned her face from one to the other of us, an uncomprehending Valkyr to whom at length the magic sounds gave pause, so that she also stood rigid.

Pelagueya sat white-faced, her hands clasped about her knees.

All this I noted, and then ceased to note as the singing of the nightingales issued from the cypress grove remote at the end of the garden and flowed outward and upward to us, and changed from dun red to a mistiness of purple, and was colour and line, singing and music and poetry in one synthesis. It swept up through the silence like the chorusing from a night-time cave on the slopes of Olympus when gods and men were young, and the world pristine, and there was wonder and wild delight, ceaseless and unsatiated, in that early earth. Youth, it sang, and desire undefiled, consummated and never-wearying, fairy and no illusion. . . . So the singing of Gault's nightingales came and held us and then stopped in perhaps less than a minute; and when we shook ourselves awake we saw that the night also had crossed the deserts to listen to that singing.

In its coming we saw a figure trudging campwards from the direction of the outlands. Pelagueya broke the silence, indicating him.

"Poor Georgios!"

She laughed, and then, suddenly and shockingly, was weeping.

Subchapter iii

"Princess!"

Pelagueya shook off my hand, laughed again, stood up.

"I'm all right." She dabbed at her eyes with a handkerchief. She walked to the edge of the parapet and leant her arms on it, not looking at us. "Sorry, all of you. It is long since I heard a nightingale."

Huebsch, half in dusk, creaked in his basket-chair. "Think I know what you feel, anyway, Princess. I was mighty near to weeping myself."

Quaritch turned back from where he stood, so that he fronted Pelagueya. "Rot! It wasn't the nightingale only. It was because she saw the Greek and thought of the contrast between his music and those damned fowls' as hysterically ludicrous. . . . Wasn't it ?"

"Of course. Or between what the nightingales sang and what you sing in your books."

I could not see his face, but I knew that he blushed then, furiously, boyishly. "Do you think I wouldn't follow the first—the nightingale's—if I could ?"

Pelagueya left her stance and strolled back towards the chair beside me. "Both you and Georgios will have to wait for the millennium—or the Lost Trumpet, Mr. Huebsch ? . . . Anton, stop dreaming !"

I looked up at her. "I was dreaming," I confessed. "What would each of us do—if we found the Lost Trumpet and it was as powerful as in the days of Joshua ?"

"That will make a very pretty after-tea game." She sank down in the chair beside me. I held a match for the cigarette she put between her lips. "You first, please, Mr. Huebsch. What would you do if you found the Lost Trumpet and a blast of it could flatten out your enemies ?"

"Like frogs under a road-roller," supplemented Marrot, helpfully.

The great Jew entered into the game. He flung back his head, consideringly. "Well, I guess I'd do one or two things. I'd clear the Arabs out of Palestine and establish a real Jewish State. I'd bring power from the mountains and the Dead Sea and corn back into the lowlands. . . . Yes, that'd be my fairy-story, Princess. I'd build Jerusalem."

"And you, Mr. Marrot ?"

"I'd pull it down again. Blast the militarists and
financiers from the face of the earth. End classes and
masses and all their dirty squabblings for ever. I'd
establish the World-State. And in the process pay
back a few scores for those starved East Anglian
ancestors of mine."

Pelagueya was remorseless : "And Aslaug ?"

"Really, I don't know. . . . Well, if it was mine
I'd—I'd make it help me find my brother's murderer
and have her punished."

Pelagueya quivered a little by my side. It was
with suppressed mirth. She said, in a strangled
voice : "And you, Anton ?"

For some reason the atmosphere of our idle tea-
table talk had acquired an unwarranted intensity. I
felt more than a reluctance to speak : it was a posi-
tive distaste. "There is still Mr. Quaritch."

"So there is. What would you do, Mr. Novelist ?"

"Really, shock you awfully, I'm afraid, Princess.
Like Marrot, I'd burst your damn civilization to
fragments. But not to bring in the soviets. To bring
instead the days of primitive anarchy, when each man
stood for himself and took what he wanted of women
and wine and life and lust, and there were weaklings
in neither top-hats nor top-boots. I'd restore the
world of 25,000 B.C."

"You'd find it difficult to write your dirty books
then," interpolated Marrot, acidly.

"In your soviet state I'd write nothing else."

Huebsch boomed out into the midst of this puppy-snarling, soothingly.

"Well, well, but what about you, Colonel ?"

"Me ? But nothing. I should not use it."

"Eh ?"

"I should not blow the Lost Trumpet, having no particular hate or love or frenzy to urge upon the world. I should merely pawn it in Cairo, and build a house in that field of Hanna's that we are now disturbing, and have tea every afternoon with the Princess."

"Good for you, Colonel."

Pelagueya's cigarette sailed through the darkness and fell like a little star over the roof-parapet.

"Bad for him, Mr. Huebsch ! Tea every afternoon——"

She was quite speechless for a moment. So I proffered her another cigarette. "And what would be your play ?" I asked.

She said in that clear voice of hers, but with the little stammer in it that comes if she is angered or excited :

"*I* would blow it. I'd clear your beastly communist friends out of Russia—make it a clean and lovely country again, with order and dignity, pride and blood."

Aslaug Simonssen spoke puzzledly. "But, Princess, you said that night in Cairo that the Bolsheviks weren't beasts."

"Oh, Aslaug ! . . . Merely bores—the most stupendous moral bores the world has ever seen.

Except that he hasn't got enough energy to attempt boring, Colonel Saloney's a good specimen."

"That, anyway, sir," remarked young Quaritch to me, casually and clearly, "is a damned lie."

I think that Pelagueya, unused to such frontal attacks from a mere man, was more astonished than ever before in her life. Huebsch again saved the situation with his tolerant boom.

"Well, well, Princess. Perhaps it's as well none of us have the Lost Trumpet to play about with, and all the walls that hem us in are still standing."

"Especially," I thought aloud, "as not one of us was sure that he meant what he said."

"How's that?" The boy had taken me under his protection. I found the others listening with unexpected attention.

"Mr. Huebsch and his Jerusalem—more or less he believes that that is what he would do. But he would pause in indecision with the Trumpet in his hand. So would all of us before we might blow the Trumpet with the single-mindedness and faith of Joshua. Saying: 'I, Anton Saloney, would do thus and this,' I lie—or at least may be wildly mistaken. For, as none of you have ever known your real selves, I have never known Anton Saloney. He is hid behind walls of custom and use and reserve and frustration that tower to heaven."

"Dr. Adler, sir?"

I think I was a little nettled at that, but I had the grace to laugh. Pelagueya touched my knee, and spoke idle words.

"Perhaps it is these very walls that the Trumpet would overthrow ! . . . People, it's too late to go back to your camp. You must stay to dinner, all three of you. Like to come down and see my garden ?"

Subchapter iv

We had lost the others—Marrot and Huebsch among the moonlight of the cypresses, intent on both seeing and hearing a nightingale ; Aslaug and Quaritch abandoned in a maze and some argument by the far desert hedgings. Now, under the lee of Gault's house, Pelagueya and I stood in the midst of the rose garden.

Revived by the night, they poured forth their smell. Like the darkness, it was a soft and kindly smell. Pelagueya bent her head towards a dim cluster, and closed her eyes, and felt against her cheek the soft, shy curl of petals.

"Smell, Anton."

The scent came up into our faces, our nostrils. Pelagueya stood utterly quiet. Then as she stood erect one of the roses broke and showered her with petals. I could see them upon her, her face and neck, ghostly sprinklings. She gave a little wriggle and a strange, sweet laugh.

"Affectionate thing."

"What is ?" I asked.

One of the rose petals had slipped into the bosom of her dress——

We stood and listened in the silver fall of moonlight. Nothing to hear. The rose-scent rippled over us in little wavelets. Pelagueya was very near. That rose-petal——

Nights and days of weariness; year on long dragging year, with ways and faces and bodies over-familiar, and the chirp of the grasshopper deafening in the ears of both of us. I knew the tale, I knew the tale! This was a moment's madness, dead and dreadful and a weary thing already in the womb of to-morrow. Moonlight and a rose-leaf's wanderings——

I put Pelagueya away from me then. She laughed, sobbingly. And then, as we stared at each other mutely the banal clangour of the dinner-bell came echoing down the garden.

Subchapter v

We went back to the camp across a stillness of white, moonlighted lands. Huebsch and Marrot walked in advance. Quaritch beside me, I remember, had a face streaked and bedaubed with moonlight shadow like a pen and ink sketch. It was that kind of moonlight, caricaturing the earth and all things that on it moved. Quaritch's voice, snapping the silence, startled me out of a dreary pondering. Which the reality—the moonlighted world or the sun-lighted?

"That girl back there, sir—Aslaug Simonssen. Why hasn't somebody seduced her before this?"

I had grown accustomed to him. I lighted my pipe. "Perhaps she has no fondness for being seduced."

The boy kicked at a stone. "I'd leave Abu Zabal to-morrow if it wasn't that she's here."

"Why should that detain you?" An obvious answer came from his silence. I stopped. "Not——?"

"Not that I've fallen in love? Nothing so complicated." He gave his young satyr's laugh. "My intentions are much simpler and my plans don't envisage either a marriage service or a maintenance allowance. . . . Look here, sir, keep your damned hands off me!"

I dropped him to the ground. He got up and dusted himself. Huebsch and Marrot were out of sight, hearing nothing of this passage. The boy's hand was in the pocket of his jacket and that jacket bulged forward in my direction.

"I wouldn't do that again, Colonel Saloney. The Wagh el Berka has taught me a trick worth two of that. As for Aslaug Simonssen, she'll come to me to-morrow if I so much as snap my fingers."

I dusted my hands. "She will not come to you twice," I promised. "Or at least on the second occasion it will be merely in order to view your corpse."

"Look here, sir. You're honest enough in most things. Too honest. That's why I like you. . . . If I want this girl—it's my look-out. If she wants me —it's hers. D'you mean you'd try to prevent our coming together because I've no intention of marrying her?"

"I mean to say that I'll prevent it for the simple reason that you have no love for her. Marriage? You might live with her in a desert hut and father fourteen children and the two of you refuse all marriage sanctions in the world—and it would be nothing to me. This is a different matter."

He went forward again. Perforce I went with him. When next he spoke it was in the tone of a casual acquaintance.

"What is she in Egypt for?"

"Her brother was murdered at Rashida—by his mistress, she suspects. She has come here to hound on the gendarmes in search for the woman."

"What was her name?"

"The woman's? Some Egyptian name. She was blind."

"Blind?" He stopped and stared at me. I halted, impatiently.

"Yes, blind. Some Egyptian prostitute. . . . I remember the name Miss Simonssen told me. Huth Rizq."

"Huth Rizq? Thought so. I know her."

CHAPTER THE FIFTEENTH

'He had turned aside into the entrance of the Wagh el Berka. I caught his arm. "What, *here*?"'

Subchapter i

HE would tell me nothing more. We came to the camp then and he went to his place in the labourers' marquee. I, in my tent, tossed and turned and found little sleep for many hours. Not that the matters of either Huth Rizq's whereabouts or Aslaug Simonssen's danger so vexed me. I was remembering instead that scene in the rose-garden with Pelagueya.

Getting up, some long time after midnight, I saw a light burning high up there in Gault's castle. Pelagueya—wakeful like myself?

Or Aslaug Simonssen? But that was unbelievable. Pelagueya it must be. Why not then do the obvious and shining thing? Dress and go out across the desert half-mile to her house and fling sand up against her window and bring her down to me? She would stand a little back, her lips parted with surprise and the haste of descent, and then laughter would come in her eyes and her hands in mine would give them a little shake, and she would cry: "Oh, Anton!" and turn back with her hand in mine, into the indigo shadows, and so up those stairs to the roof and the stars and her touch and the secret journeyings of that rose-petal——

Somewhere, out in the wastes, a jackal was baying and I listened to that baying and smiled. Jackal. The Death of the old Egyptians. No lion or eagle or wild and tremendous, dark and sombre beast, did they envisage it. Only carrion and a carrion-grubber. So this desire of mine, as Quaritch's. The mean whining of carrion-starved animals under the jeering indifference of the stars . . .

Quaritch. I switched my mind to that young satyr face and the tale from its lips of knowing Huth Rizq. What was to be done in the matter? Tell Aslaug Simonssen? She would report the fact to the Cairene police and have the woman arrested. Provided Quaritch would reveal the refugee's where-abouts.

Which, if I could prevent him, he would not do.

For that embodiment of heavy, unimaginative girlhood had long ceased to rouse my sympathy. How could it have aroused in Quaritch something stronger? She had better, and speedily, return to her England or Scotland and there wed with some bourgeois of her own type and class than stray in Egyptian deserts in search of a clownish revenge and in danger from such amoral possessive obsessions as the young novelist's——

I rose again, and searched for my pipe and matches, and saw, looking out, a thing I did not expect. Some-one, clearly enough to be discerned, was approaching the camp from the direction of Gault's castle. He came through the moonlight with a brisk enough step, and I put my hand below my pillow and drew out the revolver that lay there, standing and watching him from the eminence of the tent. Then he turned aside towards the labourers' fire, and poked that fire, and I saw his face.

It was Esdras Quaritch.

Subchapter ii

Huebsch called to me as I came from my tent towards the breakfast table. He sat there himself, not alone, but in the company of Quaritch. He said: "You want to go up to Cairo to-day, Colonel?"

I said that I had so far gone unaware of the want. It was then that the boy looked up. He had been drinking again, and was not yet sober. About him was the sickly-sweet smell of arrack. He grinned at me, heavy-eyed.

"Morning, sir. All right?" He turned to Huebsch. He sneered unpleasantly. "My God, the Israelite brain! How odd of God to choose the Jews! Haven't I explained that as yet Colonel Saloney knows nothing of the business—except that last night he told me Aslaug Simonssen was searching for Huth Rizq? Now, I know Huth. Rather! So after you two and the Colonel were in bed I went back to that house that looks like a pepper-pot gone wrong, and woke up the Simonssen girl, and made a little bargain with her. . . . Blushing, sir? Tut,

tut ! . . . Well, by the terms of my agreement with
Miss Simonssen, I'm going in to Cairo to fetch Huth
Rizq down here. Huth'll come, guilty or not——"

He would apparently have rambled on at length,
his over-bright, young, malignant eyes on the Jew.
But the latter interrupted him, slowly but decisively.
"And what has all this to do with Colonel Saloney ?"

"Oh, he's her local guardian—Miss Simonssen's,
I mean. And she insists the Colonel must accompany
me on this expedition. Believe she thinks I might
otherwise brutally maltreat Huth and drag her out
here tied to the auto axle. . . . Coming, sir ?"

I disregarded him and addressed my employer.
"If it is convenient for you, Mr. Huebsch, I would
like to resign my work here and leave to-day."

He paused in the act of decapitating an egg, large
and smooth and oddly like his head. Marrot came
out from his tent and sat down, and poured himself
a cup of coffee. Huebsch was considering me with
immense intentness.

"Say, that's a bit unpremeditated, isn't it ? Don't
we pay you enough money ?"

"It is not that," I said. "Nor any question of the
work or the personality of either yourself or Mr.
Marrot. I like both of you—very much. It is a
private matter——"

Marrot handed me a cup of coffee. "In fact, it's
the matter of the Russian Princess. Quite right to
go if you want to, Saloney. And why the devil
should you provide us with reasons ? Are you a
damned helot ?"

"Well, well, Colonel, we won't keep you against your will. But I thought you and the Princess Bourrin were by way of being friends ?"

"I think I will go and pack my luggage now," I said. "Perhaps I can take it into Cairo in the provision tender ?"

Huebsch had resumed in his egg. He did not look up. "Sure," he remarked.

So that, I reflected, turning away and disregarding again the inane grin of the boy, was that. And I felt a little disappointed. Their indifference made me realize how little my going mattered—so far as archæological research went. Kalaun could take my place at the head of the third squad and do my work with enough competence. So, like myself, my employers realized.

Now, standing in my tent, I stared with no enthusiasm at my scattered belongings. I felt in no mood at all for the agile manœuvrings and hot-faced bouncings of packing an inadequate suit-case over-adequately. But there was now no other course. Without pleasure I set to work.

Huebsch's voice made me wheel round. "You didn't breakfast, Colonel, so I'm telling Georgios to bring you some up here. And here is your salary up to the end of the contract."

I protested. "But that is too generous. I shall require payment only for the period in which I have been employed."

"Well, well, Colonel, it's your legal right. You'll have to take it." He turned away heavily, and then, a bull-god of the Semites, slowly levered himself round again. "Of course you understand that Marrot and I will sue you?"

"Eh?" I had not understood that at all.

"Why, sure. You've broken your contract and landed us in a fix, and we've no other course. Well, bye-bye, Colonel."

I shrugged aside his proffered hand and kicked my suit-case under the string-bed. I looked at him. Something rippled about the lines of his massive lips. I watched it, fascinated, comber to cheek and chin. His jaw fell, his head jerked back. He laughed, boomingly, like the salute of an ancient cannon. There was nothing for me but to join in the laugh, so thunderous and naïve and pleased it was.

"Say, think we're going to have you leave us because you got out of bed grumpy this morning?" He shook the egg-shaped head in immense negation. Then peered at me, a fatherly Baal. The camp was already astir, Marrot striding down towards the new excavations, Georgios singing at his work—an improper song in the Chian dialect. From the west there drifted a ghostly thing, extinguished in a moment, the damp smell of the morning crops. . . . It had grown to be home, this camp, I understood without amazement. Gault's crouched there in the sunrise. I should hate to leave before the search was over. . . . Huebsch talking to me, slowly and justly.

". . . that talk of yours last night—never having known the real Saloney. Well, well, I guess we're

all like that, and it frets us at times, and we want to
pack and clear out and go blundering off somewhere
else. D'you know, I've felt like that in some of the
times that have been the best in my life—in that
Jericho discovery, f'r instance. And what more than
that could an archæologist want ? . . . And it
seemed to me it was nothing at all and I'd never any
real interest in it. . . . Or Marrot either—Marrot,
the best man out East. But what else can we do,
except forget and get down to the work in
hand ?"

"Nothing else," I assented. "Yours is the voice
of sanity, Mr. Huebsch. I think I wanted to act the
deserter. But there is no desertion from that unease.
I will resume with my gang."

"Well—say, take a day off. We'll want our
permits restamped at the Ministry in a day or so,
anyway. Take them in and have them restamped
now. You needn't associate with the writer boy
unless you want to." He indicated the waiting
tender below and the slim, slouching figure of the
novelist. "Riding the rum-wagon pretty fast, I
guess. . . . Wonder what Jew he once fell foul of
—and can't forgive me because of it ?"

I also had wondered that. Huebsch waved his
hand, called a last injunction about the permits, and
strode away Marrotwards. I changed my jacket,
went to the store-tent, secured the permits, and
walked to where the tender stood. Kalaun was at
the wheel, Quaritch already aboard.

"Ready, khawaga ?"

Subchapter iii

Quaritch, who had obviously been drinking yet
again, sprawled opposite me as the tender jerked and
galumphed towards Cairo under the unskilful urgings
of Kalaun. For myself, I looked back at the camp
with thoughts wry enough. It seemed a far cry to
the Saloney who had wakened that Sunday morning
in Heliopolis and listened to the chirping of the
immortal grasshopper. Of late it seemed to me I
had taken to acting like the veriest tyro on the verge
of life, instead of the footsore Third Brother with
the greater stretch of that dreary plain behind him.

But, come what might, I would not see Pelagueya
again . . .

I found the eyes of the drunken boy upon me,
over-bright, mocking, reckless. "So you've left the
service of Solomon's by-blow ?"

He had amused me ; he had faintly shocked me ;
even, perhaps, he had stirred me to some liking of
him. Looking at him now, I found all three emotions
sunk in an acute distaste.

"I am still in Mr. Huebsch's employment, if that
is what you refer to."

"What else ? And still a Huebschian ? You can
have no very high regard for elementary hygiene.
. . . I say— Sorry, I'm going to be sick."

He was, composedly. He crawled back to his
former position, regarding me as brightly as ever.

"Where were we ? Oh, yes. By the by, sir, this
may interest you before we begin our talk."

He brought an automatic pistol out of his jacket-pocket and swung it idly to and fro on his finger-tip, presently, I think, a little piqued at my indifference and casual question :

"And why should this interest me ?"

"Because we've still details of this jaunt to discuss ; and you might lose your temper again."

"I have no details at all to discuss with you."

"Not even as Aslaug's guardian ?"

I said nothing. He moved into a more easy position. "Like to hear what we arranged when I paid her that visit last night ?"

I stared backwards, paying him no heed. He began to whistle, and then to hum in a voice that had lilt and youthfulness enough, spite the fact that it was a drunkard's voice :

> " 'Oh, what's the greatest pleasure
>   The tongue o' man can name ?
> 'Tis to kiss a bonny lassie
>   When the kye come hame !'

"My job to-night, Colonel Saloney. What a treat for the Abu Zabal cows ! No more good material going waste. What are you going to do about it ?"

I looked at him then. "Last night I told you what would happen if you interfered with Miss Simonssen. And that can still happen." Abruptly I took his right arm and twisted it behind him. He struggled ineffectually. The Browning automatic lay in my hand. An instant more and it had sailed over the tail-board of the tender.

I released the young Englishman. He righted himself, philosophically.

"More disarmament, eh ? . . . I think I'm going to be sick again. . . . Thanks awfully. . . . Right."

He breathed heavily, resuming his place, his young face with the rigidity and un-fleshlike seeming of a death-mask. "Always affects me that way, booze. No stomach for it. And no liking either. Right. Where were we ? Oh, yes. Going to help me carry out my part of the compact—so that Aslaug may carry out hers ?"

"Help ?"

"Quite. Come and help me induce Huth Rizq to make a trip to Abu Zabal."

"And what will happen then ?"

"Eh ? I told you in the camp. Aslaug will put Huth to the question and hand her over to the Gyppo gendarmes if she's guilty of Carl Simonssen's murder —which of course she isn't. Huth a murderess ! Really a great joke—and she loves jokes."

"Very well. I shall come with you when you go to this woman."

"Splendid. Exactly what I wanted."

"And I'll question her myself. If it is obvious she had no connection with the murder, she stays where she is."

"And upset my opera-plot, The Rape of the Valkyr, complete with Wagnerian music ? Really, sir, it can't be done. I'm going to have Aslaug Simonssen whatever happens."

I considered him with the troubled amazement

one might bestow on a goat in a garden struggling through a canebrake to reach at a distant flower.

"And what is this concern to possess Miss Simonssen? If it is a matter of simply serving your appetites you can serve them—to satiety—in the place where the Princess and I originally found you."

"Colonel, you'll move me in a moment to making obscene jests. And I'd hate to do that. . . . Oh, dammit, I'm going to be sick again!"

Subchapter iv

He had turned aside into the entrance of the Wagh el Berka. I caught his arm. "What, *here*?"

"Eh? Of course. She's an inmate of one of the licensed houses."

We went forward into the dun, evil-smelling street under the cold and cod-like scrutiny of the English military policeman . . .

Our tender awaited us at Bulaq. We had left it there with Kalaun, the while Quaritch disappeared on some errand of his own and I went to the Ministry of the Interior to have the camp permits restamped. Coming out, I had found Quaritch awaiting me.

"Lunch, sir?"

"I have no great fancy for lunching with you."

"All the better reason for you lunching with me." He smiled, a young satyr whom I could not hate. "You can consider it the bridal feast."

"'Or Belshazzar's."

"'Staggered by this allusive and literary repartee,

our hero maintained a grave silence. . . .' Come
along. In here ? Right."

We had sat at the same table in the restaurant
without exchanging a word, had paid our bills
separately, and had emerged into the siesta-daze of
the afternoon. The boy had glanced at me mockingly.

"I'm for Huth Rizq."

"So, unfortunately, am I."

Through the squalor and sin of the Sharia
Muhammud Ali, down the Muski with its little
inlettings of dukanin where the stout and bearded
slept and exuded perspiration, and tame pigeons
pecked and fluttered over spilt rice far back in the
deeps of unsavoury shoplets. Drowsy drivers of
street-cars nodded at their posts as they swept past ;
in crevices and corners, sprawling even athwart the
sidewalks, beggars lay sleeping. It was an hour
and a city that seemed to hold no purposeful beings
but ourselves.

Through the Khalig and so at last to the Street of
Shame whereto I had once led Pelagueya that she
might read it a mighty stanza in the saga of life. Its
cobbles rose moist and slippery under our feet, and
rounding into the main stretch of it we saw it dusty
and deserted, with a foul haze brooding over it like
a miasma. I noted that we passed the house from
which Pelagueya and I had been witnesses of the
novelist's abrupt evacuation. Here, it appeared, his
acquaintance was wide and varied.

I felt distaste in my mouth again, realizing that
and keeping pace with his slouch-shouldered walk.

This foul thing beside me and his straying, undisci-
plined lusts that he crowned as expeditions in search
of reality ! Now it became obvious to me that he was
of a type fairly common in Cairo, and indeed in all
the towns of the Mediterranean littoral; the sex-
perverted adolescent who makes of such streets a
shameful necessity and of that necessity a shameful
jesting——

He had swung aside again, into an open doorway,
up dank stairs such as once I had climbed to the
room of the tragic Connan in the Khalig.* The
sunshine vanished. It was so dark, coming from its
dazzle, that I had to claw at the wall, blinded and
cautious, as I followed Quaritch's footsteps. I knew
something of the structure of such houses and how,
frequently enough, the stairs had the merest wisps
of wood or iron for banisters, and sometimes lacked
them altogether.

"Tired, sir ?" Quaritch's voice, mocking, but,
for some reason, friendly still, was caught and echoed
and re-echoed throughout the sweating tomb of a
house. He was a flight above me and had evidently
halted. "Or turning back ?"

"Neither. Is that the door ?"

"What else ? Journeys end in clients meeting,
how much to-night, my pretty sweeting ? . . .
Mind that beam there."

He raised his hand in the semi-darkness, found a
knocker and knocked thunderously.

*See "The Calends of Cairo."

CHAPTER THE SIXTEENTH

' "Oh, yes . . . I killed him that morning before I left Rashida." '

Subchapter i

A METALLIC wash of sound-waves ebbed out from the knocker, flowed across our heads, and fell down the foul well of the stair in a faint, thundering splash. The boy knocked again, and at that we heard a shuffling on the other side of the door. Then, to the right of the knocker, appeared a parallelogram of light : daylight. A small panel had been slipped aside.

A face appeared in it—a small, Mongolian face, with brooding brows and pallid cheeks and a small, button-like nose. A Japanese face ; the face of a Japanese prostitute, the original brown of the skin hidden under layers of porcelain powder.

"Kota—it's Esdras Quaritch."

He spoke in French. The eyes stared slantingly, unwinking, levered from one to the other of us by slow movements of the head crowned with dead black hair. Then the button-like nose slowly ascended the face and sank into position again. She had smiled at us.

Suddenly the panel became a portion of the door again. The door itself opened.

I followed Quaritch. The Japanese, squat and yet
slim, with demure gestures and heavy-lidded eyes,
closed the door and surveyed us, smiling blandly.
And then I saw the room.

It was a large room—as they go in houses of that
shameful street, a room longer than broad, with two
beds and by each bed a heaped and untidy table, a
chair, a screen. Mid-way the room was another
table, round and ancient, with claw-like legs pro-
truding. A bowl of dusty flowers stood in the midst
of it. Near the door, to the left, was a large teak
cupboard. To the right an oil-stove. A heaping of
unidentifiable litter under the window. Nothing else.

Quaritch was shaking the girl's hand. "Where's
Huth ?"

The Japanese waved us to the chairs. Quaritch
caught them up and set them side by side near the
table. I knit my brows to follow a peculiar French
that both whined and purred.

"She has gone out—down to the sick woman in
room eight. Yes. But she will soon be back. But
yes. You want her ? And the poor girl in the far
end house—She is better ?"

Something like this she said, indifferently,
friendlily, her lips hardly moving. The boy, sitting
down, glanced sideways at me. It struck me, absurdly,
that he was flushing. Also, the peculiar French seemed
to have enticed his own tongue from plain articu-
lation. He muttered unintelligibly.

The Japanese sat down on the side of the nearer
bed. Me she treated to a drowsy appraisal.

"And you are a friend of Esdras ? Then you will know what we call him and what he has done."

Quaritch made a sudden movement. "Taisez-vous !"

Inviting some recital of the unclean, I could not stay my own questioning.

"What has he done ?"

She raised tired brows. "Then you do not know ? He brings doctors here to tend the sick. Yes. Down in the lowest house he himself nursed a girl who had fever-madness. She tried to have him poisoned, the patronne of that house. . . . And other things. He brings his pistol into the Street every evening and clients have learnt it is unwise to cheat or play the beast too greatly when he is within call. For nearly a year now, until the last week, this has been so." She turned those never-awaking eyes on Quaritch. "Where did you go ? We were frightened you had been killed. But the English policeman was with Huth, and he told her he saw you pass out of the Street unharmed."

But I was holding my head. Here was something inexplicable. "And he has done these things for the women of the Street—why ?"

"To get copy, of course." But his face was flushed and uneasy. The girl lighted another cigarette.

"Why ? There are fools like that. Always there have been these fools, is it not so ? Our Lord Buddha —he was such. And the Christ of the Copti. . . ,

Yes. There have been many like Esdras. Even clients. Me, I do not understand them."

I took Quaritch by the shoulders and swung him round to face me. This boy of the obscene speech and intention a Buddha or a Christ! "Then even when Pelagueya and I saw you thrown out of a house——"

"I had been sick-nursing a prostitute. Exactly. Peculiar hobby. And I'd got half-drunk to help me carry the business through. You might as well know. What now?"

"I should like to shake hands with you," I said.

"No you wouldn't, sir." He thrust his hands deep in his pockets. "Mind if we speak English? Right. . . ." He thrust his pale face close to mine. "There's still Aslaug. Do you think because of the accident of Kota blabbing I'm going to change my intentions about her? Not though the heavens fall! She's my surety that I'm alive, the one taste of golden life that I'm going to taste before I come back again to this leprous charnel-house crawl. Listen: Two years I've had of this: London, Alexandria, Cairo. . . . Hellish, Dellish stuff, isn't it? The Prostitutes' Friend. . . . The Little Brother of the Brothel. . . . I've never known a harlot in my life in the sense that your Biblical crony Huebsch would understand the word.

"Nor any other woman but one. A girl. A student in London. Younger than me. And she died before my eyes in a hospital ward. Horribly, sickeningly. Murdered by the lust of a filthy Jew who stole her

from me. . . . Oh, damn, damn, why did I ever
start telling you this? The shame that it is to be a
woman! I've been haunted ever since, I'll be haunted
all my life—and these streets are my life. . . . But
for that interlude out in the desert there, Colonel
Saloney, and neither you nor anyone else will rob
me of that."

He shook off my hands, jumped up, and began to
walk about the room. "I looked at her up there that
evening—when was it? Only last evening!—and
knew she was for me more certainly than I ever
knew anything in my life. She's a guerdon for these
ghastly rooms and streets and sickening women.
Out of them for a moment, sir—and you'd deny me
that moment! I'm to live again—a minute, five
minutes, and then back to this. Do you think I'm
likely to forgo the only touch of clean lust and pain
and passion that's ever likely to come my way again?"

He stopped in front of me, glaring at me. The
Japanese girl removed the scented cigarette from
between her lips and regarded us incuriously, her
head cocked to one side.

"That is Huth coming up the stairs."

Subchapter ii

She was perhaps five feet three inches in height,
an Egyptian peasant woman with the peasant tattoo-
markings. So deeply black were her eyes that they
minded me of some animal's, so steady and happy
their look that, holding her hand, I smiled politely

thinking she smiled at me. Then I remembered she
was blind and saw the gravity of her lips. She stood
still in that grey wrapping of hers and put out a
hand and touched my face.

"This is a man I know, Huth." It was the boy's
voice behind us. "Colonel Anton Saloney, a Russian."

"And why have you brought him here, Esdras ?
Is he a client ?" She spoke French easily, effortlessly,
and now did indeed smile up at me, cheerfully. But
I dropped her hand as though it had been unclean.

"My goodness, no !" Quaritch pushed me aside,
flashed me a wry smile. "He is a gentleman, Huth.
Almost as though he were English. Believes prostitutes are wicked and filthy people who have taken to
their job for love of lucre."

The woman crossed towards the bed. A prostitute. It seemed to me I had seen many gracious
women walk like that. . . . She sat down and put
up a hand to the shawl and so, free of that, turned
her head and smiled at us.

It was no longer the cheerful smile of the professional harlot. It was a smile I had seen on the
face of Pelagueya . . . on many faces . . . I drew
out my handkerchief and dabbed at my forehead as
she spoke.

"Then why bring him ?"

The boy stood easily in front of her, yet, it seemed
to me, with an odd respect.

"As a matter of fact, we've come to arrest you on
a suspicion of murder. Rather a joke, Huth. I'll
explain it in a moment. You can help me."

"Some woman, Esdras ?"

"How did you know ?"

"It is always either a woman or God." And she lighted a cigarette and curled her feet up beneath her. "Tell me."

He was telling her, succinctly. And I could not take my eyes off this woman of the Wagh el Berka. . . . Certainly I must be near to an attack of fever, for it seemed to me, in despite her blindness, that her glances in my direction were definitely the glances of one who *saw*. . . . She was nodding to Quaritch.

"And you want me to help ? But I shall ! What is it you wish ?"

"This woman I'm going to take—it seems she had a brother who lived at Rashida, a Carl Simonssen. It seems some woman Huth Rizq lived with him. Was it you ?"

"It was I."

The boy's laugh had a ring of triumph in it. "That's splendid. Listen. This man's sister thinks you were the murderess. That's amusing enough. But if I can find you and take you to her I fulfil my part of the bargain. Will you come ?"

The prostitute picked up her shawl. She did it without any of the tentative gropings of the blind. "Yes, I'll come." She mused. "Carl Simonssen ?"

But I also had stood up. It seemed to me time to end this mad conversation. "Carl Simonssen," I said, slowly and distinctly. "And this sister believes you murdered him."

She turned her head with its unwinking, laughing

eyes towards me. She nodded. "Oh, yes. I was
his mistress. I killed him that morning before I left
Rashida."

Subchapter iii

I think that was probably as strange a procession
as ever threaded the Warrens and came at length out
into the sunshine and the waning afternoon of the
Esbekieh Gardens—the Russian *emigré*-dragoman,
the Egyptian prostitute-murderess, the English
novelist. I walked in front through the narrow lanes
and though I had believed I was far enough from
days of such prudery a ghostly, shamefaced self of
other years whispered at my shoulder. Once or
twice I glanced back. The boy, white-faced, was
engaged as he had been ever since we left the house
in the Wagh el Berka—in attempting to induce the
woman to return.

She seemed genuinely puzzled at his reluctances.
"But you wanted me, Esdras. So I come with you."

"But you don't realize—look here, you must go
back. Murder! My God, I can't believe that of
you !"

"But why not ? And it will help you. . . . Here
is the sun again, and the Esbekieh Gardens. I can
smell them. And the tall man has stopped. Have
you money, Esdras ?"

He jingled coins in his pocket. She sighed satis-
fiedly between the two of us, smiling up at him
gravely, her unwinking eyes merry. "That is good,

for I am very hungry. Abu Zabal? It is a long distance there."

"You have been there before?" I asked. She nodded, her sightless eyes on the Garden.

"But often."

I glanced at the boy, troubled and distraught almost as was he himself. The woman moved forward.

"There is a fine restaurant just here and I love its honey cakes. Take me to it, Esdras."

It seemed to me that she was guiding him, not he her, up to the door of the Petrograd. At that door stood the commissionaire, a Greek, portentous and proud. Walking behind the two others, I expected the inevitable. No street-woman was allowed in the Petrograd. But the Greek made no objection. He drew back, bowed, and swung open the door.

We went in. The restaurant was crowded, the early dinner of prosperous Greek and Europeanized Egyptian much in progress and evidence. In the midst of the room stood one table unoccupied and conspicuous. Towards it Quaritch steered our charge and found a chair for her and himself sat down. Sitting myself, I raised my gaze expecting to find a battery of astounded eyes upon us. But except for a French-woman near at hand, who was regarding us with the casual intentness of the absent-minded, not one of the diners appeared to pay us any heed.

"Anything wrong, sir? You don't look well."

I found the boy, his worriment over Huth Rizq for a moment in abeyance, staring at me concernedly.

At that I pulled myself out of the mental fog that threatened to engulf me and beckoned to a waiter.

"Nothing is wrong. What will both of you eat?"

She sat between us and ate like a hungry child, deftly, with none of the groping motions of the blind, and talked of the sick girl in the first Wagh house, and of a client she herself had had the previous evening, and of one occasion when she had visited Abu Zabal. "There was a block-house there, and soldiers. One of them took me out to a nullah and we watched all night the fires of the coming army from the south——"

"But a block-house? There is no block-house at Abu Zabal," I protested.

"No? It was long ago. . . . Ah, listen!"

All the Petrograd was listening. In the distance had arisen the monotonous beating of a native drum. It grew in volume, drawing nearer. So did other sounds—the voices of marchers uplifted unintelligibly in some Eastern song.

Presently the first of the marchers came in sight. It was no student procession, but a march of the Cairene Labour Unions. Clerks and such-like folk, in shoddy European garb and tarbouches, marched side by side with labourers in breech-clouts and soiled turbans, and the end of the procession was brought up by a rabble without name or classification. Half-naked, half-human things, seldom seen in the modern quarters, were there; maimed and brutalized by disease and want, their faces unhealed sores, they looked their hate at us who watched.

Abandoned of God and man these, the cheated of the sunlight, parading through the streets the awful indictment of their being.

Dourly all marched, spite their song. Overhead flapped great banners scrawled with Arabic symbols. In front, the drum beat out its threat through the silenced street.

Scorn, disgust, fear; the looks I saw on the faces in the Petrograd as the marchers went by. Except on one face; the prostitute from the Wagh el Berka who sat beside me was weeping.

"Huth!"

"Oh, Esdras, I heard them! They have none but me to help them." She half-rose up. "I must go."

The boy held her down, a hand on her shoulder. "If you go, you can't go with these chaps. There'll be rioting and the gendarmes trying to disperse them in another street or so. . . . Look here, I'll see you back to the Street myself."

"Ah, but I had forgotten. I am going with you to Abu Zabal. Let us go now."

I had finished. Quaritch had eaten hardly any-thing. Suddenly he shrugged and his face lightened.

"Let's go then. It's all part of the dirty insanity of things to find you—a murderess. You! Whatever did you do it for?"

"He was dirty, so I killed him. It was great fun, until he began to scream. Then I was sorry for him—a little. I thought I would stay and tell people, but that seemed foolish, for he was not worth the

trouble, being so dirty. So I walked to the gendarmes,
and they let me go, for I was their friend. And I
walked away from Rashida and took a train to
Cairo. . . . Now I will come and meet his sister."

It seemed to me either the patter of a maudlin
child—or something far worse. I said : "Please
listen. Quaritch does not seem to have made the
matter plain. If you killed Simonssen and you had
good reasons for doing so, why do you confess it
now ?"

"But what harm can it do ?"

"When Simonssen's sister hands you over to the
police they will kill you."

"Kill me ?" She laughed with genuine amusement. "He is a droll, the tall man, Esdras."

I made a gesture of despair and summoned the
waiter. Quaritch, with an equally despairing shrug,
helped Huth Rizq to her feet and guided her out
of the Petrograd.

Subchapter iv

I sat beside Kalaun on the Abu Zabalward journey,
the while the Englishman and the woman from the
Street rode behind us in the body of the tender.
Occasionally the murmur of their voices would come
to us. Once I heard the woman's laughter, clear
and joyous. But for the most part I kept my attention
on the erratic driving of the grinning Kalaun who
loved a scandal and scented one—if not two—
ensconced in the tender behind him.

We rode through an evening that paced and padded to the left of us, hesitatingly, like a black panther, for mile on mile. The sun waited above that West that Old Egypt believed the abode of the dead—as indeed it had been, for on the Nile left bank they had been wont to bury their dead. . . . And succeeding years and generations had made of that simple necessity and happening a mysterious, symbolic thing, transplanting the dead to the western sky out of the sand and shingly Nilotic loam. To what effect and what gain ? Little enough, I remember thinking wryly. If we had kept the ancient way of Adrian's Golden Hunters it had been better for all mankind . . .

I think I must have sat dozing then, for an hour almost. But it seemed only a moment later when Kalaun shook me urgently by the shoulder.

"Look, khawaga !"

CHAPTER THE SEVENTEENTH

'There could be no doubt of that Shape.'

Subchapter i

I SAT erect. We were near to Abu Zabal. And in
the sky a strange radiance was blossoming. I
peered across the bent tip of Kalaun's nose. Night
had quite descended and we slid along the yellow
canals of our head-lights. Meantime, that soft glow
persisted in the sky and then suddenly betook itself
to earth. While I stared towards it Quaritch's voice
spoke from the opening above my head.

"That must be the Princess's house on fire, sir."

"Eh ?"

"Or something in the camp. Too far in the west
to come from Abu Zabal proper."

He was right. I caught the wheel from Kalaun.
"Change places."

He crawled behind me, squeezing himself into
small bulk to make the passage. I put my foot on
the accelerator. The light-channel through which
we rushed quivered itself into swifter flow. Little
stones pattered against the wind-screen, ping, pong,
slowly at first, but presently as a rattling hail. Ahead
grew the lights of Abu Zabal, and the dim markings
of the by-road that led to the camp and Gault's.

And now the true cause of the glare in the sky was obtrusive. Three great fires burned amid the excavations.

"Must be the tents," commented Quaritch from over the heads of Kalaun and myself.

So I also thought. The great fires whoomed up against the sky. What accident or series of accidents had led to this catastrophe ? I demanded of myself, foolishly, and swung the tender rightwards, down the Gault road. The torn, fire-illumined lands of the excavations rushed upwards at that move, and beyond them steadier lights in Gault's house swayed and stumbled us-ward. I gave a sigh of relief.

It was not the tents.

They stood safe and unharmed, as we could see now. The three great fires loomed nearer at hand, amid the scene of the more recent excavations. One was at either end of the great trench on which we had left the archæologists engaged that morning ; the third burned near to Georgios' cooking-shed, which was also the store-tent. And between and around the fires, silhouettes in copper against the disturbed Egyptian night, a multitude of figures engaged in mysterious activity.

I swung the tender out of the road and into the field, and when we had come to a halt Georgios I discovered panting by the side of the vehicle. I shouted to ask the reason of the fires.

"Discoveries, mon colonel, and there is great excitement. But with that I have no concern. You will have dinner ?"

"Dinner ? . . . What has been discovered ?"

He spread out his hands and shrugged his shoulders. "To me they appear as fragments of utensils privy to the bedroom. But M. Huebsch— he is in ecstasies. M. Marrot—he makes the cool smile. They believe more discoveries will be made and M. Huebsch had fuel borrowed from the Princess's house and all our petrol poured out to make those fires. . . . But I have kept dinner for you, mon colonel."

"That was thoughtful of you, Georgios," I said, coming to the ground and treading into the light of the bonfires. "I will eat it as soon as I have spoken to M. Huebsch."

But I was not at once to have speech with him. As I hurried past the near fire one, whom I took to be a labourer, and who was bent over a number of dim, asymmetrical shapes laid on a piece of sacking, called out to me.

"Anton !"

"Princess !"

She was clad in dusty overalls. Her hair fluffed out above the neck of the absurd jacket. Arms akimbo, she stood and looked up at me, smiling, her eyes lighted either with amusement or the flame of the fires that roared near at hand and were scaring far-away jackals in Georgios' nullah to voice hysteric protests to the skies.

"Isn't it fun ! Some discoveries at last—though not the Lost Trumpet. What do you think of them ?"

I looked down at the fragments of painted earthen-ware, as I then saw them to be, picked up one fragment—and replaced it hastily. Pelagueya gurgled. I dusted my hands and looked at her.

"I would not say it to the good Huebsch, but I feel he has been indiscreet. But why are you here?"

"Am I such a vexing sight?" She thrust her arm in mine. "Why not? Anything for a change. They sent to borrow fuel for the bonfires, and I accompanied it back."

"When was this?"

"Oh, an hour or so ago. And now I've been deputed to guard the finds. So at last I'm a worker, Anton, and you should smile at me and recite some Karl Liebknecht—or is it Marx?"

"But why?"

"But obviously. I've been worrying over you, Anton. Why ever did you leave Russia? You'd have enjoyed yourself there, making yourself miserable in order that the future might be happy. Pfuu! . . . And *do* leave me a cigarette. And there's Mr. Huebsch calling to you."

I lighted the cigarette for her and hasted towards the far fire, and then remembered something and turned to call to the guardian of the treasure.

"Is Miss Simonssen with you?"

"Goodness, no. Fast asleep, I should think. Much too proper to wander about archæological camps at night."

Huebsch I found, his immense face glistening with sweat, drinking water from a goatskin with sounds reminiscent of the Nile descending the Fourth Cataract. He looked at me sideways across the inverted skin.

"Hello, Colonel! Get our passes restamped? Well, well. Not that we'll need them now. We're on the trail at last."

His great face worked with emotion. He flung down the goatskin and caught my arm.

"Come and see."

Now by the light of the near bonfire I could indeed see something new. Near its eastern tip the great trench had at length ploughed its way into the midst of the treasure and there had halted and broadened out and betaken to itself, it seemed to me, the likeness of a volcanic eruption. Nearly all the labourers were engaged here. Marrot, in shirt and shorts and a pent-up energy, was toiling with sieve and basket in the strongest light from the fire. Others cut and hewed, and yet others, with faces now familiar enough to me though I had never learned their names, lifted small oblongs carefully aside and peered into the holes thus excavated, and all the while kept up a thin twitter of admonition and excitement. I bent down and examined the stacked oblongs and then turned to Huebsch.

"But what is it you have discovered?"

"A house—a block-house, I guess, by the shape of it."

"A block-house?" My mind went back to the words of Huth Rizq. "Then it is modern?"

"Modern?" He stared at me. "Well, well, nothing

so very ancient. Sixth or seventh century B.C. by the shape and baking of its bricks."

It was my turn to stare. "Then—but that is impossible. I have just talked to a woman who remembers the block-house here."

"Well, well, she's a long memory, Colonel."

It was obvious that the matter did not interest him. A block-house of the sixth or seventh century of the last pre-Christian millennium? I thought aloud: "Then it was built after the Temple treasures were stolen and hidden."

"Long after." His immense laugh boomed out with a new, vibrant note in it. So one of those curved-nosed, curved-sworded Semites might have laughed as Jericho's high walls toppled and reeled and crumbled thunderously to dust. "*And* it was built on top of the spot where the Levite buried the Trumpet."

"But how can you know?"

"A hunch of mine, Colonel—a hunch of all of us. Look at us!"

I felt some contagion of his own confidence. "And you have found Jewish relics?"

"Not a darned fragment yet. Don't expect any— after the brooch. He wasn't loaded with pottery, that priest who stole and buried the Trumpet. The stuff you've just seen is common Egyptian ware." He paused, frowning benevolently, looking towards Pelagueya's dim, slim figure. "Guess I'll have to go and catalogue it all the same."

I took off my coat. "I will take your place in charge of this sector."

Subchapter ii

So I had done, working without result for many minutes. While others hewed them out, I set the oblong bricks in neat walls, keeping the while a careful eye on each wielder of pick and mattock. And presently that vigilance was rewarded. Something in the deeps of the loam crackled under a heavy blow. I jumped down into the excavation and put the labourer aside and searched in the earth with my fingers. The thing came out in my hand in two pieces.

It was some three feet in length. I carried it over towards Marrot and his sand-sievings by the fire.

"Hello, Saloney. What's that ?"

"A statuette," I said, and knelt down to put the fragments together, upright, against a bank of earth. Then I stood up and together we looked down at the newly risen deity, as I supposed it to be. Marrot knelt where I had been and nodded a confirmatory head.

"Human-headed household Hathor. Very worn."

"Huthor," he pronounced it. Some dim association of names jangled in my mind, vexing me. The worn soapstone eyes of the goddess regarded us unblinkingly. And suddenly I remembered the reason for the familiar sound of the unfamiliar pronunciation. "Hathor ? The goddess of love ?"

"That's the lady. Why ?"

"Nothing." I shook myself. Absurdest of fancies

that which had been with me. . . . Marrot had gathered up the statuette again.

"Send it over to Huebsch, will you ? And you'd better get back to that bit of digging there—if you want to. Damned if I know why you should at this hour of night, on the starvation wages we pay you. Damned if I know why any of these labourers are such fools as to be out here at this time of night——"

"I think I could tell you," I said, "so you seek damnation unnecessarily. They are here for the worst of reasons from the point of view of a good proletarian ; because they like their employers, you and Mr. Huebsch. But why are the excavations going on ? Would it not have been better to wait until the daytime ?"

"Of course it would. But that won't do for Huebsch. He's possessed by one of the Semite demons —Ialdabaoth, I guess. Swears we'll dig and find the Lost Trumpet to-night. Lost grandmothers. But we'll probably find something of interest in this late Dynasty block-house. Keep a sharp look-out for more gods and for the love of all their modern manifestations try and get them unbroken."

I went back to the excavating of the eastern wing. We were down to hard sand level again, and for minute after minute nothing of interest came from the pits. I had straightened up after five minutes of brick-building when Pelagueya's voice spoke at my shoulder.

"This *is* you, Anton ? Georgios was frantic, so I've brought you your dinner."

I turned to find her standing with a tray in her

hands. I attempted to take that from her, but she backed away.

"Sit down. See, I'll put it here. Now you'll see what to eat. And I'll have a cup of coffee, please, though you haven't asked me."

She sat down beside me, in that sudden crumpling of limbs and body that was so oddly child-like and charming. I found my cigarette-case again and handed it to her the while I ate of Georgios' excellent chicken. Pelagueya blew smoke-rings through her nose and cupped her hands in the attitude she loved. "Anton, I believe Mr. Huebsch is right. I have the same feeling."

"About what?"

"About the Lost Trumpet—that it is going to be found to-night."

"Was there ever a Trumpet to lose?"

"Oh, Anton, don't be so prosaic and world-weary. You are the oddest mixture these days. At one moment—out of Lermontov; at another—that dreary Feodor. And once you were entirely Pushkin. . . . I don't suppose there ever *was* a Trumpet—unless it's that one that Dr. Adrian talked about. Remember him?—the voice of human sanity that's never been quite stilled. Perhaps we're digging for that, all of us——"

She shivered. I put my hand on her shoulder, and so on her uncovered neck. But she was warm enough. I said: "You should go to bed. You are dreaming awake. What has this lost Jewish relic—even if it exists—to do with these things?"

"Nothing at all, Anton. Or something. Let's say both. . . . Perhaps there was nothing peculiar in the essence of the Trumpet that overthrew Jericho. The miracle happened through the faith that Joshua brought to the blowing of it."

"I am very dull."

"You are very dear. And this is fun—even if nothing else comes of it. Oh, did you bring back the English novelist with you ? What is the matter ?"

I had almost dropped my coffee-cup. I had only then recollected the two who had ridden from Cairo in the body of the tender. I explained to Pelagueya and she stood up.

"A prostitute—and Carl Simonssen's murderess ! Pfuu ! Still, she must be hungry, poor thing. Give me your tray, Anton, and I'll go get Georgios give her some food. . . . And do shout to me if you discover the Trumpet."

The Trumpet ! Turning to work, I realized that my stay in Abu Zabal must now be short enough, Trumpet or no Trumpet. And no doubt it would be no Trumpet. Unless something of importance was found under this block-house I was sure that Marrot, at least, would close down the excavations, and I be freed from the web and tangle in which I had been drawn. And then——

I began brick-building again with unnecessary speed. And then—why, I would return to Cairo as a dragoman and tramp the sands and bazaars with tourists and listen until the croaking of the grass-hopper had become a madness inside my brain.

Subchapter iii

Midnight passed and still we dug and laboured at removing the shattered debris of the block-house. It had been built strongly and securely in those far-off times. And then, in some convulsion of war or riot, an enemy had entered it and burned it to the ground . . .

"*There was a block-house there, and soldiers. One of them took me out to a nullah and we watched all night the fires of the coming army from the south——*"

Insanity to remember that. Were there such things ? Such things that a modern prostitute had the stony grace of an ancient statuette—*was* that ancient statuette—and remembered back across such gulf of years as seventy-five generations might not span——

Under layers of ashes our gang presently came upon bones—the dismembered bones of a man who had either died fighting, or else died even more horribly, for Marrot said that these bones had not mouldered apart in the years. They had been severed from the trunk by the blows of heavy weapons, maces or axes. And up out of that ashen pit rose another thing that made me smile for that glamour of the ancient historical world of which the little novelists write—a smell of decay and death, dank and vile and sickening. . . . Between one and two o'clock in the morning Huebsch called a halt to the labour of the gangs, and we sat and ate and drank in the waning light of the bonfires. The enthusiasm of most of us was waning in like manner.

But not of Huebsch. His immense voice boomed out across the excavations in instructions for replenishing the fires with all the spare camp-props that could be gathered. It was obvious that he would sacrifice tents and tender if that should prove necessary, and Marrot's acid suggestion that the great Jew might add himself as a supreme auto-da-fé produced nothing more than a kindly, considering stare and a maelstrom-ripple of smile. Then we started again, tiredly, and at length the whole of the block-house and its outbuildings had been cleared away. It had been a very small block-house.

Below was the basic sand. Huebsch and Marrot cleared the labourers off the ground of the pit and then with level and tape marked out the lines of a great St. Andrew's cross. Along those lines Kalaun and his companions were set to the digging of two fresh intersecting trenches. I had had enough for the time being, and sat to smoke a pipe and watch the hasty stridings to and fro of the great Jew and his tall, slim secretary. Pelagueya had elected herself to this post and followed Huebsch everywhere, importantly, notebook in hand, her clear voice, with a note of excitement in it, raised in an occasional suggestion towards which the ovoid head of her companion would be readily inclined. Huebsch had found a fellow-enthusiast.

Once, as Pelagueya passed and I looked after her amusedly, I remembered my companions of the journey from Cairo and called a question.

"They've gone," Pelagueya called back.

"Gone where ?"

"Down to my house to arouse Aslaug, I suppose. At least, Georgios says that the Englishman drove the tender down there. We here were all too busied to note."

Down to Gault's ? . . . I looked towards the two lights that had shone all night from rooms high up in the walls of the house. What was happening there now ? Aslaug Simonssen, her brother's murderess, her would-be seducer. . . . Had I better go there and find out ?

Pelagueya's voice broke in upon my thoughts. I became aware of a hush in all the camp.

"Anton, come quickly !"

Subchapter iv

Huebsch knelt on the ground at the bottom of the pit, Marrot peered over his shoulder, the feeble beam of his electric torch directed into a jagged hole newly opened. Pelagueya was at the other side of the pit ; Kalaun had just withdrawn his pick. The lights of the bonfires were dying and I stumbled amid heaps of earth as I made towards the grouping—at a run, as I noted with a twinge of amusement.

"What is it ?"

The groups of labourers broke apart as I jumped down. Pelagueya caught my sleeve.

"Sh !"

Huebsch had squatted above the dark hole, lowered his immense, gorilla-like arms and inserted

his hands, and grappled with some hidden thing.
He pulled. The thing refused to budge. His legs
and arms straining and up-bulging in muscle, the
great Jew made another attempt. A dark, shapeless
mass was slowly emerging. Marrot backed away
and swung down his torch-beam upon it. A final
tug and the sand-stained, sand-preserved object was
lifted in Huebsch's hands.

A great sigh went up from all of us ! A little
early wind came shining through the dimness. Far
in Abu Zabal a cock began to crow. Huebsch,
breathing immensely, shook sand and mould from
his discovery and peered at it nearsightedly in the
light of Marrot's electric torch. It was the latter who
spoke first, and in a voice strangely high-pitched.

"Leather : a leather sack somehow preserved.
Soaked in gums, perhaps."

"That, and the sands themselves." Huebsch's
voice, surprisingly, was quite calm, even slightly
flat. "Thank God that's done. You can dismiss all
the boys, Colonel. There'll be nothing more to-night.
Nor, of course, to-morrow."

I had come forward to look at the find. "But
are you certain this is the——?"

The near fire spiralled a final column of light.
Huebsch held up the leather sack and crumpled the
leather roughly into the curved shape of the object
hidden in its folds.

"Look."

We looked, Pelagueya and Marrot and I, first at
the object and then at each other. It was impossible

—a boy's treasure-tale come true—but there could be no doubt of that shape. . . . The fire fluffed down into darkness. We began to shiver in the chill air, and I put my arm round Pelagueya, and she stopped shivering and turned her face, a dim, sweet face, to thank me. Then:

"We'll all die of pneumonia if we remain here. And your tents are too uncomfortable after such a night. And you've no electric light with which to examine the Thing. The three of you must bring it over to my house and must stop to breakfast."

Huebsch slung the object under his armpit, turning his great, slow head upon his temporary secretary.

"That'll be fine, Princess," he agreed.

CHAPTER THE EIGHTEENTH

' "We will see if one of us can blow the Lost
Trumpet." '

Subchapter i

WE walked into the blow of that faint dawn-
wind, side by side, the three of us. Behind us
the night. But the day was not due for another hour
yet. A hasting shadow in front went Georgios on
his mission to rouse the Bourrin household with the
news of our coming, and himself to prepare breakfast in the Princess Pelagueya's kitchen.

Pelagueya had abandoned the shelter of my arm.
She walked by my side and I saw her head dimly
downbent against the great moving shadow that was
the head of Huebsch. Presently Marrot began to
whistle underbreath, and broke off, and made a
strange sound that startled us all from reverie. It
was a portentous yawn.

"I could yawn my skin off and walk about in my
skeleton," he confessed.

"So could I," said Pelagueya. "Especially as I'm
told I have a good skeleton. . . . Horribly sleepy.
But I'm not going to sleep—yet. Waken up, Anton!
You're stumbling in your tracks."

"In my sleep."

Huebsch swung his burden under the other arm. "Well, well. Emotional excitement. I guess that's what's tired us. It kept us up during the search and now——"

Marrot said : "Hell, listen to the jackals !"

They were moaning eerily enough ; a final chorussing away in the west before the day came. In that hesitating hour it was an uncanny and fearsome sound. In some mythologies there are beasts that devour the daylight, and gods and culture-heroes who slay the beasts. Unendingly, day after day. And the little anthropologists have poked and questioned and queried and made plain the meaning of that ceaseless conflict, bringing it from dusty legends of the outer world into its ancient birthplace and lodging, the human brain. Day was God ; the beasts and night were Evil. The immortal struggle in each human being. And how false alike mythology and interpretation !——

I had been again "stumbling in my tracks." Pelagueya's hand came on my arm.

"Not ill, Anton ?"

"I was thinking out a new mythology."

"Then you *do* want breakfast. I always think out that kind of thing myself when I'm very hungry." Her teasing sounded as vivacious as ever. She had indeed wells of vitality to unseal for every possible emergency. "And now we're here. You three will want to bathe. I do. Ibrahim will see to you."

Subchapter ii

Ibrahim did, his eyes still rimed with the frosts of sleep. It appeared that Georgios, however, had had no need to awaken the household. The "young khawaga" had seen to that some time earlier. And where now was the "young khawaga"? Ibrahim did not know; perhaps on the roof still, looking at the stars. It was there he had betaken himself. As for the harlot, she was with the Sitt I-sloog——

I dismissed Ibrahim then and in company with my employers in that very expensive bathroom set to cleansing from my person the evidences of the night's toil—or at least such evidences as soap and water and perfumed pumicestone might remove. Huebsch had deposited the leather sack inside the bathroom entrance, and even while, like a great river beast, he plunged and swayed above his basin, kept a close regard on that sack. Drying my face on Pelagueya's over-frilled towels I caught that straying of his eye doorward. He smiled slowly, consideringly.

"Guess we'll keep a sharp eye on it till we've made sure of the contents."

"But I had thought you were sure?"

"Well, well. What was it the writer boy was saying the other evening here? That there's nothing so admirable as inconsistency. . . . Very human, anyway. Pass me that brush and comb, Colonel."

So, a little refreshed and I at least very hungry, we presently betook ourselves to the room that

Ibrahim indicated—that same room where I had dined with Pelagueya on the first night of the expedition in Abu Zabal. The table was set very gleamingly with napery and cutlery and the essentials of one of Georgios' inimitable breakfasts. Pelagueya was waiting for us, transformed, in a short skirt and that article of attire which I believe is called, mysteriously, a jumper. It was morning garb; and indeed the morning was now undistant.

Through the eastward-facing window I saw the darkness speckled with light as though a drizzling snowstorm were passing across those winterless lands. The long escarpment of light on the horizon had broadened a little. Abu Zabal roofs were etched in a broken sierra against that whiteness. Marrot went to the window and peered out, and turned back and grinned at us, acidly.

" 'Came the Dawn'—a very good movie scene, though a bit overdone."

Pelagueya waved us to the table. She was less familiar than I with transatlantic references. "Yes, it will soon be morning. And I feel very excited. Do you, Mr. Huebsch?"

The great Jew levered himself ponderously into the indicated chair. "Not too greatly to neglect enjoying your hospitality, Princess, or Georgios' cooking."

Pelagueya was absent-minded. "Perfect jewel, isn't he? I think I'll engage him to cook for this place when you people break up your expedition. Unless——"

I made the obvious urging. "Unless what ?"

She started. It had been no designed pause. "What ? I don't know. Eat breakfast, Anton. Coffee, Mr. Marrot ? Oh, we're forgetting the others. Ibrahim—go and find Mr. Quaritch. He's still on the roof ; I smelt his tobacco. And if Miss Simonssen's awake ask if she'd like to breakfast now."

The boy came in a moment later, slim shoulders slouching, his face curiously flushed. He bowed to Pelagueya's gesture, smiled faintly at me, and sat down and drank coffee and ate nothing, staring out of the window but starting every now and then at the footsteps heard outside the door. Then that door opened and Aslaug Simonssen came in, so pale that Pelagueya ceased to poke uninterestedly at the fish on her plate.

"Aslaug ! What's wrong ?"

"Nothing, Princess." But there was something very much. She sat down in silence, took the food Ibrahim placed in front of her, and made a pretence at eating. Quaritch never took his eyes from her. Abruptly she raised her head and looked at him. And I sat amazed. It was a glance of sheer fear that each exchanged . . .

Pelagueya had finally desisted from her tormentings of Georgios' carefully cooked fish ; Marrot was crumbling a roll over and over on his plate, and scowling now and then towards that window-scene that reminded him of a moving-picture caption. I myself found my appetite had declined sadly when

brought to the test. Even Huebsch, eating immensely
and competently, seemed without enthusiasm in the
business. . . . And all of us had been so hungry

Humanity in little, I decided, this odd breakfast
table company in an hour on the verge of dawn!
We had no leisure or appetite to eat or drink of life,
four-fifths of us, because to-morrow we were to be
killed or raped or have our mothers die of cancer.
Or God was to come shining from the clouds and
reveal a new and tortuous way of forgoing appetite.
Or wonder was to come and make appetite unnecessary. Or we had fed all appetites to sickness and
satiety. Or we feared or loved too much that which
we longed to devour——

"Goodness, we are all very silent! And no one
is eating. It's that Thing in the sack, Mr. Huebsch.
When are you going to bring it out?"

Huebsch had finished. He tended this thick lips
with his napkin, and glanced towards the black
leather sack to which the sand and mould still clung.
"As soon as we've all finished and the table's been
cleared, Princess."

"Yes? Ibrahim, get them to clear the table."

Huebsch rose up from his chair and crossed
towards the leather bag. "And you might get them
to bring a knife, Princess. Or a dagger. Something
with a sharp point and an edge as well."

Quaritch stirred a little, his boy-face wrinkled in
a questioning sneer as he looked at the Jew. "Found
the Temple treasures, eh?"

"He is about to bring out the Lost Trumpet," I

said, and only then realized that neither Quaritch nor Aslaug Simonssen had heard of the discovery. Both stared at Huebsch. The novelist gave a short laugh.

"That so, sir? Careful folk, the sheenies. Always find what they've lost. . . . Let's have a look."

Huebsch was carrying the stained leather sack to the table. He waved Quaritch aside.

"In a minute, maybe, young man. . . . Ah, here's the knife."

It was brightly sharp-pointed and two-edged, a Tuareg knife that had once belonged to Gault. Even so, and even in Huebsch's immense clutch, it seemed to make little or no impression on the tough and ancient leather buried these twenty-five centuries. I remembered the Carthaginian breastplates that had been made of rhinoceros-hide and steeped in gums to make them arrow-proof. This leather also the sands or ancient art must have treated in some such fashion. We crowded round to look.

Finally, with a strong downward thrust, Huebsch drove home the point of the knife, shortened the blade, and then ripped a wide slit in the sack. Thereon he dropped the knife, smiled benevolently at Pelagueya, hostess and most faithful fellow-enthusiast, and upended the sack upon the table.

Subchapter iii

Something heavy fell out and rolled a little and shoggled to a standstill. A minute brown powdering sprayed across the table. There was a general intake of breath ; and we all stood motionless, looking at the thing.

It was the Lost Trumpet. Huebsch's faith and enthusiasm had been justified. There was no mistaking the antiquity of the instrument lying before us—even as it was difficult to see in it anything unusual. It was a ram's horn, perhaps a foot and a half in length, dark brown in colour, streaked and scoriated in faint red lines. At either end it was circled by a metal band. That at the mouthpiece I knew was gold ; I had seen much of ancient gold excavated from the gold-littered soil of Egypt. But the larger circle was of other metal.

I think I was the first to move after the Trumpet had dropped on the table. I bent down to examine the larger circle, and thereat, like automata released by the snapping of a thread, the others moved also.

"So that's the Lost Trumpet," said Pelagueya, wide-eyed.

Marrot smiled at her. "Disappointed ?"

"Not so much as you are, Mr. Marrot."

He flushed, surprisingly. Aslaug Simonssen bent over the table. "Will it blow ?"

Before anyone could prevent him, the boy had snatched up the Trumpet. "The planet to blazes, they say. Let's try !"

And, with a reckless laugh, he put the ancient mouthpiece to his lips, and out-curved his cheeks, and blew immensely.

A little puff of dust sprayed out, descending on

Marrot, who cursed vigorously and stepped aside. But there was a more unexpected happening. Quaritch dropped the Trumpet as though it were alive. It clattered and rang as it hit the table again. The boy had covered his ears with his hands.

"God, I've gone deaf !"

I caught his arm. "What is it ? Have you swallowed dust from the mouthpiece ?"

He peered at me exasperatedly ; shook his head. He was quite obviously deafened. Huebsch picked up the Trumpet. The rest of us stood and stared at the novelist, Aslaug Simonssen putting out a tentative hand to him and then withdrawing it sharply. He beat at his ears.

"What are you saying ? Really, this is quite damnable. . . . Ugh ! it's passing."

It was most curious. He took his hands from his ears. The look of apprehension still remained in his eyes. He shook his head to our questions.

"Happened ? I don't know. Just that I couldn't hear. My ear drums closed up."

"You distended your cheeks over-much," I suggested.

He sat down. "I feel damn rotten, anyhow."

Huebsch, immense and grave, had carried the ancient instrument over to the window, and, having shaken more dust from its choked interior, was now engaged in wiping the mouthpiece with his handkerchief. Pelagueya had sat down again and was looking at him, head on one side, cheeks a little flushed with excitement. Marrot was embracing the back of a

chair and regarding his colleague closely. Aslaug
Simonssen, a strayed daughter of the vikings, stared
at the Jew with her lips a little apart. It was Marrot
who broke the silence.

"Problem : What is the difference between a
white elephant and a Lost Trumpet found ? What
are you going to do with the thing, Huebsch ?"

"Well, well, read the inscription, I guess, so
soon as I can see it through this coating of grime."

Marrot was at his side in a moment. "Inscription ?
H'm. So there is."

The window circle collected all of us, except
Quaritch, who still sat and rubbed his ears. Looking
through the window I saw the day very close by
then, and the cypress boughs waving in the coming
of the morning wind. Pelagueya's shoulder touched
mine and I glanced down at her face, sweet and
eager as her body. . . . It was pity Rodin had died
without knowing Pelagueya. 'Eternal Spring-
time'—she would have made a fine woman counter-
part of that. . . . Huebsch was muttering to himself.

"Not much of it. And plain enough."

Pelagueya shook his arm. "Then do read it."

"Eh ? Sure. Something like this, Princess :
The Trumpet of God's Man."

Subchapter iv

The electric light had grown pallid, almost green.
Now that zone of daylight widened ever more
quickly in the sky. And I saw the roofs of Abu Zabal

caught and painted in a something that was not a colour, but the ghost of cobalt. The curved block lettering on the mouthpiece of the Lost Trumpet winked up at us, rune-like, and I handed on the instrument, and Aslaug Simonssen, the next to receive it, bent her gaze on the runes, young and unintelligent. "God's man?"

Marrot's voice was as cool and acid as ever. "Then undoubtedly it's meant for you, Huebsch, seeing you're the only Jew here—and an Ancient Unorthodox one to boot."

"No such thing." It was Quaritch's voice from his seat beside the table. "God's Man—obvious enough."

"Not obvious at all, Mr. Quaritch," said Pelagueya. "Instead, dreadfully dim. So enlighten us."

"Pleased, Princess. God's Man—who hasn't heard of all the ideal nationals as God's Englishman, God's German, God's Spaniard—maybe even God's American, though I can hardly believe that. God's Man is the synthesis of the lot." He regarded us with young, jeering eyes. "So which of you is going to blow the thing? And I shouldn't think women are excluded. . . . Like me to toss up for you?"

Huebsch, reclaiming the Trumpet from Aslaug Simonssen, considered the Englishman hugely, benevolently, and shook his head.

"Guess you're taking a fragment too much on yourself, young man. I'll stage-manage whatever trifle of drama we decide on for our entertainment." He turned, a portentous bull-god, archaic and

Assyrian, upon Pelagueya. "That is, with your permission, Princess."

"But granted ooith pleasure, Mr. Huebsch," she said, in that rounded uncertainty of the "w" which assailed her English in moments of excitement. "And what is the entertainment going to be?"

"We will see if one of us can blow the Lost Trumpet."

CHAPTER THE NINETEENTH

'She set the Trumpet to her lips.'

Subchapter i

WE had, all of us, known that the thing would be attempted. But, put in words, it was a breath-taking proposal. The Lost Trumpet! What would happen? In the grip of fantastic imaginings I glanced up at the ceiling. Pelagueya caught my glance, and laughed, and glanced up at the ceiling herself.

"Anton thinks you may endanger the architecture, Mr. Huebsch. What do *you* think will happen?"

"Not an idea, Princess. But we'll go outside if you prefer it."

Marrot spoke then, scowling at Huebsch and the Trumpet, dully gleaming with either metal band. "Anyway, there's something in Saloney's uneasiness. It's possible the damn thing has some twist of construction that may set up unusual sound-waves——"

"Well, well, that's fine for a materialist. You think that, apart from it being a genuine relic, it may have genuine powers?"

Marrot shrugged his shoulders contemptuously. "Think what you like I think. Anyway, here's someone who's an authority on trumpets, ancient and modern. Try it out on him."

There had been a knock at the door, and Georgios Papadrapoulnakophitos stood bowing before us.

Subchapter ii

"The breakfast—it was satisfactory, madame ?"

Always polite, Georgios disregarded his employers and stood questioning Pelagueya, who stared at him remotely. Then, realizing that this was the visit of a noted chef to a patronne, acted accordingly.

"It was admirable, Georgios. We were about to send you our congratulations."

The little Greek bowed, beamingly, and was about to turn away when Marrot caught his arm.

"Wait a bit, Georgios. You're a musician. Did you ever see an instrument like this ?"

Georgios took the ancient shape of the Lost Trumpet into his hands gingerly, consideringly. "It is a horn, M'sieu', and is very unclean."

"It's a Trumpet, we've been led to believe. One that produced quite unique music in its day. Do you think you could blow it ?"

"M'sicu', I am the master of the bugle, the trumpet, the fife——"

"Then just give a little toot on this thing."

Just as the little Greek was about to obey, Marrot snatched the Lost Trumpet out of his hands, angrily. "No. Don't. I've changed my mind. Sorry, Georgios."

"It is very well, M'sieu'."

Georgios retired, puzzledly. Marrot wheeled on the rest of us. "Why the devil didn't you try to stop me?"

"Stop you?" I echoed.

"Of course. Oh, a damned dirty trick. Trying to amuse ourselves at the expense of one we consider a social inferior." He glowered at Pelagueya. "*You*, anyway, might have told me it was a scoundrelly thing."

Pelagueya nodded. "It was. But I was like yourself, Mr. Marrot—a scoundrel who didn't think. Now you've made me. Thank you."

"Well, well, it was a mistake," said Huebsch, pacifyingly. "And since Georgios is out of the running I might as well try it myself."

And so saying, he picked up the Trumpet, caressed it for a moment, then set the worn gold band to his lips.

I looked away from him. My eyes were towards the window. And suddenly, on the horizon, I saw the flicker of sheet lightning, and realized the nearness of a sand-storm because of that sudden oppression in my head. Almost instantly the oppression lifted. I turned back. Huebsch had lowered the Trumpet and was looking at it queerly. Marrot was wiping his forehead. On Pelagueya's temples I saw stand beads of perspiration. Quaritch prowled to the window.

"Storm coming up. Anyone else see that lightning flash?"

"I've a headache," Pelagueya said. "Unless——"

But she did not finish what she had thought to say. Instead, she left my side and crossed to Huebsch, and held out her hand.

"Shall I try?"

He smiled at her. It seemed to me that a great weariness had suddenly been imprinted upon his face. "Well, well, why shouldn't you play with the toy, Princess?"

She raised the Trumpet, and smiled over at me, a smile I knew, and set the mouthpiece to her lips. We waited, I with a quickly beating heart. There came not a scrap of sound. Laughing, but white-faced, Pelagueya lowered the thing.

"I'm utterly useless. And I thought there was to be some fun. What a bore—like everything else. . . . Who is next? Aslaug—catch!"

Aslaug disturbed another little cloud of dust that settled on Quaritch. Thereat she stood staring at him affrightedly, so that even Pelagueya noted the stare and moved irritably, questioningly. But no sound had come from the Lost Trumpet. I saw the day near to breaking then. The promise of the sandstorm had not been fulfilled, and the lightning in the sky had been but a solitary flicker. I turned back again at sound of Pelagueya's voice.

"The thing is a fraud, Mr. Marrot. . . . Eaogh! Sorry. I'm sleepy. There, we've all tried now, so Mr. Huebsch will have to take it away and sell it in a museum."

Marrot was withdrawing his lips from the Trumpet though not his eyes.

"The damn nonsense it is." He muttered unintelligibly. Then glanced round the room. "All tried? What's the matter with Saloney?"

"No, no. It will be useless."

Marrot raised sardonic brows at his hostess. "Well, if the Colonel's useless, so are we all. See no reason why you shouldn't have a go, Saloney."

Pelagueya spoke in a strained, queer voice. "Anton, I beg that you won't try."

I stood with the Trumpet grasped foolishly in my hand, myself absurdly troubled and undecided. Pelagueya's hands were clenched below her chin. She shook her head at the question in my eyes, and gave a little laugh.

"No, I've no reason. Only—Pfuu! the thing is both useless and uncanny. Put it away, Anton dear."

Huebsch had been considering the two of us, wearily benevolent. "Oh, Princess, I guess it'll do no harm. So if the Colonel would like to——"

Quaritch broke in impatiently. "Do go ahead, sir."

I know nothing of such wind instruments. But I raised it to my lips as I had seen the others do and set my lips against its cold, grained mouthpiece, and drew a deep breath, and breathed in it, gently enough at first and then with increasing force and volume. And the thing against my lips resisted soundlessly, with immense strength as it seemed to me. I tried again, and at that, for the fraction of a second, that resistance seemed to wilt a little. . . . I took the Trumpet from my lips, shakily. The others were staring

towards the window. Huebsch swung round, weary
brows corrugated in thought.

"Nothing doing, Colonel ? See that flash out there
on the horizon ? There's a bad storm coming up."

"It's stifling, isn't it ?" Aslaug Simonssen brought
out a handkerchief and dabbed at her forehead. I
laid down the Trumpet. Outside in the garden an
early insect had begun to chirp, devilishly. I
shivered, and found Quaritch looking over my
shoulder with a strange intentness.

"Here's your guest, Miss Simonssen."

All our eyes went to the doorway then, I think.
And in the doorway stood the woman Huth Rizq.

Subchapter iii

None of us spoke, but she had heard Quaritch's
voice. She came forward into the room, walking
with an easy grace, her hands held in front of her.
She halted, touching the table with her finger-tips.

"You are here, are you not, Esdras ? And others ?"
Her head turned from side to side, the reckless
laughter shining in the blind eyes. "I grew tired
waiting for the girl to come back ; I had told her
all about poor Carl and why I killed him. Now I
must go."

Pelagueya said, coldly, from her stance by the
window : "A friend of yours, Mr. Quaritch ?"

"I have never denied her, Princess."

He was sitting at the table again. I glanced at
Aslaug Simonssen. She was pale as death and kept

glancing from Quaritch to Huth Rizq with the strangest, most hunted look in her eyes. She spoke at last, in a voice so low that I could hardly hear it.

"Mr. Quaritch brought this woman to see me, Princess. She knows about how my brother was killed. She—she works in Cairo."

Huth turned her face towards the speaker. It was evident that she understood English. "Why are you so troubled ? I not only know about your brother. I killed him, I tell you." I saw the flicker of a little smile pass across her grave lips. "And as for my work in Cairo, I am a prostitute, and must go back because my clients will come looking for me this evening." She began to walk towards the window. "There is a window here, is it not ? I can feel the morning air."

Marrot drew back to let her pass. Pelagueya, with a shudder, also drew aside. The Wagh el Berka prostitute stopped and also turned her sightless eyes.

"Why did you do that ? And why do you not speak to me ?"

Pelagueya said : "I—I have seen you before. Where was it ? . . . And I am sorry I was discourteous. I am tired."

Huth Rizq shook her head. "You are unhappy. Weary and uncertain. Now when I have smelt the garden wind I must leave."

Pelagueya gave a sign and Marrot pulled open the window, and the air flowed in coldly, as though liquid, till the room was flooded with its coming. Suddenly Quaritch reached across the table, as he

had done earlier in the evening, snatched up the
Trumpet, got to his feet, and in three strides had
crossed the room to the side of Huth Rizq.

"Here, Huth. Sound this."

I think there were three of us who made movements to stop him, and then refrained. It did not
matter. Huth Rizq raised her head, down-bent as it
had been in sightless scrutiny of the thing in her
hand. And I clenched my own hands, seeing her in
that attitude, remembering the attitude of the soapstone Hathor excavated from the block-house ashes.
She smiled at Quaritch. But it seemed to me that
the unconscious, reckless mirth had vanished from
her eyes.

"What is it ?"

"A ram's horn trumpet. Blow it."

"I will try. But only for a moment. It will soon
be morning, and I must go."

Then, as each and all of us in that room had done,
one after the other, she set the Trumpet to her lips.

CHAPTER THE TWENTIETH

'Except the coming of that flash.'

Subchapter i

I DO not know how I may tell of the thing that happened then, how gather in any coherent recital the multitudes of whirling plot-items that blew to being in that crowded little room. For each of us later had a different tale, or no tale at all, or a denial of anything extraordinary—except the coming of that flash.

Of the coming of that flash none of us had any doubt. One moment we stood in the electric-lighted room, with the day striding towards us from the horizon and the form of the Wagh el Berka prostitute outlined against that pale, hurrying approach. The next there was a blinding dance of arrowed lightnings, a crash that seemed to shake to its foundations the Turkish castle of Gault, a drifting onrush of fire-smell, then darkness dead and complete . . .

And because there is no other for whom I can vouch, this is my tale. In the moment of that flash and roar I heard and saw the Volga. Very clearly and distinctly it came to me in vision. Autumn on the Volga and morning among the tamarisks and a kingfisher sliding across the grey ripple of waters,

and Pelagueya, hair wind-blown, backgrounded with
that green and grey. . . . That, and a sudden loosening and freeing of the blood in every vein of my
body. I was neither blinded nor stunned. Instead,
suddenly happy and impatient in a breath. I stood
still, impatiently, and then the darkness that had
succeeded the flash and roar suddenly passed and the
room was flooded with the sunshine of the morning.

Not a yard from me stood Pelagueya, her hands
at her eyes. I caught those hands and she blinked up
at me as one slowly returning to the world.

"Princess—you are unharmed? Pelagueya—only
now I've thought—what nonsense to call you
Princess, what nonsense I've always talked to you!
Often and always, never saying the things I have
wanted to say and was meant to say. But now—We
are going to be married. To-day, if we can."

"*Anton*——"

"And not for romance or remembrance or honour.
Because I love you and desire you and have envied
every lost rose petal that ever knew you. Married.
But not for Egypt——"

Her arms round my neck then. "I know. It
came to me in a flash just now—in that flash. And
we're talking our life-secrets to everybody, and what
does it matter? . . . *Back to Russia, both of us*. And
I don't care though they set me to cleaning latrines or
fighting provocateurs or polishing Stalin's top-
boots. The fun of it—to work and talk and fight
for daylight and sanity! Anton, why haven't we gone
before?"

"Because I have been a deserter, a fugitive from life. But I am going to live again. Kazan Gymnasium—Lunacharsky has talked of me, Gorki—We'll work at anything. Give: I who have never done anything but take . . ."

We were Russians again, speaking in Russian, our faces flushed, Abu Zabal forgotten. Pelagueya laughed at me.

"You have never done anything but give. It is I who have done the taking. But that's over. Back to Russia with not a piastre-piece we're going, Anton—and I'll kiss the slimy streets of Odessa when we land. The fool I've been——"

"Dear fool."

"*Anton, what happened to that woman and the Lost Trumpet?*"

Subchapter ii

The shielding flame of excitement dropped from about us. We turned to look at the room.

Our movement started others to life. Marrot, nearest to us, not looking at us, but window-ward, sprang towards that window.

"My God!"

We went forward and looked in silence. Huth Rizq lay crumpled on the floor, face dead and calm and content. There could be no doubt as to how she had died. The breath of a great fire had smitten and killed and stripped her. She lay in the window-fall of sunshine. She had gone home with the morning.

. . . I knelt and put my hand upon her heart and found no movement there, and had a sudden thought and glanced round the room.

"The Lost Trumpet—where is the Trumpet ?"

It was nowhere near Huth Rizq. But the others fell back and I saw midway the room a little heap of powder and dust and charred metal. Marrot was speaking in a strange, strained voice.

"That flash of lightning must have fused the thing utterly."

"*Lightning?*"

"Of course. What else ? Lightning. Didn't you see it strike through the window the moment she lifted the Trumpet to her lips ? . . . Murdered to make an archæologists' holiday. We killed her, Huebsch and I, playing with those damned toys on which I have wasted my life. But it's the last. I've finished with archæology. I'm going back to America to do real work, to fight all the insane cruelties of ignorance and folly that murder such harmless folk as this. . . . God, why haven't I gone before ? Afraid of sneers and laughter, afraid of my reputation. . . . Huebsch, I'm going. I'll help you clear the camp and the Institute'll soon send you another assistant——"

Some words like these poured from him. And then we became aware of Huebsch. He stood beside us and looked down at Huth Rizq, his face singularly clear and expressionless and unexcited. At Marrot's words he smiled, gently, amusedly, no longer weariedly.

"Well, well, there'll be no need for an assistant.
This is my last venture as well, Marrot. I'm going
back."

"What—to America ?"

"America ? No. Remember that little colony up
from the Dead Sea ? I'm going there, to my own
people. Always wanted to, I think. . . . Jerusalem."
He turned away with dreaming eyes. "They can build
that everywhere, I suppose. But I'm going to help
the job in its original country. . . . What was that
poem, Miss Simonssen ?"

"Look at the morning," I said. "Who ever saw
it so clear ?"

Something disturbed the dead woman at our feet
—the woman we were so strangely and yet uncal-
lously disregarding. "A moment, sir. She is mine
to look after."

It was the boy. Flush and pallor alike had gone
from his face. He picked up the body of Huth Rizq
and laid it on a couch, and knelt by it. And suddenly
the grip of Pelagueya's fingers tightened on my
wrist.

Aslaug Simonssen stood mid-way the room, looking at the prostitute and the poet. Such look it was
as I shall long remember—such look as once I would
have turned my eyes from, such look as a day before
would have shocked the soul of Aslaug Simonssen
into self-horror and disgust. So for the barest
moment she stood and then was at the side of
Quaritch.

"Esdras !"

He looked up at her remotely, and smiled. Her
tongue stumbled among unaccustomed sincerities.

"Esdras, I *want* you to ! I'm not afraid of the
bargain. Always I've lied to myself. . . . This
woman said you were to go back to your work in
the streets of Cairo, but I—oh, you cannot leave me
either !"

He stood up then. "Aslaug !"

They were quite unconscious of us. The boy
held her and smiled down into her eyes. "I've
searched so far for reality, but I think I've heard it
this morning——"

"Listen !" I said.

It was only the sigh of the morning wind. But
no such wind comes to any city but Cairo and the
little towns that squat at her feet on the desert hem.
It grew and grew, coming from the sands—as a
sleepy boy, roused in some desert lair, uplifting a
moment a sounding Trumpet above the sunrise
roofs of Abu Zabal. Once, twice, thrice, he blew.
Then the wind had passed on to Cairo and day had
come upon Egypt.

EPILUDE : UNENDING MORNING

I COULD not sleep these last two hours. It was after midnight when I awoke, finding myself very sharply awake, trailing no little mists out of dreams, which is unusual with me. I lay long then in the darkness, seeing the moonlight deep in the great embrasures of the window, for these walls have the thickness of castle walls. My left arm was cramped and for a little I lay and rubbed it to bring back the blood. But I moved it gently because of the sleeper beside me. And then, on that instant, I heard a camel's bell on the road to Cairo.

It was a sound that came through the waning moonlight, unloosing such trooping host of memories as set my mind quivering as one quivers to the sound of marching men. So I knew then that for me to-night there was no possibility of more sleep, albeit, as I came from the bed, I found myself still drowsy. Only here, in this room next door, did that drowsiness pass. For I found myself at the window, looking out at the sheen and play of moon-mist, listening. At the bend of the road I would hear it again.

And presently so I did—that faint, austere tinkle of the journeying caravan. If Gault could hear it now from his grave in the lost mountains of Mesheen !

Below the window I could smell the last of the

roses. A faint, shy phantasma of a wind moved the
green cloaks of the garden plants ; in the moonlight
I saw the cypress grove rise and pause, as though
startled, looking desertward, it may be, on that last
road its owner took. Gault—who also perhaps had
heard the Lost Trumpet.

I have sat here at my desk since then, waiting for
the morning, re-reading scraps of the record I have
made in my diary-English, pausing in indecision
over the telling here and there. Were indeed things
so and thus ? The Lost Trumpet—a Jewish relic
that a flash of lightning destroyed, or——?

Huth Rizq—how, after all, might anything but the
most fantastic dreaming associate a peasant prostitute
with the Hathor of Love, sounding a lost clarion-call
in a house in the desert ?

Huebsch, Marrot, Quaritch, Aslaug, Pelagueya and
myself—surely it was only the horror and startlement of the accident that swept us all to actions and
decisions we had long premeditated ? The camp
below this house lies bare and deserted now and
those others have scattered on their missions and
lives as that morning revealed them. And to-day
Pelagueya and I leave for Russia—we, the aristos,
who know that our lives will lack meaning and
sweetness till the day of our deaths if we return not
and share in that dream against which we struggled
and fought, believing it a nightmare . . .

Very near to morning now. In a moment I shall
hear Pelagueya awake and go to her—she, who has
been so miraculously, intimately mine that I have

surely known the beating of her heart in my own body
—and she will put her arms on my shoulders, half-
asleep, yet excitement-quivering, and cry: "Oh,
Anton! To-day!" And all my dreaming life in this
most ancient of lands will cease and pass and I be
gone : into life and reality.

But I know that the Lost Trumpet was blown. I
believe it lies unblown in every troubled human
heart. I believe that that morning we heard it there
rose in each of us the golden ghosts of ancient times
of whom Adrian talked, who lie chained and prisoners,
but undying and unslayable, simple and splendid,
kindly and gracious, behind the walls of pride and
race and creed.

THE END

J. LESLIE MITCHELL

AN APPRECIATION*

by

John Lindsey

¶ I came across the work of Leslie Mitchell entirely by accident and I was struck immediately by its authenticity and realness.

His first novel, "Stained Radiance", was avowedly destructive. An orgy of destruction ran through the whole book. His characters destroyed one another mercilessly—they destroyed God, society, sex. And Leslie Mitchell let them do it. They seemed to horrify him as, perhaps, all mankind had horrified him by its unimaginative lusts and frightful, unthinking cruelties, and its appalling hypocrisy.

The book wept and raged with pain so that one felt that here was a man who had indeed been down into the pit, who had seen all the baseness of which man is capable, the poverty, degradation, the wounding laughter : man crucifying man. It was the cry of the over-sensitive artist against the wrongs of the world.

Time and again I wanted to put the book down. I felt that I could not go on : that the pain it engendered in me was too intense, too excruciating to be borne. But I did not put it down. I was forced to continue : even, as it seemed, against my will ; because here was something real, that compelled my attention.

And somehow, out of all the pain and suffering in the book, there emerged another thing for which I could find no name for the moment. It was too small, too flickering a light for hope . . .

"Stained Radiance" had many faults. It was over-written. It was restless, allowing the reader no respite ; set at too high an emotional pitch, so that one thought, "This cannot go on" ; but it did go on, and something else happened ! A new idea or thought had to be brought in, thrown before the reader for consideration, snatched away only that another might take its place—another thing that the author was forced to say——

¶ But in his second novel, "The Thirteenth Disciple", he has definitely found that something that flickered in "Stained Radiance". His new

* Reprinted from *The Twentieth Century*.

characters have found something too : they are in the round, instead of, as in the first book, appearing as flat drawings. The pain is still there, but it is not so intense. The rage is still there, only now it is suffused with pity. The wild anger has gone. There is still anger, but this time Mr. Mitchell has not set out to destroy only. He wants to construct, and, in a large measure, he succeeds.

In "Stained Radiance" he is horrified by sex, it has got muddied like everything else. He hates "strange and disgusting changes in her body". In "The Thirteenth Disciple" he is no longer horrified, except in so far as people make sex cheap and pornographic by clothing it with rose-buds and soft-coloured lights.

The form of "The Thirteenth Disciple" is different : a friend writing the biography of a friend, having had access to certain documents, but, inevitably, restricted in his knowledge of that friend's mentality and emotions. I have read the book through carefully twice. I cannot find that in any single instance has the author stepped beyond those things of which he was allowed to know.

Then again, the book is filled with an amazing "sense of place". To confine oneself to those chapters dealing with Leekan Valley, one is struck by the author's ability to recreate not only the actual scenery of the place, but the implied scenery : the undercurrent of feeling and sensitiveness which this bleak country engenders.

The book is sub-titled "Portrait and Saga of Malcom Maudslay in his Adventure through the Dark Corridor." And I suppose that the word Tragedy would be used to describe it. But it is more than Tragedy in the sense that the book has fulfilment, that Maudslay himself is fulfilled. Out of the "agony in stony places" something new is born, and the whole book is illuminated in the light of this fulfilment.

In his third book, "The Calends of Cairo", a story-cycle, he has deserted —only for a holiday, I think—the urgencies of the Western world. Here is the Modern East : the whole book saturated in a strange, wild spirit—a spirit of unrest and yet tranquillity in the midst of that unrest ; full of colour and a noble searching after meaning.

On these three books alone it seems to me that Leslie Mitchell has justified his inclusion among the very few people—men or women— writing to-day whose work we cannot spare. The work is individual : perhaps almost annoyingly so. It demands a certain mental adjustment on the part of the reader. But, granted that adjustment, it is important work, indicating a certain line of thought that is too seldom treated of : *a certain freedom from preconceived notions of what is right and wrong.* And the explorer along that line of thought is, I am sure, a writer who will have an influence, and that a very definite one, on the thought and literature of the twentieth century.